Blinding
Lies

AMY CRONIN

This book is a work of fiction. The names, characters, places, businesses, organisations and incidents portrayed in it are either the product of the author's imagination or are used fictitiously. Any resemblance to actual persons, living or dead, events or locales is entirely coincidental.

Published 2020 by Crimson
an imprint of Poolbeg Press Ltd.
123 Grange Hill, Baldoyle,
Dublin 13, Ireland
Email: poolbeg@poolbeg.com

© Amy Cronin 2020

The moral right of the author has been asserted.

© Poolbeg Press Ltd, 2020, copyright for editing, typesetting, layout, design, ebook

A catalogue record for this book is available from the British Library.

ISBN 978178199-427-6

www.poolbeg.com

About the Author

Amy Cronin lives in Cork, Ireland, with her husband and two children. Having obtained an MBS in Management from Cork Institute of Technology, Amy worked in a variety of jobs before deciding to write full-time.

Blinding Lies is her debut novel, the first part of a trilogy.

Acknowledgements

To Paula Campbell, Gaye Shortland and all the team at Poolbeg – thank you for a warm welcome, kindness and enthusiasm for my writing.

Every time a dream comes true there are supportive people behind the one daring to give it a go – those who listen, cajole and cheerlead. I owe a debt of gratitude to Valerie and Will, my first readers and proud supporters. To Linda, Elaine and Stephanie for listening and for your endless encouragement. To Sandra for answering multiple questions patiently and with enthusiasm. To my wonderful friends and family. And to Kevin: the very first reader, an excellent plot-hole finder, and the most steadfast supporter of all.

This book is based in Cork city and county, but I should mention that the Lee Street Garda Station and the names of some businesses are fictional – as are the characters, of course!

Having been an avid reader all my life, it is a profound privilege to write my own book and be in a position to offer it to readers – I truly hope you enjoy this sliver of my imagination!

Dedication

For Kevin

Prologue

When the bullet pierced his neck, blood erupted in a vivid red mist, staining the wall behind him. Kate watched as his hands went to the wound, but it was futile. A crimson river flowed quickly, pulsing between his fingers, and dripped onto his white shirt.

David's blue eyes bulged, and his knees gave way. He looked at Kate in a silent plea for help. Even in his desperate state he must have known she would never save him. Immediately, it seemed, the front of his shirt was covered in blood. He was dying. His hands dropped, giving in to the inevitable, and he collapsed back onto the carpet.

Quickly, she threw the gun she was holding onto the floor. She hadn't heard the gunshot – perhaps she was in shock? Her throat ached where David had squeezed it, trying to crush the life out of her, the way he had done to her sister for almost four years.

She had finished packing. When David had let himself into the house her suitcase was standing ready in the hall with her passport resting on top. She hadn't realised he had

1

a key but later she would guess he had taken her sister's set.

David had been frantic, searching for a gear bag that he accused her of taking. He had screamed that the Germans were in the city, looking for him, looking for *it*. She had never seen David Gallagher scared. She had expected anger, but his state of mind both frightened and intrigued her. David had promised that his brother John was on his way here, and together they would peel the flesh from her bones until she handed it over. She believed his threat – she had borne witness to the Gallaghers' sadistic capabilities for far too long.

She stood over David Gallagher as he lay dead on her living-room floor. She felt … nothing. She had imagined this day many times and had thought she would feel triumph and relief. Instead, she felt empty. It was over. The nightmare was over.

A pounding at her front door, violent thumping on wood, made her jump.

John!

Grabbing her jacket, hat and scarf, and slinging a red satchel over her shoulder, she moved quickly to the backdoor. Her suitcase and passport forgotten, she fled her home.

Perhaps the nightmare was only just beginning.

1

Thursday

The office was cold that morning, the November chill pervading every available space. Plug-in heaters warmed the corners of the open-plan room. The early arrivals kept their coats on and shivered, shaking away the morning commute as they switched on computers and printers.

Anna sat at her desk, hands cradling a cardboard coffee cup, slowly thawing as the heat penetrated her gloves. She savoured the café latte as she did every morning; the coffee shop across the street, Victus, was a staple in her morning routine. The Lee Street Garda Station, the newest of the Cork city stations, had been built less than four years before, owing to the huge increase in both crime and population in Ireland's largest county. When Anna had moved to the building three years ago, it had still had that brand-new smell. As a member of Garda staff, providing clerical and administrative support to the Gardaí, she worked on the ground floor, and was usually first at her desk. She liked to begin the journey from her home in Kinsale as early as possible, to beat the infamous morning rush-hour commute. This morning, as with every other, the office slowly came to life around her and she greeted her colleagues with a smile.

Today, though, Anna felt slightly on edge, her smile tight. She hadn't slept well. The strands of an idea, a theory, had been pulling at the corners of her mind since she had begun to type up her work notes yesterday evening. She was naturally a logical thinker – her analytical approach at work hadn't gone unnoticed in the three years she had worked in the busy station. That, and her post-graduate diploma in statistics had led to her being tasked with organising and collating files from Garda stations throughout the county. And yesterday she had noticed a thread that just might sew some unsolved cases together.

A few days ago, there had been a break-in at a house near her own home. The victims were her elderly neighbours. She had been given the report on the crime to add to the statistical analysis files she compiled weekly, and it was ready to be logged into the national security system.

But details of the report rankled Anna. It wasn't the fact that the address of the break-in was in a house near her own semi-detached house in the coastal town of Kinsale that had caused her heart to skip a beat. She had typed reports similar to this many times – burglaries were common in every town. It was the subsequent crime that she felt certain would follow, in the same geographical area, that caused her breath to catch in her throat.

A tower of files was stacked precariously to her left, an ominous reminder of work awaiting attention. Post-it notes and memos were tacked to the padded cubicle walls, listing daily tasks and reports to follow up. Yet she knew she wouldn't be able to concentrate on anything other than the theory that had caused such broken sleep the night before. Finishing her latte, Anna decided she would get nothing else done until she had examined the previous cases and tested her idea. Her mother had always told her to trust her gut instincts – and if she was right, a serial sex-offender could be finally apprehended.

Her computer was on and her files almost loaded. She shrugged off her coat and pulled off her gloves, drumming her fingers impatiently until the blinking cursor indicated the system was ready. Pulling a notebook and pen towards her, she began. Accessing archived reports that she had analysed and categorised over the last three years, she made notes – dates, addresses, the fine details, linking it all with lines and arrows. There was a connection here somewhere and she was determined to find it. She opened Google Maps, and cross-referenced addresses, ticking them off her list. She was looking for the thread that connected it all, methodically working through each point, each crime. Every time she found it her excitement grew. These reports were detailing crimes from all over the city and county; while the crimes were geographically dispersed, they all landed on Anna's desk in the city centre at some point. And now she knew she was right. There *was* a pattern!

From time to time she sat back and reread her notes, just to be sure. Finally, she closed the last report, her heart pounding. Confidence pulsed through her. What had been merely a hunch, gnawing at her, prodding her subconscious until she paid attention, was now a sure connection.

She looked up from her notes. The office was almost full, clerical support staff and administrators milling in to start a new day. The city station was a busy place, and soon, by nine o'clock, the buzz of activity would be a steady throb.

Lately, it was even busier than usual. A political conference was taking place in the city in less than a week, and every available space within the station was taken up with extra bodies. Brexit was on everyone's mind. In the midst of their busy schedule, several politicians had decided to organise what they called a 'Unity Conference' in the newly built event centre in the city. Gardaí had been drafted in from other city stations, Dublin and Limerick, a myriad of detectives and undercover officers from stations throughout the country. Personnel were dispersed across the city's stations to ensure the event ran smoothly. The Events Unit and its team were more visible every day, the Events Coordinator ever present. Every corner of the room had a desk squeezed into it; every available plug was powering a new device. There was a long list of domestic and foreign politicians attending the conference, arriving into the city in a matter of days, and the tension in the station had been palpable for weeks. The Chief Superintendent, Janet McCarthy, was engaged in meetings every hour of every day, it seemed to Anna. She didn't know how the Chief Super could get anything else done.

Anna's experience in the station over the last three years led her to believe a political conference meant nothing to the city's ordinary criminals – crime never stopped, certainly not for visiting dignitaries. The report on her desk detailed a violent robbery. And with growing certainty, she knew an even more sinister crime would follow.

Anna provided clerical support to some of the detectives in the Garda Station, and she remembered the name of the one who was investigating the latest in this list of unsolved attacks – Detective Sergeant William Ryan. He had taken over the investigation after the retirement of the previous detective. DS Ryan had only been involved in the most recent case. Anna liked him. He was recently transferred into the city station and seemed to be enthusiastic about the job.

"Hi, Anna!"

Her colleague Lauren breezed past and started unwrapping herself from her layers of winter clothes. Her desk chair was soon laden with her coat, heavy cardigan and blanket-sized scarf. She pulled off her hat, her dark bob fizzing with static, her multiple bracelets tinkling. Lauren spotted the takeaway coffee cup Anna had left on her desk and smiled warmly at her friend.

"*Ooh*, thanks! Did you get me anything nice?"

Anna grinned and tossed a paper bag across the small gap between their desks.

Lauren Doyle had started in the station a week before Anna, and they had quickly bonded over some of the worst aspects of the job – perpetually grumpy detectives, the more macabre case details, and the shocking lack of staff parking.

Lauren pulled a chocolate croissant from the bag and squealed in delight. She looked around the room. Most of the Garda staff – the civilians – started work before nine, to avoid the city traffic and grab a parking space. Lauren, with an apartment nearby, was almost always the last to arrive.

"Any news?"

Anna grabbed her notebook and scooted across the small distance between their desks on her wheeled swivel chair. She felt a trembling excitement at finding a potential lead and hoped her friend would see the same link she had.

"Will you take a look at this with me? I was typing up the report on the break-in at a house in Willow Rise yesterday evening when I came across something."

"That's near where you live, isn't it?" Lauren said, wiping croissant pastry flakes from her lips. Her black-framed glasses had slipped down her nose and she pushed them up with her little finger.

"It is! The Pearsons live at Number 3. My house is behind theirs." Anna shuddered involuntarily.

She had read the report; it had been a horrendous ordeal for her elderly neighbour and his wife. Their house had been broken into in the middle of the night by two men. Mr.

Pearson had been punched and kicked before the house was ransacked. Reading the report of the attack had left Anna shaken – she could only imagine how traumatised her neighbours must be.

"So," she continued, "something about these cases was gnawing at me and I want to get your opinion. I had to look back over the other cases to see if I was remembering correctly, and I am."

"What other cases?"

"The unsolved sexual assault cases."

Lauren's hand paused, her coffee cup suspended in mid-air. Her blue eyes had grown huge behind her glasses.

"The six sexual assaults over the last three years?"

"Seven actually. I looked over the files and, as I thought, the general addresses are all the same. Obviously, in a big county like Cork, there are house break-ins every week; it's a regular occurrence. But in a number of *these* cases, a woman has been assaulted in a house close by within a few days. First, there's a break-in. Elderly people, couples or singles – there's no connection there, except that none of them had a house alarm. Then a few days later, a young woman is sexually assaulted in a different house nearby."

"It must be a coincidence!"

Anna suppressed a sigh of annoyance. "Seven coincidences? I don't think so! And besides, there are no such things as coincidences, Lauren! There are only facts, patterns, and logic."

Lauren smiled patiently at her friend – she and Anna had had this conversation many times. Lauren made decisions based on the zodiac and moon phases, Anna on weighted logic. They had long ago agreed to disagree and salvage their friendship.

"I've checked Google Maps to be sure," said Anna. "In two cases, the house that was broken into looks directly into the house where the victim of the assault lives. In the others, the houses are close by."

Lauren gasped and Anna's heart leapt – there *was* something worth exploring here.

"Do you think the burglar is the rapist?" Lauren asked, her voice low.

Anna shook her head. "No. The Guards have made arrests for most of the robberies. A few of them were kids, some were drug addicts – they're not connected. The robbery at the Pearsons' was committed by two men who were wanted for a lot of other crimes throughout the county – theft, arson and so on – forensics have their DNA."

"But there's no DNA match for the sexual attacker on file." Lauren was familiar with the crimes too.

"Yes, that's right."

Lauren furrowed her brow. "You've lost me now."

"If you look at this from the angle of the sexual assault, it becomes clearer. It's a stand-alone, seemingly random crime, right? Except, within a week prior to it occurring, a house nearby is broken into, where the owners had no security alarms in place. In the transcript from their statements they were all asked and confirmed they didn't have one. Most of them mentioned they were planning to get one now that they had been robbed. It's unusual these days not to have one."

Anna paused and took a deep breath before quickly laying out her theory.

"What if the attacker is from the alarm company? What if he's the guy who installed the alarms? It would give him plenty of opportunity to scope out the estate, check if there's any woman alone at night. All the sexual assault victims lived alone, or their partners or housemates worked nights. The alarm guy could have figured that out if he was watching the area, and spending time there by day installing alarms. And if his DNA isn't on file, the Guards have no way of catching him."

Lauren gulped her coffee loudly, wincing slightly as it scalded her throat. To Anna, she looked a bit sceptical.

Anna ploughed on, speaking in a rush. "There's never been a link between the assault victims. No common relationships or club memberships, nothing. Now there is. Even though the crimes have taken place throughout the city and county, there *is* one thing they all have in common – they all live close to a house that was recently broken into. With *no* house alarm. And if all of those homeowners subsequently got an alarm installed, and used the same company …"

Anna spread her arms wide and watched the gears of cognition click into place in Lauren's mind.

"*Jesus!*" Lauren spluttered around a mouthful of croissant. "You have to talk to the detective about this. I mean, it's a long shot, but there could be something in it!"

Anna nodded and frowned. "Detective Ryan. I haven't seen him around for a few days."

"Oh, he had appendicitis! He's been out for over a week." Lauren always had the gossip on the detectives in Lee Street Station. She took pride in knowing everyone's movements.

"You know, if the time frame between the break-in and the sexual assault is only a few days, you'll have to go over his head. An attack could happen soon. Oh my God, Anna, so close to your own house!"

Anna nodded. She had been thinking the very same thing.

"Clever to spread out the crimes," said Lauren. "Geographically, I mean. Except that they all end up here at some point."

Anna looked at her towering pile of files and muttered, "Indeed."

Cold air assailed them at the entrance to the room. Detective Superintendent Frank Doherty had pushed the double doors in and strode purposefully through the desks and staff which supported his team. He looked straight ahead, offering no greeting, his face a bullish shade of red. The Detective Superintendent was a large man; tall and broad, his shirt buttons were perpetually strained against his stomach. He was unpopular among the Garda staff, never satisfied with anything less than an immediate result. He was a man who demanded answers but offered little in the way of support and encouragement. Lately, he had begun to resent the job more than at any other time in his life. His wife, Noreen, had been making his life miserable, demanding he take early retirement. They had a villa in France that she was keen to live in permanently – there was a vineyard close by she was fond of. Now that their youngest had finished college and was working in Dublin, Noreen saw no reason why Frank should stay. He had "served his time" as she put it and could draw his pension. Daily she nagged and moaned until he approached head office about retirement, to placate her more than anything.

As soon as Frank Doherty's retirement date was set, he found he had begun to lose interest in the job. Noreen was making plans for redecorating the villa and Frank found himself growing excited at the prospect of leaving this city behind. He was counting down the days and was relying heavily on blood-pressure tablets to get him to the end. The political conference, with its security demands and the constant emails and phone calls it necessitated, was a highly inconvenient blemish on his intention to coast into retirement.

Anna groaned as she met Lauren's eyes. She had no choice but to speak to the detective about her theory. He was Detective Sergeant Ryan's supervisor in the Special Protection Unit – it made sense to take her suspicions to him. Lauren nodded to Anna in silent agreement, her eyes full of sympathy. DS Doherty was generally considered unapproachable. He had yet to speak to most of the pool of clerical support staff, despite the years they had worked together, other than to issue demands. He had no time for them, and the civilian staff dreaded any direct interactions with the man. When he had once taken to issuing a morning greeting, it had been to call out "Good morning, Nametags!" as he strode through the room, smirking to himself. Someone had had a word, and the derogatory salutation had ceased, but Frank Doherty remained as gruff as ever.

Anna stood up, notebook in hand, a feeling of dread overtaking her previous excitement. She had to jog slightly to keep up with the long strides of the Detective Superintendent.

"Sir?" she called, hoping to gain his attention. She wasn't in the least surprised when he ignored her.

"Detective Superintendent Doherty!" she called a little louder.

The detective, his hand on the door to the stairwell, paused and looked around. His eyes settled on the short young woman in front of him and his expression darkened. Anna was aware of the eyes and ears of the full office behind her. Her mouth went dry.

"What is it?" he asked, in the tone of irritability Anna and her colleagues had grown accustomed to.

Anna cleared her throat. "I have a theory on the series of unsolved sexual assaults, and I was hoping to speak to you about it. I think –"

She stopped abruptly as the detective rolled his eyes and sighed. She immediately regretted her decision to speak to the man. But she had no choice but to continue now. Feeling foolish and embarrassed at the edge of the open-plan room, she willed her voice to be steady.

"Detective Superintendent Doherty, I really think –"

The man pushed open the door to the stairwell and then turned to look down at her again. His face was a crimson shade, his eyes bulging.

"Am I missing something? The last time I checked you worked in the typing pool. Now all of a sudden you think you're Nancy Drew. You have a *theory*?" He shook his head as he turned to go.

Anna persisted. "I would take it to Detective Sergeant Ryan, but he is out sick. Anyway, time is really important in this situation and –"

Frank Doherty sighed again and pinched the bridge of his nose, clearly fighting to remain patient. Anna felt her cheeks flame.

"Let me spell it out for you. The detectives in my unit are doing a fine job, we don't need some typist getting her knickers in a twist and telling us how to do it! The political conference is happening next week, in case you hadn't noticed, and we are all up to our necks in security and detail – no one has time to entertain your *theories*. Why don't you do me a favour and get back to your desk like a good girl. Leave the theories to the detectives, eh?" Muttering under his breath, he continued on his journey to his office, letting the stairwell door slam behind him.

Anna stood facing the closed door for a few moments after Doherty had gone. Tears sprang to her eyes, but she breathed deeply and calmed herself down. This wasn't the first time Frank Doherty had made her feel small and insignificant, and she vowed not to let him get to her. He was but one avenue to exploring her theory, and hopefully bringing these unsolved cases to a close. His dismissal stung though – had he just called her *a good girl*? She thought of her ash-blonde hair tied up in a ponytail, her pale-pink blouse and navy work trousers, and realised she looked a lot younger than twenty-six. A good girl?

Squaring her shoulders, she turned and walked back to her desk. The room was warm now, and noisy. Telephones and fax machines beeped and clicked, voices rose and fell – the bustle of detective work at its best.

Lauren's eyes met hers, and the embarrassment of the encounter passed unspoken between them. As Anna passed her desk, Lauren grasped her hand, her bracelets jangling.

"Are you OK?"

Anna nodded and took a deep, steadying breath. She sat at her desk.

Lauren rolled her chair in closer; she had gossip to share.

"I expect he's rattled by the shooting. I just heard – Tom Gallagher's son David is dead! Shot dead in a house in Wilton!"

"Wow!" Anna was momentarily distracted from her humiliation. Tom Gallagher was arguably the city's most prolific criminal, a drain on Garda resources and a very dangerous man. She felt a sense of dread wash over her. The station was already carrying a tangible pulse of tension due to the political conference – the shooting of a gangster's son would surely add to the chaos.

"You're teaching tonight, aren't you?" Lauren prodded gently. "That'll help you forget about *him*." Her mouth curled in distaste as she nodded in the direction Doherty had just gone.

"Thanks, Lauren." Anna smiled warmly at her friend. Thinking of her class of eager six-year-olds, she relaxed even further. Teaching Taekwon-Do brought her huge joy. She was a first-degree black belt and still training. She had assisted her own instructor Jason in teaching Taekwon-Do for almost a year now. The martial art had been her father's passion, and she always felt close to him when she put on her white suit and wrapped the belt around her waist.

14

She felt eyes on her and looked up. A man of her own age, his long frame looking cramped around his makeshift desk, met her gaze. His brown eyes were friendly. She recognised him as Myles Henderson, of the Special Detective Unit; they had been introduced yesterday. He was one of the detectives looking after security detail for the visiting dignitaries next week.

Anna could feel sympathy radiating from him – no doubt he had noticed her rebuff from Doherty. She groaned inwardly and turned back to her computer. She didn't want anyone's sympathy. She had reports to type.

2

A ringing telephone.

"Natalie, what's up?"

"Kate!" It was a hushed whisper, urgent – she sounded terrified. "Kate, there's someone in the house, I think it's him!"

"Are you sure?"

"Where are you? Oh God, he's coming up the stairs, I can hear him coming!"

Natalie was beginning to cry and was growing hysterical.

"Alright, I'll be there soon. Lock the door, OK? Natalie? Natalie!"

"Oh God, the twins!"

"Lock the door!"

Sometimes, a locked door didn't keep the monster out.

Kate woke from the nightmare with her heart racing and her skin glistening from a sheen of sweat. Bedsheets were tangled around her legs. She sat up, switched on the bedside light, and breathed deeply, the way the victim support officer had shown her once – in through her nose and out through her mouth.

The hotel room was bland, and she struggled to recall where she was. She was seized by panic. Then the events of yesterday afternoon came crashing around her and she fought to swallow the nausea that crept up her throat.

She leapt from the small bed and ran the short distance to the bathroom, vomiting into the sink. She retched until her stomach was empty, and crouched there, gasping for air. When she straightened up, she was confronted with her appearance in the mirror, and she was momentarily shocked by what she saw. Her face was tearstained and ghostly white, her red hair a tangled mess. Her reflection in the mirror matched how she felt; she looked pale and drawn, stressed and tired. And the face she saw there bore the evidence of the nightmare events of yesterday – her jaw was bruised, her neck red where David Gallagher had put his hands around her throat.

She lowered her eyes, no longer able to look at the evidence of what had happened. She turned on the taps and concentrated on cleaning the sink, washing away all trace of her vomit and upset. Her whole body hurt – her arms and legs ached, and her lower back throbbed. The heaving as she had vomited a few minutes ago had caused her left side to cramp; she wondered if she had a broken rib. A tremor in her hands frightened her – she looked at them, shaking. These hands had killed a man.

Stepping from the bathroom, she took in her surroundings. Beige carpet, beige quilt cover, beige blanket … an orange throw to add a splash of colour, which seemed garish in the light from the bedside lamp. The hotel room was tiny. She felt claustrophobic and lonely in the small space. She knew she would have to leave soon and escape the city.

Moving back to the bed, she began to pick at a cut on her hand, thinking. She no longer had a mobile phone or purse – she had left almost everything behind when she fled her house yesterday. Neither did she have her wristwatch but, to her surprise, the cheap hotel offered a bedside clock and telephone.

She hoped Natalie might already be awake and up with the twins. She was – she answered on the second ring.

"*Kate! Thank God!*" There was no need to ask who it was; no one else had Natalie's number.

Kate felt better just for hearing her sister's voice. Her heart rate steadied, and she lay back on the bed against the pillows.

"Where are you?"

"I'm still in Cork."

"What!"

"Natalie, don't worry, it's not for long," she whispered, closing her eyes against the harsh bedside light. "I had a nightmare and needed to know you're OK. Are you safe? How are the twins?"

"We're fine, the girls are just having breakfast. Rachel, Rhea – say hi to Aunty Kate."

She knew Natalie had turned the phone in her nieces' direction. There was a chorus of "*Hi, Aunty Kate!*" from the girls on the other end. She could picture them sitting at the kitchen table, legs not quite reaching the floor, devouring their breakfast, identical blue teddy bears under their arms. She smiled into the receiver.

"I miss you, guys. I'll see you soon."

Natalie put the phone back to her ear and spoke in hushed tones.

"Really? How soon?"

She ignored the question. "Are you set up?"

"I guess so. I found the hotel OK. The apartments they offer are small, but it feels too big without you. There's a market nearby where I picked up some supplies and the girls are being so good. We just need you to get here! What happened? I thought you were right behind me!"

She eyed the red satchel she had grabbed yesterday, grateful she'd had the presence of mind to bring it with her. She could picture Natalie chewing on a thumbnail the way she did when she was worried and trying to think.

"Things went … wrong. David came to the house. Don't worry, I'm fine, and I should be able to leave the city very soon." She didn't know whether this was in any way true. She needed things to settle down. She thought of her passport, sitting on top of her hastily packed suitcase in the hallway of her rented semi-detached, and sighed wearily. Things had gone so horribly wrong and now David Gallagher was dead. She couldn't bring herself to tell Natalie just yet. She needed to get to France and join her sister – but how could she do that without a passport? She imagined her house was crawling with detectives and forensics people by now and, knowing the Gallaghers, they would be staking it out too, waiting for her to return.

There was no way she could go home.

She tried to put as much confidence as she could into her voice as she said, "I'll figure something out!"

"OK. But this wasn't the plan …" Natalie's voice trembled and trailed off.

Kate felt wretched and couldn't think of anything to say.

"Please stay in touch, OK? And be careful, Kate – we need you!"

"I will, I always am. And you're sure they're safe?"

"Positive, they never leave my side."

"Love you, Nat."

"Love you too, Kate."

She lay there against the pillows, thinking. To say she would join them very soon was probably an untruth. But there was no way she could tell her twin sister what she was thinking right now, nor what she planned to do. Things were too dangerous. Natalie had been through enough.

She resolved to press on. She needed to end this nightmare. She had learned that time waited for no one, and that she had to take care of unpleasant things herself. She headed for the shower, determined to move things forward. David Gallagher had been an abusive monster, but he had proved useful in the end. He had contacts, people that had access to all sorts of things ... even fake documents. After all he had put them through, she was determined to make use of his resources and leave his twisted world far behind.

The first thing she had to do was change her hair – the fiery red curls stood out and, now more than ever, she needed to blend in. She would dye it and cut it short – isn't that what women always did in the movies when they needed to disappear?

At midday, she exited her hotel prison with bated breath. A quick trip to a nearby supermarket to purchase hair dye, large scissors and a few other essentials had almost caused her heart to constrict with tension. But it had been worth it – her hair was short and dark-brown and she looked nothing like her old self. She resolved to replace the light red jacket she had grabbed as she fled the house – the threat of being spotted grew with every step into the heart of the city. She knew who the Gallaghers were, and she knew that they would be looking for her. Tom Gallagher's henchmen were probably watching her house, and no doubt combing the city streets. Not to mention the Gardaí. She had to get out of Cork. Of Ireland. She knew her only way out was with a passport, so she had no choice but to leave the hotel again and venture into the city. She knew of no other way to get what she needed.

It was blustery and very cold. Winter had arrived and she was glad of it, glad of the opportunity to huddle under layers of clothing. Her scarf and hat were useful tools to further disguise herself. Blending into the crowd was her best chance of survival. She had the wispy strands of her hair tucked into her hat, hands jammed into the pockets of her red jacket, as she strode quickly forward. She needed food. It had been hours since she had eaten. She forced her weak legs to keep going, one in front of the other.

Within a few hundred metres was a greasy spoon café with booths and windows that were fogged with condensation. It was perfect. She made no eye contact as she headed for a booth near the door, thinking it was best to stay near the exit in case she needed a quick getaway. The café served an all-day breakfast, so she ordered a full Irish and a pot of coffee. While she waited, she carefully observed the customers, relieved there were few. Perhaps the cold was deterring people from venturing out for lunch, she mused. She was grateful.

She took a small notebook from her jeans. It was well-worn, thumbed through many times. It had belonged to David Gallagher … now it was hers.

She quickly found the page she needed, read David's scrawled note.

Nick @ the Mad Hatter, docs, p/p, x, cards, cash

She had heard of the infamous Nick before. He could supply anything required of him, for the right price of course. The Mad Hatter was owned by a businessman in the city, and was in competition with the Gallaghers when it came to clubs and bars. David and Natalie had socialised there occasionally; David liked to check out the competition. Judging by the notes in his notebook, he also liked to keep tabs on what Nick could supply. The bar opened at ten o'clock each morning to cater for the brunch trade and the usual barstool philosophers. Today, she had little choice but to join them.

She had run through this problem over and over – she could not return home to get her passport or driving licence. And she could not leave the country without identification. She had no other choice but to try to buy documents from the only source she knew of, and fast, before the Gardaí and the Gallaghers closed in. She knew the Gallaghers could have put the word out, that all the businesses in the city could be keeping a lookout for her by now. But she hoped her drastically different appearance, and the fact that the Gallaghers were probably reeling from the shooting of their son, might provide a distraction and buy her some time.

She tried not to devour her food when it arrived so as not to draw attention to herself, but she was starving. The hotel she was staying in, if you could call it a hotel, didn't serve food, and she had been too scared to leave for longer than necessary. She knew though that hiding under the duvet wasn't a long-term option. She longed to leave Ireland and the Gallaghers behind, to join her sister, and forget this whole affair. The need to escape was palpable and growing in intensity every hour. With each mouthful she felt revived and felt her strength and determination return.

She had passed the Gate cinema on the short walk to the café and knew it was open. She wasn't ready to call on Nick just yet and needed to further steady her nerves. The cinema would be warm inside, and more importantly, dark. She could sit in peace and think her plan through. Placing a ten-euro note on the table, she quickly left the café, making her way to the cinema, her eyes darting left and right, alert for anyone that looked like one of David Gallagher's gang. They had a stereotypical "tough guy" look; tight hair and tattoos, and usually wore dark jeans and coats. They weren't exactly subtle. She had socialised with some of them before while Natalie had been seeing David

Gallagher. She would recognise them instantly if she saw them again, she was sure of it.

The wind stung her cheeks and whipped her scarf around her. This part of the city was busier; shoppers were out in droves, despite the cold. She moved between them to her destination, shivering with cold and tension, ready to run.

The cinema was as warm and dark as she'd hoped. She purchased a large coffee and sat in the back row, to be near the exit. The movie was a thriller of some sort; she made no attempt to follow the plot. She didn't know if it was the coffee coursing through her veins, trepidation at what she was about to do, or trauma from the events of yesterday, but she felt pumped full of adrenaline. She could not sit still. Her eyes darted around constantly, and she shifted in her seat. The cinema was almost completely empty, just her and two elderly gentlemen, but still she could not relax. Images played in her mind, a horror movie of her own making. David Gallagher laughing as he punched and kicked, his voice screaming *"I'll fucking do it, I swear!"*, the look on his face as he fell backwards, blood spurting from his neck. Try as she might, she could not erase her memories. And her fear. She had been part of David Gallagher's life for many years now, and she knew what he had been capable of, what his family was still capable of. She needed to escape.

After the movie she freshened up in the ladies'. She took her time in there, although she knew no place would be safe from her attackers if they found her. She was aware she was dragging out the inevitable, the trip to the Mad Hatter. David Gallagher's world scared her. Her reflection frightened her too – there were deep lines under her eyes, and she was deathly pale. Exhaustion and fear were taking their toll. She did what she could with her appearance, but she had haphazardly hacked off her long hair and it stood up in wispy tufts. She hardly recognised herself. The bruise on her jaw was getting darker. She had bought concealer together with the hair dye, and applied more now, desperate not to draw attention to herself. Her hands shook as she dabbed on the pale liquid.

Across the street from the cinema was a department store. She moved through the crowds of eager shoppers, browsing the hangers and shelves, hoping to go unnoticed. She purchased a knee-length black winter coat, a scarf and a hat, avoiding eye contact with the cashier. In a toilet cubicle at the back of the store she put on her new things, transferring her old ones into the large shopping bag – she would dump them as soon as she could. On the second floor she found a passport-photo booth and ducked inside. Before the camera flashed, she tried to arrange her hair into something that resembled a style. Pushing it this way and that, she thought that Natalie wouldn't recognise her if she saw her now – her identical twin had never looked so different.

Realising she had no choice, and could no longer delay the unavoidable, she made her way to the Mad Hatter. She walked briskly and covered the distance within ten minutes. Steeling herself, she knew she would need to be extra-careful. She thought of Tom Gallagher, head of the family. His son was shot dead in her house – the man was certain to be looking for her. She hoped he was too preoccupied to do it just yet.

It was dark inside the Mad Hatter. The venue's few customers were clustered at the long bar with pints of lager in front of them. It looked like they were settling in for the day. A few of them turned in her direction to check out the door when it opened but returned to their drinks and muted chat with disinterest. She took a deep breath and sat near the door, shoving her shopping bag under the table.

A waitress arrived shortly, with a laminated menu tucked

under her arm. She looked to be in her forties, with smudged eyeliner and an impossibly short skirt. Her nametag read "*Betsy*".

"You having food?" she asked, chewing gum and looking bored.

"Just coffee," Kate answered. "Is Nick working today?"

Betsy looked her up and down, chewing, her eyes narrowed. She blew a large pink bubble-gum bubble and let it pop, before slowly drawing the gum back into her mouth, and resumed chewing again. Eventually she answered, "I'll check", and she moved away.

Kate gulped for air as she waited. This was so dangerous – it seemed she was making a habit of putting her life at risk. Her palms were sweating, and she rubbed them together under the table. Betsy had made her feel uncomfortable and she had a feeling her encounter with Nick wouldn't go much better.

She had kept her coat, scarf and hat on – nausea crept up her throat as sweat began to pool on her upper lip. After a few minutes Betsy brought her coffee, then turned and strode away again, never mentioning whether Nick was in or not. She sipped the coffee. It was awful; she winced as she swallowed. Time ticked on, and no one approached her. But she was keenly aware she was being watched. The tiny hairs on the back of her neck stood to attention, and her heart raced to the point where she felt she would explode with tension. She almost fled – this was surely suicide? Nick could contact the Gardaí, or the Gallaghers, at any time! But she had no choice. She knew of nowhere else to get the documents she needed to leave. And she couldn't go to the Gardaí and appeal for help – for a long time now she had suspected David Gallagher had a Garda on his payroll. Besides, they would surely arrest her the minute she walked into the station.

Eventually, a heavy-set man made his way towards her table from a door marked "**Staff Only**". He had his eyes fixed on her, and walked slowly, like a predator sizing up its prey. His arms were huge, his muscles bulging below the rolled-up sleeves of his shirt. Sweat glistened on his bald head. He sat opposite her.

"What do you want?" he asked in a flat, monotone voice.

She felt the room spin and gripped the edge of the greasy table.

"Are you Nick?" she asked, her voice barely above a whisper.

"What do you want?" the man repeated.

She took a deep breath and made eye contact.

"I want a passport. I can pay cash." She slid her passport photos across the table.

Nick raised one eyebrow – he seemed to be assessing her, this nervous woman sitting in front of him, with her hair bundled into a hat, a heavy coat and scarf almost obscuring her completely. Perhaps he was worried she might be an undercover Garda.

Eventually, he picked up the photos and nodded.

"It will take two days. And it will not be cheap. Ten grand. Cash. This is risky for me, you understand?"

She couldn't place his accent; she nodded to show that she did understand.

"Saturday night, ten o'clock. Sit here, order a drink," he instructed, appraising her with his eyes, making her skin crawl. "Do not wear so many clothes. I'll find you." He smirked.

He picked up the photos and walked away, back through to the staff area, passing Betsy who was wiping tables nearby.

Once he was out of sight, Kate exhaled deeply. Her adrenaline now depleted, she felt completely drained.

Dropping five euro on the table, she abandoned the coffee, grabbed her shopping bag and made her way back outside. She longed for the sanctuary of the hotel again. She set off, eyes darting left and right for any sign of Gallagher's men or the Gardaí. Her eyes stung from the biting wind and with tears of fear and frustration. Two days! She had no choice but to hope that wasn't too long. She felt vulnerable and exposed on the city streets – but she told herself she had better get used to it. There was much to do.

In the back office of the Mad Hatter Nick was sitting with his phone in his hand. He had called it in. A young woman, looking for documents. Mr. Gallagher's man Murray had given a description to all the clubs and bars and, although the woman had been almost completely covered in her winter clothes, Nick knew better than to ignore the possibility that this was who Tom Gallagher was looking for. He had texted a photograph of the passport photos the woman had supplied. He looked forward to his reward.

Outside, Betsy was on her cigarette break. She leant against the wall, cigarette hanging from her lips, and pulled her thin coat around her. She thought for a few minutes, about how much trouble she could get in, but also about how much she *owed*. The woman looking for Nick haunted her – she was clearly terrified. It wasn't every day a young woman came in here looking to buy a passport. Betsy knew the look of a woman in trouble – she had felt that level of terror before and had been given a second, even a third chance.

It didn't take Betsy long to decide what to do. Pulling out her mobile phone, she selected the right number and waited. After a few seconds on hold the call was transferred and answered.

"Detective Sergeant Elise Taylor, how can I help you?"

3

At lunch, in the staff canteen, Lauren and Anna sat together as they always did. Lauren munched on her sandwich and filled Anna in on some of the office gossip she had managed to glean that morning.

"Your detective, the one with the appendicitis? He's due back tomorrow from sick leave."

She pushed her glasses back up her nose.

Anna nodded, feeling relief course through her. She would approach him first thing in the morning then. She had thought about requesting to speak to the Chief Superintendent, but Janet McCarthy was in meetings all day with the Special Events Team – no doubt pertaining to the latest crisis in the city. Anna surmised that the shooting and the political conference would be taking up all of her available time.

Lauren lowered her voice and leant closer to Anna. "There's only one suspect for the shooting of David Gallagher apparently – a woman. He was found dead in the woman's house and she's missing. I don't have any more details yet."

Anna felt sure it wouldn't take her friend long to have the whole story.

"It's probably gang-related, you know what the Gallaghers are like," Lauren said confidently.

Unfortunately, Anna *did* know what the Gallaghers were like. From her experience typing up and collating reports, a large number of the criminal dealings in the city were somehow linked to them.

Lauren brightened as she moved on to another topic.

"Have you seen the new guy from the Special Detective Unit? His name's Myles Henderson. He's down here from Dublin, doing some technical stuff for the conference. He's *gorgeous*!"

"Aren't you taken?" Anna asked, looking pointedly at the diamond that sparkled on Lauren's ring finger.

"A girl can still look!"

Anna erupted into laughter. Lauren was always so much fun to be around.

As they made their way back to their desks, they passed Myles at his own, typing furiously, lost in the details of his report. Anna remembered his warm smile of support that morning. Lauren elbowed her in the ribs as they passed him, and Anna laughed and nudged her back.

"You're such a child," she muttered, laughing.

Her laughter quickly dried on her lips as she approached her desk, realising that Detective Superintendent Doherty was standing there. Beside him was Detective Sergeant Elise Taylor from the Protective Service Unit. Doherty was Elise Taylor's supervisor.

Elise cut a smart figure, in a black trouser suit and sharp blonde bob. She appeared tired though; her eyes were red-rimmed, and her face pale. She had the appearance of a woman who hadn't slept in a long time.

Anna couldn't help but overhear their conversation as she sat down at her desk.

"The property is rented by a woman named Kate Crowley. It looks like a brawl went down at the house. We've checked all the hospitals but there's no sign of any injured woman matching her description."

"Right," Doherty said with obvious disinterest.

The hairs on the back of Anna's neck stood up and her hands froze over the keyboard. *Kate Crowley*. She knew that name. It was the name of one of her childhood friends. If it was the same Kate Crowley, she and Anna had been in school together, losing touch when Kate's parents separated, and she and her sister moved to Dublin with their mother. However, the name was a very common one in Cork.

"We need to move fast on this," Elise went on. "Gallagher's own house looks like it's been ransacked. I'm waiting on the forensics report but that'll take some time – there's a lot to go through."

"Sure." Doherty pulled a small plastic tub from his trouser pocket and shook out a tiny white pill. He ground it between his teeth.

"I've also heard John Gallagher is missing. I think it's all connected."

Detective Sergeant Taylor finally had her supervisor's attention.

Doherty's eyes bulged slightly.

"Tom Gallagher's son?"

"Yes, his older son."

"Well, maybe this Kate girl killed them both?" Doherty sounded smug as he said, "Kill two birds with one stone, eh?"

Anna looked up and supressed a smile as she watched Elise's face darken in exasperation. She clearly was in no mood for Doherty and his clichés. Doherty sounded bored; the gravitas of the situation was lost on him.

Elise pressed on. "One of my contacts informed me a woman has set up a meeting in a bar in the city with a man named Nick – he's the manager there. She's trying to buy a passport apparently. I'd like to station some men inside and bring her in for questioning. Not to mention catch the sale of illegal documents in the process. Perhaps it's our shooter."

"Why would she be looking for a passport?" Doherty sounded sceptical.

"Perhaps it's because she just killed a man and needs a way out of the country!" DS Taylor sounded as though she was fighting to remain cool. She sighed audibly. "We have a chance to find out, if you give the go-ahead to bring her in. If it is our main suspect, she is mixed up with the victim's family – her sister is David Gallagher's partner, and mother to his children. Gallagher was abusive."

Frank Doherty exhaled loudly at this. He did recall some details of reports to that effect.

"There's something else," she went on. "We received an intel bulletin Tuesday morning from the Federal Police in Germany. They have been tracking international movements of suspected criminals, including a family called the Meiers. They were observed boarding a flight to Cork Airport. It might have nothing to do with what's happening with the Gallaghers, but with everything going on –"

"Here she is, our very own Nancy Drew!" Doherty had a habit of cutting people off mid-sentence when he was bored. He snatched the file from Taylor's hand and turned to Anna with a sneer. "Type this up like a good girl."

He flung the file onto her desk where it landed with a thump, toppling the stack of files to Anna's left. Then he was gone, his large frame thundering through the open-plan room.

Elise watched her supervisor go, her face twisted in surprise and anger. She turned to Anna.

31

"Don't let him get to you," she said tightly, helping Anna to gather up the files.

"It's hard not to!" Anna replied, aware her face was bright red. She wasn't embarrassed, she was angry. "I'm twenty-six years old! I've a BA in mathematics and a post-graduate diploma in statistics. And that's twice today he's called me 'a good girl'!" She slammed the last of the files on top of the pile Elise had helped to create, almost toppling it again.

Anna met the Detective Sergeant's eyes and smiled apologetically.

"I need these notes typed up and brought to the incident room when you're done." Elise eyed the pile of reports on the table. "It takes priority."

Anna nodded. She had worked with Elise on and off over the last few years. The detective was normally polite, if somewhat aloof.

Elise ran a hand over her tired face and headed for the stairs.

Anna sat down again, only too eager to get into the heart of this story. This was the shooting Lauren had told her about earlier. The opening set of notes appeared to be the minutes of a meeting held between Elise Taylor, Doherty, Janet McCarthy, and several other detectives Anna was familiar with. She began to read, her horror growing with every sentence.

At a time to be determined, but sometime late afternoon the day before, as estimated by the State Pathologist, a man identified as David Gallagher was killed in a house in the city suburbs, in Brook Valley near Wilton. It appeared he had died from a single gunshot wound to the neck. There were signs of a struggle in the house – furniture was knocked over, glasses were smashed, and there was blood on several surfaces. There was also a packed suitcase and passport belonging to a woman named Kate Crowley in the hallway. The house, a three-bedroom semi-detached in a large housing estate, was rented by the same woman. Neighbours told detectives Kate had lived there for the last three years – the landlord was being contacted to confirm. The dwelling was empty when the Gardaí arrived, responding to a call from a neighbour after hearing what sounded like a gunshot. It seemed to Anna that Kate was unlucky enough to live next door to a "nosy-neighbour" type, Steven Smith. The pensioner seemed to have nothing better to do than keep tabs on the comings and goings of his neighbours – he told Gardaí that Kate had left the house before 8 a.m. but had returned just before lunchtime. Shortly afterwards, a car pulled into the drive behind her Volvo, and a man exited. That car was confirmed as registered to David Gallagher. Both cars remained in the driveway.

Anna sighed loudly, her heart pounding in her ears. The Gardaí assigned to the case had already covered a lot of ground, and it looked very bad for Kate Crowley. She was missing, and there was a dead man in her house. Possibly, a *murdered* man.

The next page detailed what information was available or known on her. Anna read with fevered interest, praying it was not the Kate Crowley she remembered. However, soon her worst fears were confirmed. It *was* her old friend. Kate Crowley had a twin sister Natalie – now Anna had no doubt it was her. The twins had been born and raised in Cork, before moving to Dublin while they were in their teens. Kate worked as a graphic designer for City Graphics. She was good at her job, respected, but had left her office abruptly the morning of the shooting, without a word to anyone. A colleague had been interviewed and stated that she had been at her desk early that morning but had taken a phone call and left unexpectedly before lunchtime. She had not returned.

Anna remembered the Crowley sisters. They had attended the same primary school as she had, St. Catherine's in Kinsale. The girls had all been close friends, until going their separate ways.

Anna read on with a growing sense of panic. There was a report from the Protective Service Unit, in which Detective Sergeant Elise Taylor served. It listed twenty dates over three years on which Kate Crowley had filed a complaint of assault against David Gallagher. But Gallagher hadn't assaulted her – Natalie was the victim of the attacks. Anna winced. She remembered Natalie. She had been shy, quieter than her outgoing sister. It pained Anna to think of her being abused. Reading on, she realised Natalie Crowley and David Gallagher were known to be in a relationship and had twin daughters together. She couldn't imagine how mild-mannered Natalie Crowley had got mixed up with a criminal like David Gallagher.

It appeared no charges were ever filed against David Gallagher for domestic abuse. Anna knew it was tough to intervene in these cases without the co-operation of the victim. She rubbed her forehead with a growing sense of foreboding, dreading to turn the pages and keep reading, but unable to stop.

The following page detailed a transcript of an incident involving David Gallagher and Natalie Crowley. Gallagher had assaulted Natalie at their home in the city, and taken their two children, toddlers Rhea and Rachel. He had driven them to the quays by the Marina in the city, then he rang Natalie and claimed he was planning to drive into the water. Kate, who was by now with Natalie at her home, called the Gardaí, who had quickly averted the impending crisis. It was noted that David Gallagher appeared heavily intoxicated at the scene. He was detained but released the following morning for a psychiatric assessment. Anna had seen this before – a Gallagher wriggling out of trouble thanks to their solicitors making demands.

Anna was growing extremely uncomfortable, the seriousness of the situation dawning on her, weighing her down. She realised that what she had just read was a major problem for Kate; it was motive to want David Gallagher dead.

She read on. There was a one-paragraph summary of David Gallagher and his family, headed by Tom Gallagher. It contained no new information for Anna – she had typed up many reports relating to the Gallaghers.

For some time, the Gallagher family had been gaining ground in the city. Tom Gallagher and his two sons had been expanding their territory over the last few years. The Gallaghers had been a growing problem for the Gardaí in Lee Street. They were suspected of trading in weapons, drugs, liquor – whatever was profitable on any given day. Anna knew the Gardaí had achieved a few minor convictions against some of Gallagher's associates but never any of the Gallaghers or their inner circle. No convictions had yet been made against the immediate members of the family. Only Tom Gallagher's niece had been caught with irrefutable evidence and she was serving a five-year prison sentence in Limerick prison. From what Anna had heard in the office, she wouldn't be getting out early on account of good behaviour.

Anna was aware the Gallaghers owned a number of bars and clubs in Cork, and they controlled the family business from Tom Gallagher's offices spread around the venues. He kept his family life separate as much as possible, secluding his wife in their house in South Rise, overlooking the city. The Gallaghers had no competition that Anna could think of. Anyone that looked to be a threat to them had already, and sometimes suddenly, left the area. The Lee Street Gardaí had cleaned blood from the streets many times after David Gallagher and his brother John. They dealt harshly with people that owed them money or people they thought were trying to invade their territory. The Gallaghers took up a vast amount of Garda resources. But they were armed with expensive solicitors. So far, they had proved organised, very clever and one step ahead of the Gardaí. Anna felt sorry for Kate Crowley – through her sister, she had found herself mixed up in a nightmare.

One sentence, highlighted in yellow at the bottom of the page, caused Anna to draw her breath in sharply – John Gallagher was missing. His car had been found by the quays at the Marina. His wallet and phone were inside. It was not known when the car had been abandoned. No-one believed he had entered the river, but the question remained – where was John Gallagher? Was this all connected? The source of this intelligence was listed as "intel" only – there had been no missing person's report, which didn't surprise Anna. The Gallaghers didn't turn to the Gardaí to solve their problems.

Anna could only imagine Tom Gallagher's fury. One son was shot dead. Another was missing. There could be war on the city streets if this was not resolved soon.

She read on. The next page detailed that members of a suspected criminal gang had entered Cork from Germany. She knew that intelligence bulletins were often received relating to movement of known or suspected criminals. The German Federal Police had supplied a flight number and time – Tuesday morning. Did this gang have anything to do with the frightening situation unfolding? She continued reading, feeling queasy, desperate to reach the end of the scrawled notes.

A printout from a separate report was stapled to the page, offering details on the Meier brothers from Munich. There were four brothers in the Meier family, but photographs were only included for two of them – Tobias and Leon, both in their thirties. There had been minor convictions against them for drug offences but, much like the Gallaghers, they remained on the edge of law-enforcement, never getting caught in the act. Their suspected enterprises included selling and distributing drugs, but they also appeared to have connections to other gangs in Russia and the Ukraine. They were being monitored, but so far had done nothing to raise the level of concern. The note finished by stating there was no known connection between the Meiers and the Gallaghers, but the timing of their arrival coincided with David Gallagher's death and John Gallagher's disappearance. All avenues were to be investigated, particularly in light of the political conference in the city later in the week.

The final paragraph of Elise's notes said that she had received a call from an informer just this afternoon. A woman who might be Kate Crowley had set up a meeting in a club in the city, the Mad Hatter, for Saturday night. The woman was reportedly seeking to buy a false passport. Elise was requesting undercover detectives be stationed inside.

How was Kate wrapped up in the shooting of David Gallagher – was it self-defence? He had a history of violence against her sister. Maybe he had attacked Kate? And if that was the case, why didn't she hand herself in to the Gardaí? Obviously, she was trying to leave the city – attempting to buy a fake passport was a crime in itself. And where were Natalie and her two children?

Anna felt the pull of a migraine as she tried to comprehend all that she had read, and all the questions that yet remained to be answered. As she began to type up the job book, detailing the tasks to be completed in the case, her hands shook. She could fully appreciate the tension in the office in the last twenty-four hours. The political conference was fast approaching; Cork city would host over a dozen heads of state. There were a number of unsolved sexual assaults in the city, the attacker striking at random every few months. A major criminal had been shot dead, and his brother was missing. Now, a suspected criminal gang from Germany had flown in. And Anna was at the heart of it all, typing up notes and memos, absorbing all the chilling details. She felt genuinely scared for her old friends Kate and Natalie – they had got themselves mixed up in something that could get them killed.

As Anna typed, she became aware her breath was coming short and shallow and she forced herself to stop. Her Taekwon-Do training took over. She sat into the back of her seat, the weight of it against her back a grounding force. She took a series of deep breaths in through her nose, and out through her mouth. Slowly she felt her nerves relax and her shoulders loosen. With steadier hands, she was able to continue.

When Anna brought the completed job book to the incident room, she was rooted to the spot by the large photograph on the wall of Kate Crowley.

She was the same age as Anna, twenty-six. She hadn't changed much, physically. She still had the same long, wild, red hair and bright-green eyes. Beside her photograph there was another – a dark-haired man, thickset, in his early thirties. David Gallagher. Anna looked at Gallagher's face on the screen. To her he looked like a normal guy; clearly, from the notes she had just typed up, he was capable of terrible things. She imagined him now, dead on a slab, being attended to by the State Pathologist, and shivered.

4

"It's very simple," there was a pause, a sigh, an expression of exasperation. "I want what was agreed. The item is of great importance. Our employer negotiated a fair price with your brother, and we have come to collect. No lies, no excuses."

John Gallagher, tied to a wooden chair by his wrists and ankles, was long past panic. He had been beaten for hours now. Days maybe; time rolled into itself and he couldn't tell. He thought it was Thursday but couldn't be sure. He had been bundled into a car yesterday, or maybe the day before that? They had driven for hours, or so it seemed to him, before arriving at what appeared to be an old farmhouse. It terrified him that they didn't care to use a blindfold and didn't seem bothered that he could identify them. What terrified him more was their accents – eastern European perhaps. Possibly German.

They had hauled him into a room, tied him to a chair, and the interrogation began. He could no longer open his left eye, and his jaw ached. He was spent.

There were four of them, and they wanted their

merchandise. John was certain he was being beaten to a pulp by the Meier brothers.

John Gallagher and his family had been holding goods for the Meier brothers for a few years – weapons, drugs, cash – anything that needed hiding for a while before it was moved across the Irish Sea or back into mainland Europe. Lately, they had begun to deal in stolen diamonds – as far as John was concerned, it was none of his business as long as they paid their holding fee. The Gallaghers didn't ask questions, so long as the money kept coming. None of the Gallaghers had ever met the Meiers in person and, as far as John was aware, the Meier brothers had never set foot in Cork city before, which suited him fine. They were known sadists, brutally violent when necessary – but they paid well, and Tom Gallagher, head of the family, had always kept them sweet. Until now.

John lifted his head and registered the man's words: *"Our employer negotiated a fair price with your brother."*

David had been put in charge of dealings with the Meiers recently. But the price for holding their goods had been set by their father at the start of the arrangement – had David tried to renegotiate the deal?

Fist hit cheekbone with a sickening thud.

John coughed and fought to control his voice. "I told you!" he rasped. "David was killed by Kate Crowley – he told me she stole from him, from us. She will have what you're looking for!" He coughed again, spitting out the blood that was pooling inside his mouth. His body sagged against the restraints; he was utterly exhausted. He stared at the ground, his head bent, his blood a steady drip onto the floor.

"My employer has already paid half. I cannot return to him empty-handed. Do you understand?"

John heard a tremor in the man's voice, a pulse of fear

that added menace to the words. He didn't raise his head –
he had no energy left. And he hadn't the faintest idea what
the man was talking about.

His attacker sighed again and turned to his brother,
standing a short distance away, observing the beating with
folded arms.

"Leon," he said, in a voice so soft it terrified John, "bring
the tools. Tomorrow, Mama Gallagher will get a present
from her son."

5

Anna shuddered as she made her way to the staff car park at half past four. She walked hurriedly, hunching slightly against the wind which stung her cheeks. It was late November and brutally cold; despite her coat and scarf she was freezing, assailed by the bite of the chill air.

The day had exhausted her. From examining the sexual-assault cases, her encounter with Doherty, and typing up the notes on the shooting, she was emotionally and physically drained.

She found the fact that a photograph of her old friend's face was posted onto the wall in the incident room as a person of interest in a shooting very hard to believe. She felt terrified for Kate – she couldn't stop thinking about her. If she was guilty, if she had shot David Gallagher, Anna knew Tom Gallagher would show her little mercy if he found her. She hoped it was her colleagues who found her first.

From the notes she had typed up, it seemed clear to her that self-defence was the only probable explanation. David Gallagher was a violent man – she knew that. He had been an abusive partner to Natalie Crowley. She wondered where she was. There had been nothing in Elise Taylor's handwritten notes about Natalie's whereabouts. Was she still alive? Where were her children? The weight of the situation hung over Anna like a dark cloud.

As she sat into her car, her mobile phone vibrated in her pocket as a text message came through – her brother Alex, reminding her about dinner with his family tonight and telling her to come by any time that suited her.

Chloe can't wait to show you her new pet, he had typed, finishing the text with a picture of what Anna assumed was either a guinea pig or a hamster. She smiled. The thought of her brother's cooking and her niece's infectious laugh was enough to brighten her mood and quell her growing worry.

Every Thursday evening after Anna taught Taekwon-Do Tykes in her local community hall, she always called to her brother and his family. Alex lived in the centre of Kinsale, in a new development, and Anna loved having him nearby. She and her brother were close, and she adored his wife and daughter.

But tonight, she had something she wanted to speak to him about – something that she had wanted to bring up for a while. She reached for a business card that she had put in her glove compartment a few months ago. It bore the details of *K.R. Lane, Private Investigator*.

Anna had met Kristian Lane for coffee in March, over six months ago. He had promised answers and had said that he had contacts in the Gardaí who could help him find out the truth about what had happened almost ten years ago. He was expensive, billing by the hour, but Anna figured it would be worth it. Yet she still hadn't booked his services. Perhaps she was scared of what he might find out? And she didn't know how to explain to Alex that she wanted to hire a private investigator to find out what had happened to their parents the night they had disappeared. The anniversary of their car accident and mysterious disappearance was fast approaching. With a growing sense of urgency, Anna wanted answers.

The city of Cork was the one of the largest in Ireland and considered by its inhabitants to be the country's real capital. Anna had lived there all her life and had no plans to leave. She loved everything about the city; the bustle of its streets always thrilled her. Her semi-detached house, her childhood home, was in an estate over forty minutes' drive from the city, along the Wild Atlantic route favoured by tourists. Every time she ventured into the city she felt like a tourist herself, relishing the electric buzz that flowed through the lively streets. She shopped for fresh produce in the English Market often after work, wandering slowly among the crowds. She had a full and happy life in Cork, and she never wanted to leave. She knew that was in part because she hoped her parents would return one day, and she wanted to be there if they did.

This evening, as Anna changed from her work trousers and blouse into her white pants and top, she felt the weight of the day lift from her shoulders. She and Jason greeted the children warmly as they filed into the hall, eager for today's lesson. Jason, her father's friend, was like an uncle to her. Even though he was her teacher, he was always happy to let her lead the way in their weekly classes with the kids. The youngsters loved Anna and viewed her as a "big sister". It offered her a welcome feeling of belonging to something bigger than just her and Alex's small family. The sound of their shrieks and laughter brought a smile to her face. She would soon gain control of the room – she always did. Within minutes, as the children stood in lined formation in front of her, chanting the five tenets of Taekwon-Do in their sing-song voices, she was fully relaxed – Detective Superintendent Doherty, the sexual assault cases and Kate's predicament briefly forgotten.

"*Courtesy, Integrity, Perseverance, Self-Control, Indomitable Spirit!*" she chanted with the children, smiling as the younger ones attempted to pronounce the long words.

As always, during these classes, Anna remembered her father. She recalled chanting these words with him in the garden of their home as he taught her and Alex defensive moves and encouraged them to think through the five tenets and to understand what they stood for. His words echoed in her mind. He had tried to instil in them that showing fortitude – courage in the face of danger or adversity – was a valuable attribute.

"*Never be a victim.*" His words were never far from Anna's mind. "*Protect those who cannot protect themselves.*"

The hour was always over too quickly for her. As she released the children one by one to their parents and said goodnight to Jason, she smiled as she thought of her niece Chloe. She couldn't wait for the cuddles the little girl always offered in abundance – she needed them today.

Alex greeted Anna with a hug, the aroma of his cooking enveloping her as he pulled her close. Alex Clarke was very like his younger sister physically. He was six foot tall but he shared her light-blonde hair and brown eyes. Apart from their father's eyes, they both resembled their mother.

When Anna was sixteen years old and Alex twenty-five, their world had been shattered by the disappearance of their parents. Michael and Helen Clarke's car had been found on the motorway to Dublin. There was no sign of them – and never any sign of them after – they had literally disappeared into thin air. All that remained was an obvious car accident – a badly mangled vehicle abandoned at the side of the road, with no evidence of where the occupants had got to.

Ten years later, Anna still could not understand how two adults could just vanish and leave no trace behind. Someone must know where they were – someone must be keeping this secret. Her parents' disappearance had been devastating for her, and in her eyes Alex had rebuilt her existence, piece by piece. Where any other twenty-five-year-old might have been overwhelmed by the responsibility, Alex had dedicated himself to raising his little sister. He finished his accountancy exams by night while working by day, somehow managing to help with homework and attend school plays and soccer games. He had done his best to give his sister a normal life after such a traumatic event. Anna felt an intense bond with him.

Four-year-old Chloe leapt into Anna's arms, squealing "*Anna, Anna!*", and sat at her feet in the kitchen, playing with her new pet hamster as Alex cooked and chatted.

Alex ran his own accountancy firm from home, which allowed him to take care of Chloe after playschool while his wife worked at a stockbroker's in the city. Samantha was there now, working overtime, so it was just the three of them for dinner.

Alex was filling Anna in on how busy he was at work, and Anna was happy to let him talk, to be distracted from her own job.

"It's never been more hectic. I've had to invest in a new software system, but it should take some of the pressure off. I have to keep up with the times! But it's worth it – the new system will literally take hours off my workday."

"That sounds great!" Anna said enthusiastically, twirling Chloe's light-blonde pigtails between her fingers.

"Did you hear about the shooting in Brook Valley?"

Alex asked, then smiled. "Of course you did. And don't worry, I'm not looking for any inside information!"

Anna laughed at her brother. Alex was always curious about her job, about the information she was privy to overhearing. Anna had never been tempted to gossip – even though she knew she could trust her brother. She had signed a confidentiality agreement at work and had never broken it. It wasn't in her nature to break trust – teaching her students the value of self-control on a weekly basis kept her too grounded for that.

The three of them moved to the dining table, Alex and Anna carrying their plates and tall glasses of milk; Chloe insisted on carrying her own, making Anna smile. Her niece was growing up fast!

Anna was hungry after work and teaching. She loved the flavour and heartiness of Alex's cooking – he was a good cook, and it reminded her of when it was just the two of them.

"This lasagne is lovely, Alex. And it's so nice to be served, instead of cooking for one."

Living alone, Anna never bothered with the effort Alex went to when he cooked. She was happy with ready meals and salads.

She turned to Chloe. "So, tell me, what are we calling your furry new friend?"

Chloe beamed, relishing the chance to take centre stage. Between mouthfuls of food, she debated name after name, giggling and bouncing in her seat.

Later, after reading far too many bedtime stories, Anna tucked Chloe into bed, then joined her brother for coffee in the living room downstairs. Alex had lit the fire; it crackled in the hearth and warmed the room. They sat in opposite armchairs and the conversation flowed easily between them, as it always had.

Anna cleared her throat and took a deep breath. It was just her and Alex – Samantha was still working. This was her chance.

"Alex, I've been meaning to talk to you about Mum and Dad."

Alex, stoking the flames at the hearth, looked up sharply.

"What about them?"

"Well … it's almost ten years since they disappeared. And nothing has changed. We've never moved forward. I want to give it one last shot to find answers. What do you think?"

"OK." Alex nodded slowly.

He was a measured guy, and Anna could tell he was thinking through her words.

"What do you have in mind?" he said then.

"I asked a few questions at work and found out that their disappearance will not be revisited unless a new angle is discovered, something that was missed in the initial investigation. We could do another public appeal, to try to jog people's memory, but it's a long shot. So … I want to hire a private investigator to go over the whole thing. To look over all the files, all the notes we have."

Alex swallowed hard; it was loud in the quiet room. Anna sat forward and put her hand on his arm. His eyes were filled with the anguish she still felt.

"Why do you want to go down this road, Anna? I don't understand."

"Don't you ever lie awake at night and run through all the possibilities, Alex? What if they are alive?"

"Anna," he began softly, his eyes boring into hers, "you must know there's no chance of them being alive. Every angle was covered. Every possible theory was exhausted. I'm sorry but you must accept it – they are dead. Hiring a private investigator will only prove that fact!" His tone was earnest, his eyes pleading with his sister to understand. "The detectives that worked Mum and Dad's case did their best. Sometimes, a case goes cold and there are just no leads. You have to let it go!"

Anna met his eyes and the look she saw there made her want to cry. Alex's heartbreak emanated from them. He knew her well, knew she continued to be plagued by anger and sadness that her parents had vanished, and no bodies or evidence was ever found. She knew too that Alex had lost exactly what she had, and now she was talking about opening up the wound and going through it all again. She felt a rush of guilt – but she just had to give it one more try.

For Anna, there was also the matter of their family home. She had lived there all her life and had no intention of leaving. But if their parents *were* dead, which she knew in her heart was the most likely scenario, then the house was half Alex's. He had never mentioned it and had never sought to liquidate his share of the house. Anna knew it was worth a lot, especially with it being on the Wild Atlantic Way. Although it was relatively small it was in a beautiful coastal location with a decent-sized back garden, close enough to the city to be accessible, but far enough away to be secluded. Anna had known a happy childhood there. They had been content before the accident. Now Alex had a family of his own … Anna knew the time had come to decide the future of their parents' assets once and for all.

After their disappearance everything had changed. Their father's friend from London, a man they had never known, had turned up unexpectedly. He had given them details of a trust fund their parents had set up. It contained almost five-hundred thousand euro. Alex had used his half to buy a house with Samantha. Anna still had most of hers in the bank.

Anna sat back in the armchair, feeling the familiar frustration she felt whenever this subject was raised. Alex never wanted to discuss it. He had chosen to move on. And she had reached a point in her life where she wanted to move on too, but she just couldn't accept the obvious truth. She longed for her parents to be alive and safe somewhere, but that scenario made no sense to her. Why would they leave her and Alex and start a new life somewhere else? So, she knew she must accept the most likely outcome that they were dead, their bodies never recovered. But she needed to feel she had exhausted every angle.

"Alex, believe me, it's been ten years – I too want to put this behind me. And I'm willing to move on. The house is half yours."

"I've told you, there's no need to –"

"We should move things forward legally and end this once and for all. And I'm willing to do that. But I *need* to feel I tried everything first. The investigator is good at what he does; he's a retired detective and will go over the case with fresh eyes. Will you support me on this?"

Alex stared into the dancing flames of the fire for what felt like a long time.

"I will." He finally looked up. "But you have to promise me you will accept what he finds."

Anna smiled broadly. "No problem!" She was hugely relieved. With Alex on board, she felt sure she could handle whatever Kristian Lane might uncover.

Eventually, after ten o'clock, Samantha returned. She looked weary from her long day. She hugged Anna, apologising for her lateness. Alex kissed his wife's cheek and went to the kitchen to heat up the meal she had missed.

Samantha kicked off her shoes and dropped onto the sofa. "Oh Anna, I've missed the whole evening with you, I'm sorry! God, I'm worn out! But don't tell your brother –

he thinks I'm working too much as it is!" She massaged one foot, then the other.

"Alex mentioned you have a new boss, and that he's very demanding."

Instantly she noticed the slightest shift in Samantha's mood – a tiny intake of breath, rapid blinking and a stiffening of her shoulders.

Samantha picked imaginary lint from her trousers as she answered, "Yeah, he's a nightmare! But we're working on a new client portfolio at the moment and things should ease up soon."

Clearly, Samantha's overtime was causing some tension between her and Alex. Anna decided not to mention the topic again.

Samantha smiled gratefully at her husband when he appeared with a glass of wine and a hot plate of food. Anna refused to join Alex in a glass of wine, opting instead for tea.

The rest of Anna's evening passed in easy conversation. Time slipped by and, before she knew it, it was almost midnight. She excused herself and made her way home. She lived only a ten-minute drive away and was soon parked in the driveway of her small semi-detached house.

As she sat in the driver's seat, she remembered the files on her desk, the burglary and the sexual-assault cases, as well as the shooting of David Gallagher. She had managed to forget the awful revelations of her day earlier; now, alone in the dark, they came rushing back. She felt a momentary sliver of panic – she felt vulnerable. She reminded herself she was a black belt in Taekwon-Do, and took a deep steadying breath, before pushing open the car door, alert to every sound and shadow.

The housing estate was quiet. An owl hooted in the distance; it was the only sound Anna could hear apart from her own quick breathing. The night was calm, the moon full and the sky bright with stars. The sound of her car door closing shattered the stillness and she winced.

She pushed the key into the lock in her front door and stepped inside. Immediately she felt the hairs stand up on the back of her neck as an icy chill crept down her spine. The house was freezing cold. She frowned, wondering if her heating system was broken. She reached out to drop her keys into the bowl on her hall table and jumped at the unfamiliar sound as they clattered loudly onto the wooden table surface. The bowl on her hall table had been moved – while she normally reached out from her first step inside the house and dropped her keys directly into the blue porcelain bowl, it was now further away, in the centre of the little table.

With a shaking hand, Anna felt along the wall and flicked on the lights. The hall was empty, the house quiet. She willed herself to walk through to the living room. Fully alert, she turned on lights as she went, shivering slightly in the unfamiliar cold of her house. In the living room, her eyes scanned the small space. Her bookshelves were so fully packed that it would have been impossible to tell if anything had been taken. Her father's old record player looked untouched, her mother's collection of Bach's cello classics beside it unmoved. Maybe she had imagined that the porcelain bowl was in a different position, she chided herself. And maybe the heating *was* broken.

But as she made her way into the kitchen, and shivered in the icy-cold draught, her breath caught in her throat. The sliding patio door to her kitchen was slightly ajar, the thin white curtain billowing softly.

Cursing, she moved quickly to close and lock it. That door had always been stiff and difficult to properly close.

Anna stood in her kitchen and breathed deeply, trying to

calm herself. She was trying to remember if she had opened her back door that morning before work. But it was late, and she was very tired – she just couldn't be sure.

There were only two explanations. Either she had stepped outside for some reason this morning and had forgotten to close and lock the sliding door afterwards. Or someone had been in her house.

6

Friday

Mae O'Brien had wanted for nothing since the day she married Tom Gallagher. Her mother had worried he was too rough, and from the wrong side of town. But Tom had promised her the world, and Mae had seen him keep his word. A plush house in the fanciest part of the city, fast cars, real fur coats – she had it all. But, lately, things had begun to fall apart in Mae's world. Life was spiralling out of control, and if there was one thing Tom Gallagher normally had in abundance, it was control. Drugs, cigarettes, street women – they all fell under Tom's iron fist in this town. This was *his* city. So how had he lost control so spectacularly?

First that bitch Kate Crowley had shot and killed their beloved youngest, David. Mae knew it was her – she had resented David for years – they had never got along. David was found dead in her house. To Mae, there could be no other suspect.

Mae felt raw pain, a pain that wounded her physically and cut her to the bone. She was barely managing to lift her head from the pillow to eat.

Tom had vowed to see her through it. For the last two days he had been sustaining Mae, and probably himself, with promises of vengeance. He had assured her he would let her pull the trigger when they had Kate at their mercy. But that hadn't happened yet. She had disappeared. Mae had never wanted anything more than to get her hands around Kate Crowley's throat.

Tom had put the word out – and put a price-tag on Kate's head. Thirty thousand euro for her body – fifty thousand to whoever brought her to the house alive. It was a lot of money, but Mae would have paid ten times that to see her broken and bloody on their tiled floor. The thought gave Mae comfort; it was something to focus on.

Now, however, there was another problem – John was missing. The same day David was shot, John had disappeared. He was Tom's second-in-command, his most trusted confidant; John was truly his father's right-hand man. Tall and broad like his father, John would take over the family enterprise one day, see out any pitiful competition and make it an even bigger success. Mae was certain of that. But where was he?

On Wednesday, John had telephoned his father to deliver grim news – a Garda source of John's had contacted him to tell him that a man had been shot dead in Kate Crowley's house, and it looked like David. The Garda had apologised that he didn't have more concrete information, but John had heard enough. He told his father he was on his way to the house, and he would be in touch.

Except that he wasn't in touch. His car had been found by the docks two hours later, seemingly abandoned. His keys, mobile phone and wallet were inside, the whole lot untouched, which in itself wasn't surprising – no one in this city would dare to rob a Gallagher. Mae's head hurt from trying to figure out if this was all connected – and how. She felt trapped in someone's idea of a bad joke. They should be planning to bury one son but couldn't move forward until the other was found. It was a living nightmare.

By Friday morning Tom was increasingly agitated, pacing, shouting, demanding results from his street army. He was holed up in his office at the back of the house with Murray, his trusted associate. Word on the street was that the Meiers were in town – this was a first. Tom knew David was holding stolen goods for them but couldn't fathom why they had flown into the city. If they wanted to negotiate new terms or arrange delivery of their goods, they could have gone through the usual channels. There had been an arrangement between the two families for a couple of years now; there had never been the need to meet face to face before. Tom had heard they had flown in on Tuesday, and he wondered if David had somehow fucked up. Were the Meiers responsible for John's disappearance? The thought niggled at him – why were they in Cork?

John's disappearance *did* worry him – it was so out of character. After David was shot, Tom had sent Murray to search David's house before the Gardaí got there, to remove anything incriminating. So far they had found nothing. Not a single thing. John still lived at home, and a search of his room had also yielded the same result. Nothing. Which in itself was a problem. David should have thousands of euro hidden for the Meier gang, and diamonds from a recent robbery. Although Tom had handed control for that element of his business to David, he still liked to know the ins and outs of their dealings. So where was the gear?

Someone had robbed them. Tom had no doubt it was Kate Crowley. She'd had the opportunity, and she had shot David for good measure.

Tom had no time to grieve for his son. His hands had developed a tremor; it was an agitation he knew would be healed when he had them around Kate's throat. In the meantime, he was growing tired of waiting for John to turn up – where the hell was he? John was responsible and steady compared to hot-headed David – if he said he would be in touch, then he would.

When Mae signed for a package, she had a crystal tumbler in her hand, a soothing whiskey helping to numb the pain and sickening worry. It was her customary balm these days, no matter what hour of the day.

Tom, pacing with agitation in his office, heard the smash as the crystal hit the tiles, before he heard Mae's screams. He and Murray rushed to her. She was at the large dining table, a blood-soaked handkerchief in her hand, holding what was undoubtedly a severed finger. It was a ring-finger, and on it sat a solid gold band with a perfect white diamond set in the centre, twinkling in the light – a gift from John's parents to celebrate his thirtieth birthday. It was his finger. Mae screamed and retched, before sinking down onto the floor.

Tom ran to her, cradling her in his arms.

"I promise you I'll bring him home!" he said, as rage burned inside him.

He shouted to Murray, who was hovering in the doorway.

"Assemble the men, all of them. Find the Meiers. And find the bitch that killed my son. Tell the men outside her house to keep their eyes open. And search for any friends, boyfriends, anything. We tear this city apart, do you hear me? Tear it apart!"

7

It was almost nine-thirty in the morning before Anna arrived into the city. She was in a foul mood. She had tossed and turned all night, barely able to sleep. The details of the day before had replayed in her mind like a horror film on repeat, the faces of the main characters rotating in and out of focus: Kate Crowley, David Gallagher, images from Google Maps relating to the sexual-assault cases … added to the fact she was worried someone had been in the house. Anna had scarcely managed a full hour of sleep.

When she had finally drifted into an uneasy, fitful doze, she had slept through her alarm, leaving her no time to head to the gym that morning. She had looked forward to expelling her tension into the punchbag and pushing her body, lap after lap, in the pool after. Now, she would have to carry her agitation with her into the day, an ominous thought in itself.

After doublechecking that the back door was firmly shut and locked, Anna had set out for work at her usual time, but the roads had been covered in a treacherous sheet of ice.

It had taken her double the usual length of time to get to work. She thought back to the bright moon of the night before, and the cloudless, star-filled sky. She should have anticipated the weather this morning; at this time of year, without cloud cover, it was bound to be icy in the mornings.

For most of her journey she had struggled to maintain control as her car slid on black ice. And when she had finally arrived at work, her shoulders and jaw tense, to find the carpark full, she had almost screamed.

Having finally parked in the nearby city-centre car park, for which she would have to pay the daily rate, she checked the time. For the first time in three years she was almost late for work. Screw it, she thought. She needed caffeine.

So instead of turning right and making her way to the office, Anna crossed the street and walked carefully to Victus, her favourite café. The footpath was as treacherous as the roads, and she almost lost her footing twice. She inched along, cursing herself for not taking a sick day.

The warmth of the coffee shop was a welcome balm, the familiar clink of china mugs and the aroma of roasting coffee beans soothing her frazzled nerves. It was busy, but she spotted a small table at the back. She smiled at Louisa, the barista. Anna was here every morning for her latte and croissant, and they had struck up a friendship. Louisa returned her smile and offered a thumbs-up; Anna's usual order was on its way.

Anna took a seat, unwinding her huge scarf and pulling off her woollen hat.

"Mind if I join you?"

Startled, Anna looked up into the spectacled brown eyes of Myles Henderson. She was momentarily speechless and motioned for him to sit down. He had a large coffee-to-go in one hand.

"I was getting a takeaway when I spotted you." Myles

held out one hand across the table. "Myles Henderson – we were introduced yesterday. It's Anna, isn't it?"

Anna shook his hand and smiled.

Myles was tall – she guessed six foot, the same as her brother. His unruly black curls stood out. He was wearing a thick black overcoat over black drainpipe jeans – he looked to Anna the antithesis of a traditional detective. He certainly looked cool compared to the detectives in Lee Street station.

"You're from the Detective Unit in Dublin, aren't you?"

Louisa had delivered Anna's coffee and croissant, and she sipped at the frothy latte, savouring its heat.

"That's me!" Myles smiled.

His enthusiasm and good humour were infectious, and in stark contrast to Anna's sleep-deprived mood. She felt herself brightening.

"Are you enjoying it here in Cork?"

Myles nodded. His smile really was striking – dazzling white against sallow skin.

"I am! I'm just here until the end of the conference, and I'm hoping to take a few days to explore the city and the coast. I love to surf. I've heard Garrettstown beach has some pretty decent waves!"

Anna nodded. "That's not far from my house. You should definitely check it out. Although, at this time of year, I hope you packed your wetsuit!"

Myles shivered in response to her words. "I know, it's freezing out there, right?"

Anna couldn't quite place his accent. Lauren had said he was from the Dublin branch, but Anna thought Myles had one of those accents that could be from any eastern Irish county.

"I'm staying in a nice hotel just over the bridge." Myles gestured out the window.

Anna broke off a piece of her croissant, feeling that all she had to do was listen. Myles was definitely one of those chatty-in-the-morning types.

"I'm planning to head out tomorrow night actually, there's a band playing that I like. Saber – have you heard of them? They're playing in a club called the Mad Hatter. Do you know it?"

Anna chewed her croissant slowly – with her mouth full she could only nod. It was easy to guess where this conversation was going – Myles was asking her out. Her heart was racing. Myles was asking her to go on a date to the Mad Hatter, the place where Kate Crowley was scheduled to be at the same time. This was Anna's chance – immediately, she made up her mind. She would try to connect with Kate, with her childhood friend. She would try to speak to her – though with undercover detectives on the lookout, that might be difficult. Her friendship with Kate had meant a lot to her, and she owed it to her to try to help her out now.

"Do you fancy joining me?"

With his bright smile and easy-going nature, Anna wondered if anyone ever actually said no to Myles Henderson.

8

Kate surmised that it could only be trauma that had knocked her out cold for so long. She had slept for eighteen hours. Struggling to sit up, she was again momentarily gripped by panic at the unfamiliar surroundings – could she ever get used to this? Pushing herself from the bed, she moved to the bathroom and quenched her thirst straight from the tap. Her lower back caused her to groan as she bent to the sink – she didn't dare to look at her reflection in the mirror. She touched her hand to her hair as she padded back to the bed, running her fingers through to its short ends. The back of her neck felt cold.

She thought of Natalie. She *always* thought of Natalie. To be a twin, an identical twin, was to never be separate. Two bodies, two hearts, one soul.

Throughout Kate's childhood, she had felt so special. She had a best friend and a sister rolled into one. They were inseparable; there were no arguments because they always had the same thoughts. There were no differences of opinion because her opinion was Natalie's and Natalie's was hers, and that was just … life. *Their* life. They were happy.

Even when their parents separated and the twins had to leave their home and friendships in Cork behind to move to Dublin, at least they had each other. When their father died, they leant into each other as one supportive unit. And when their mother married again, they jointly loathed their stepfather, and mutually despaired when the newlyweds moved to America. The decision to return to Cork together was easily made. She and Natalie, Natalie and her; they were one.

Until Natalie met David Gallagher.

Now she had killed him. How could she ever tell Natalie?

On her anxiety-riddled dash to the supermarket the day before she had bought some other supplies – bottles of water, painkillers and some energy bars. She swallowed two tablets now and chewed on an energy bar, her thoughts racing.

She wondered how Natalie was coping without her, and how the girls were. Her nieces were only three years old – they had already seen too much.

From under the bed she pulled out her small red satchel. She felt huge relief that she'd had the presence of mind to grab it as she fled her home Wednesday afternoon. The fact that she had failed to put her passport into it would haunt her forever – but still, she had some leverage.

She emptied the contents onto the hotel bed. Ninety thousand euro in cash … and a tiny silver, rectangular memory key.

It had been important to David Gallagher – he had been frantic when he realised it was missing. So frantic he had called to her house in a murderous rage. She had stolen it along with his money, days ago. Clearly, the memory key held something of great value to him. But without a computer she had no way of knowing what was contained inside.

63

She turned it over in her fingers.

"What are you hiding?" she murmured softly.

Rising from the bed again, she pulled open the curtains. It was a cold, icy morning. She watched the traffic crawl slowly along the city streets, drivers cautious on treacherous roads. She had to get air – the walls of the hotel room were closing in around her. She would wait until the roads had thawed before heading outside. And she would try to stay invisible as she moved through the streets – her life depended on it.

9

Lauren was surprised to see Anna stroll into work at almost ten o'clock. Her early-bird friend was skirting close to the limit on the acceptable start time. Lauren had missed the takeaway coffee cup on her desk this morning – she had assumed Anna was delayed because of the icy roads. Her face broke into a huge grin when she saw Anna finally arrive, side by side with Myles Henderson. She watched them in conversation, lingering a little before parting to go to their desks, Myles touching Anna's arm as he moved off.

As Anna arrived at her desk, she handed her friend a takeaway cappuccino.

"Ah, you're so good, you never forget me!" Lauren pulled off the plastic lid and blew into the foam. "I see you had some company this morning."

Anna smiled at her friend's teasing tone.

"Oh stop! Myles is really nice, really … easy-going. We're going out for a drink tomorrow night actually."

Lauren gagged on her first sip of coffee and foam

dripped onto her blouse. She grabbed a tissue from a box on her desk and dabbed at it.

"Do you and Robbie want to tag along?" Anna asked, but Lauren grimaced.

"No way! Just ring me Sunday morning with all the gossip. You two lovebirds are about to be split up actually – I heard the department have hired out some office space for all the extra bodies floating around here. Which makes perfect sense really – we are already cramped as it is. There isn't even a spare socket to charge your phone!"

Anna nodded at her friend. Lauren was right – it was far too cramped in the office with all the extra detectives covering security for the political conference.

"William Ryan is back in by the way – I saw him in the canteen earlier."

Anna had her computer switched on now, and paused, chewing on her bottom lip. She had been so sure yesterday about her theory linking some house break-ins and the sexual assaults. Today, she felt a little uncertain. It was a tenuous link, and if the victims of the robberies hadn't actually got alarms installed, or had all used different companies, her theory was moot. Then Anna remembered the billowing white curtain inside the open sliding door in her kitchen and made up her mind.

The majority of the detectives had larger cubicles on the second floor of the building. Grabbing her notebook with the recap of the break-ins and sexual-assault cases, Anna headed for the stairs in search of William Ryan.

Detective Sergeant William Ryan stood surveying his desk and groaned. There was an avalanche of Post-its and printouts covering his workstation. He had only been out for a week – how was it possible he had so many messages, and such a long to-do list? He rubbed his right side where the scar was forming, the skin feeling tight and itchy. His supervisor, Detective Superintendent Doherty, had made it abundantly clear his ruptured appendix was highly inconvenient. Especially with the imminent political conference. No-one had covered William's work while he was out. Now, staring at his desk, he realised he didn't know where to start.

"Excuse me?"

William turned to face the young woman standing behind him. He recognised her vaguely from the civilian staff – he had transferred into the station only six months before. He was ashamed to admit he didn't know everyone's name yet – that was normally a priority for him. The woman smiled cautiously and tucked a strand of light-blonde hair that had escaped her ponytail behind her ear. Her large brown eyes gave her an almost startled appearance, but when she smiled her whole face relaxed.

William sat down at his desk and motioned for the woman to do the same.

"I'm Anna Clarke, from the Garda staff downstairs."

"Nice to meet you, Anna. What can I do for you?"

Anna had taken the spare seat across from the detective and surveyed his desk between them. "I can see you're swamped. I'll try not to take up too much of your time. I hope you're feeling better?"

William nodded and motioned for Anna to continue.

"Well, I'm not fully sure where to begin."

"I find the start to be the best place."

"Of course!" Anna flushed and hurried on. "Part of my duties include analysing reports from other stations for statistical purposes. I was reviewing a report about a break-in a few days ago and it got me thinking. It's possible there is a connection between some house break-ins over the last three years and the seven unsolved sexual assault crimes that have occurred in the county."

Anna paused. She had spoken in a rush and wondered if it all sounded ludicrous to the detective. But she could tell she had William Ryan's attention. His eyebrows had shot up almost into his dark hair and his blue eyes had grown wide. He sat up straighter, wincing a little, elbows on the armrest of his chair, his fingers steepled under his chin.

"Tell me about the connection, please."

Adrenaline began to flow through Anna's veins – now that she had the detective's full attention, she was anxious not to waste it. She took a deep, steadying breath and cleared her throat.

"Well … there have been a lot of robberies and break-ins over the years, naturally. It's the same in every county. But in seven of those cases, a sexual assault has occurred in very close proximity to break-ins, within a few days. I've looked back over the reports – there's nothing to link the burglars to the sexual assaults. Most of the thieves have been apprehended and they are from a variety of backgrounds, and some were in custody when the sexual assaults occurred. Plus, there was DNA left at the sexual assault scenes that has no match on file. The only link, as such, is the close proximity of the attacks."

"Go on."

"In *all* seven cases, the homes that were broken into had no house alarm at the time, and they indicated a desire to have one installed to the Gardaí. I checked the transcripts to confirm that."

"And?"

"Whether they did or did not get an alarm fitted isn't documented on any of the files. But supposing they all *did* get an alarm fitted, and just happened to use the same company? And supposing the alarm company sent a guy out to install it who happens to have no previous convictions – the Guards don't have his DNA on file, and he has ample

68

opportunity to check out the area and spot potential victims."

"That's a lot of supposing." William smiled. He rubbed at his jaw with one hand. He was thinking this over. After his transfer he had dealt with one attack on a woman, living alone. It remained unsolved. He was aware there were several in the city and surrounding county that had appeared to be random, unexplained attacks. It was possible … maybe Anna Clarke was on to something.

Anna held up her notebook. "I've made some notes recapping the cases."

William straightened up and began to move things around on his desk in search of a pen. One thing he wasn't a fan of was deciphering someone else's handwriting. He preferred his own shorthand. Under the slips of paper and files awaiting his attention, finding something to write with was proving futile. Moving around was causing him to wince in pain again.

"Do you want me to grab you a pen?" Anna enquired and he nodded gratefully.

William gestured to the back of the room, and Anna noticed a tall cupboard she hadn't seen before. She had walked straight past it. Its cream door blended into the wall, only a faint wooden outline highlighting its existence. The very same storage cupboards were downstairs on Anna's floor too. They were almost completely flush with the wall, with no handle. One had to push gently against the door, and it popped open. Clever. They were deep enough to step into and lined with shelves containing an array of stationary. And she hated them. Referred to as "stealth storage" by one of her colleagues, she dreaded having to search inside them – cramped spaces like that set her nerves on edge. Lauren always fetched what Anna needed for her – and Anna figured a daily takeaway coffee for Lauren was a fair trade-off.

The storage cupboard on William Ryan's floor didn't seem to have a lightbulb, but there was plenty of light illuminating it from the main room. Anna stepped forward, pulled what she needed from a high shelf, and exited quickly, shivering involuntarily.

"I don't know if you're aware of this," William was saying from his desk, "but all the sexual assaults are linked. The DNA collected at each scene is a match to all the other assaults. We've known for a while now we are dealing with one attacker. Unfortunately, we've no idea who we're looking for." William took the pen Anna offered him with a nod of thanks and gestured to her notebook as she sat back down. "Tell me what you've got."

Anna perused her notes and leant closer.

"The first break-in on my list took place on 24th February 2016 at Number 4, Cherry Avenue, Lincoln Road. Some household items taken were recovered and an arrest was made two weeks later. The occupants of the house had no intruder-alarm in place and indicated to Gardaí their intention to get one fitted. There was no follow-up on that. Three days after the break-in, a woman living alone in Number 15, Sea View Close, was sexually assaulted overnight. The attacker had his face covered, so the victim wasn't able to identify him, but he left traces of DNA at the scene. No arrest was made in connection with the sexual assault. I checked Google maps – Cherry Avenue and Sea View Close have houses that run back to back. The house in Sea View Close is within viewing distance of the house that was broken into in Cherry Avenue. The pattern continues six more times. There is a short time span of between three and eight days between attacks in the same geographical area, none of the properties broken into had security alarms, and the victims of the sexual assault were home alone at the time of the attack." Anna met William's eyes. "I think the victims were being watched. Either the victims lived alone or their partners or housemates were all out of the house for work purposes on the night. It seems to me the attacker observed the property and noted the comings and goings, making sure he wouldn't be disturbed."

She passed her notebook to William and he jotted down the remainder of the dates and locations she had written there. He was relieved her writing was legible, and he could feel the faint stirrings of excitement in the pit of his stomach. Anna Clarke had done some quality research and was definitely on to something. The geographical proximity of the two crimes was very close and one house offered a direct view of the other in some cases. If the robbery victims had actually installed intruder alarms from the same company, he might have grounds for a search warrant. If not, William found he could be very persuasive. Maybe the alarm-company employees could be persuaded to give a DNA sample – if they were innocent, they would have nothing to worry about.

"So, the most recent attack was just a few nights ago, in … Willow Rise," he said. "Again, no house alarm. Time will be important here. If this pattern is true, an attack could take place within a few days."

"Er … that's the housing estate where I live, actually. And I live alone … so … this whole thing is making me a bit jumpy."

William's eyebrows shot up again. "I'm not surprised, I'd be jumpy too. Have you noticed any unusual activity in the estate? Any work vans with a company logo on the side?"

"Well, no, I'm at work all day so I wouldn't see anything. I *did* have an unusual experience when I got home last night. It seemed I had left my back door open – a sliding door into the garden. It was slightly ajar. Also, and I could be imagining this, but the key bowl on my hall table had moved …"

71

William dropped his pen onto the notebook and gave Anna his full attention. The serious look on his face sent a shiver down her spine.

"Tell me about the key bowl. What keys do you keep in there?"

"I … just my daily keys, for the car and front door. And a spare set for …" Anna's voice trailed off and she felt the blood drain from her face.

"Is the spare set still there, Anna?" William asked softly.

Anna could only whisper her response. "I don't know."

William wrote out his mobile number, tore the paper from the notebook and handed it to Anna. "I want to know about those keys as soon as you get home from work, OK? In one sense, if someone was in your house, they don't need the keys, because they've already found a way in. But if the keys are missing it proves someone was poking around. And I want you to take a look at your sliding-door lock. Check the outside of the lock for scratch marks or any damage."

"OK." Anna was aware her voice was shaky.

"It is a good idea to double-check all the doors and windows. Do you have a friend that could come and stay over, give you some peace of mind?"

Anna thought of Alex. He would insist she move into his house if she told him what was going on. She groaned inwardly – Alex always worried so much about her.

She nodded at William.

"Great! And leave this with me." William tapped the notes he had taken and smiled reassuringly at her. "I think you're on to something here, and I'm going to give it top priority."

10

"Tell me again what you found at the house!"

Tom Gallagher and his associate Murray were in his office at the back of his mansion on the hill. It was Friday lunchtime, and Tom felt his agitation growing. It was almost forty-eight hours since David had been shot. And almost as long since John had gone missing. The situation was dragging on, and he wanted answers. He could feel tension literally choking him with every passing second. The top button on his shirt had long ago been opened; he opened the next one down and drew in a deep, drowning-man's breath.

John's severed finger sat in its cardboard delivery box on his desk, still wrapped in the blood-soaked handkerchief. Tom couldn't bear to look at it, but it hovered on the edge of his vision, and never left his consciousness. His whole body ached to avenge his son's mutilation. His right leg bounced as he waited for Murray to fill in the gaps in what he already knew.

Tom Gallagher was a careful man, always keen to avoid

a list of enemies. A man was either on his side or out of the picture – it was safer that way. He could only assume it was the Meiers that had taken John. But the Germans had made no contact, nor had they sent a note with John's mutilated finger, leaving Tom even further in the dark. Either this was new territory for them, or they were planning a more elaborate stunt to get his attention. Tom had yet to confirm where the Meiers had travelled to in Cork; it was as if they had disappeared into thin air. If they were in the city, and had taken his son, it was a move he couldn't yet understand. They had never seen the need for a personal visit before.

David had been put in charge of their work with the Meiers shortly before his death. Tom realised now that that had been a monumental mistake. It seemed that as soon as he had given his younger son more responsibility, life had begun to spiral out of control. Now David was dead. Tom tried to focus his efforts into finding John; it was a powerful distraction from the realisation his youngest son lay on a slab in the city morgue.

And on finding Kate Crowley of course.

The Gallaghers were middlemen who had made their fortune holding goods where no-one would look. It was now merely a small part of their enterprise but it remained a lucrative one. A robbery in Dublin? Send the money to Cork, to Tom Gallagher and his sons; they would make sure it disappeared until the Gardaí had given up searching for it. A shipment of drugs bound for Belfast? Divert it to the quays of Cork, Tom Gallagher could hide it for a while. The Gallaghers took a holding fee, then returned the goods, whatever those goods might be. It was easy money, hiding the spoils of a crime they had absolutely nothing to do with.

The Meiers gave repeat business, a couple of times a year. Their reach extended across Europe and Tom was happy to facilitate them. He liked their set-up; it was much like his own, and they were careful too, never getting caught. The most recent job was so easy, so foolproof, Tom had given it to his son, to give him something to get his teeth into. It was David's apprenticeship, his training for working with John when the time came. Of course, John would take the reins; he was the logical choice. Calm and measured, John was a natural leader. Tom had planned on leaving behind a lucrative empire to John, and with David by his side, Tom was certain his legacy would be in good hands. Now one son was dead and another missing, being tortured, if the blackening finger on Tom's desk was anything to go by. The growing dread that gnawed at Tom's insides was unrelenting.

Ely Murray had come into Tom Gallagher's employment when he turned eighteen. He had watched the man grow his empire, and Murray had never wanted to be anywhere but centre stage. Thirty years later, he had worked his way to fourth in command. Now he was second in line after the boss. Unless John turned up.

The Gallagher lifestyle suited Murray, and he had the scars to prove it. A particularly nasty scar ran from his ear to his lip – Murray liked that one. He had suffered a slash to the face at a brawl in a row over territory – many wannabes had encroached on the Gallagher's territory over the years. Murray and the gang of loyal men he had amassed always set things straight – but there had been casualties along the way. Murray didn't mind the scars that added to his reputation as a hard man not to be crossed – and the ladies didn't mind them either.

Tom Gallagher had two sons of course, and Murray had been under no illusions as to who Tom intended to take over the business, who he intended would continue when he retired. John was steady and controlled, and with his father's deadly streak. David had been a different type of man altogether. David had been a hot-headed fool in Murray's opinion, and Tom had made the right choice to keep David as second-in-line after John. David had brought the Gallagher family to the attention of the Gardaí too many times. Street fights, nightclub brawls, and beating the mother of his children ... all drew too much attention. It wasn't Tom's style, nor Murray's either; it wasn't how to get ahead. Under the radar was Murray's way; he was quiet, a man who measured his temper. He wasn't loath to knife a man in the belly, but he would do it in the corners of a dark alley, not the busy dance floor of a packed nightclub. David's death had left another mess for his father to deal with, and with John missing, everything was at stake.

"We searched the whole house overnight," he said now. "A detective called Elise Taylor is handling the case by the way. We found hardly any clothes for the children or Natalie in the house – there's no sign of any passports either. She's done a runner. There was no merchandise to speak of – no cash, no drugs, nothing. You're clean. But it begs the question – where is the gear David was holding for the Meiers?"

"Kate Crowley can answer that question, I'd bet my life on it!" Tom held a pen in his fist and clicked it, on and off, over and over.

The action irritated Murray, but he said nothing. His boss, normally so calm and measured, was starting to crack under too much pressure. There were spidery red veins running through the whites of his eyes, and his body jerked in little spasms every now and then. To be in the line of Tom Gallagher's fire right now was surely suicide.

"We put the word about," he said. "Fifty grand for Kate Crowley alive – that's our preferred outcome."

"And?"

"Lots of interest – it's a lot of money – but so far nothing concrete."

"She could be anywhere – she could have even left the country!"

Murray shook his head. "There's a jumpy woman due at the Mad Hatter tomorrow night. It must be her – how many women go around looking to buy a passport? It's not an everyday occurrence. A cop I have on the inside told me Kate Crowley's passport was found inside her house, along with a packed suitcase. I'd bet she was leaving with her sister, except now she can't because she needs documents. We'll have her in our hands by tomorrow night."

"Show me the photo again!" Tom demanded and held out his hand.

Nick, the club manager, was an old mate of Murray's. He had texted on an image of the woman's passport photos. Tom studied it closely; it *could* be her. Natalie, mother of Tom's grandchildren, was her identical twin. The hair was different – short and dark – but that was easily achieved. It was the woman's bright-green eyes that gave Tom certainty that Murray was right.

Tom nodded and threw the pen onto his heavy oak desk. Murray's confidence was rubbing off on him – his dark mood was starting to shift.

"I'll handle it myself," said Murray. "I'll take a few guys to the club and bring her in."

Tom liked this plan; Murray was thorough and ruthless. If it was Kate seeking to buy a passport, she would be in his house very soon.

"Why haven't the Germans made contact?" he said. "If they are the ones that cut off John's finger, then why don't they get in touch and tell me what the fuck they want?"

"I've no idea. We never deal with them directly – we always go through Ainsley."

Tom sighed heavily; Murray was right. To further deepen the pool of deniability, the Gallaghers were only ever contacted by the Englishman, Alan Ainsley. He brokered the deals with the Meiers and a large number of other groups that needed goods to hide for a while. Ainsley kept everyone happy, and separate. Except, this time, everyone *wasn't* happy – David was dead, John was missing, and Mae was drinking herself into oblivion. Tom didn't know how to tell her David's children were gone too – her granddaughters meant almost as much to his wife as her own children.

"We need to find the gear David was holding for the Germans."

"Remind me – what was it again?"

"Cash and diamonds. Not a whole lot, less than a hundred grand."

"Why pay a personal visit for so little? Why take John when they know we can cover it? If David fucked up and hid it somewhere we can't find it, we replace it. Easily done. Why come here and take John?"

Murray could only shake his head.

"When will they release my son?"

"John?"

"David! He's been on a slab for days now. Find out when the Gardaí will be finished with him. Mae needs to put this to rest. She needs to put one piece of this to rest."

Tom ran his hand over his face and through his dark hair. Murray felt a stab of pity for his boss.

"Sir?" Jessica, the housekeeper, knocked softly on the half-open door.

Tom turned and raised his eyebrows – her creamy skin and soft curves were a balm to the soul.

"I'm so sorry to interrupt. It's Mrs. Gallagher, sir."

Jessica hovered in obvious discomfort at the door. Murray's eyes roamed over her appreciatively.

Tom got to his feet. "Keep searching the streets. I want

John back. The Meiers must be holed up somewhere. And Kate – I'll take her dead or alive!"

Tom turned to Jessica and smiled tightly. "Lead the way."

Jessica walked briskly to the front of the house, her low heels clicking on the tiled floor. Tom Gallagher liked to collect loyal people, and Jessica was one of them. He either bought or earned their loyalty, and in Jessica's case it was both. She was an immigrant, a single mother with a teenage son – she needed a well-paid job where she wasn't required to work the streets, where she could be paid off the books. Tom needed someone to run the house and keep her mouth shut. He had taken her off the streets and into his home; he paid cash and enough of it for her to stay loyal and stay quiet. She knew what would happen to her if she ever broke her silence and spoke to the Gardaí – Murray would be let off his leash for starters.

She led Tom to the living room and stayed at the doorway while he cautiously stepped inside. The smell of vomit and whiskey assailed him. Mae sat in a pool of her own filth, retching and crying in bursts.

"I want John!" she sobbed when she saw Tom standing over her. "I want my son! My David! I'm going to kill Kate Crowley – look what she's done!" Mae vomited again onto the floor.

Tom bent down and stroked her hair. "This will be over soon, my love." He turned to his housekeeper. "Take some time off. Don't come back until I tell you."

Seeing the tense set of his jaw, one hand curled into a fist at his side, Jessica quickly left the room. She had never seen the Gallaghers like this before, and it terrified her. She was happy to escape the lion's den.

She grabbed her coat and handbag from the hall closet and walked quickly from the house, without looking back.

11

Anna was grateful to be busy that morning as the threat of a sexual predator lurking near her house was thankfully pushed to the edge of her mind. It hovered there, waiting to pull her back into a state of anxiety. But it would have to wait.

The stack of files to her left resembled a very unsteady Leaning Tower of Pisa.

A new brown folder of handwritten notes had been positioned on her keyboard, with a yellow Post-it-Note on top, reading: *Priority – to incident room asap, DS Taylor*

She rolled her shoulders to loosen the knotted tension there. The fact that Detective Sergeant Taylor had put both "priority" and "asap" in one sentence left little doubt about how urgently she wanted to solve the case. Well, she needn't have worried, she thought wryly; this was one case she was just as keen as the detective to see filed away and resolved.

She quickly read the notes. Just this morning Elise had received confirmation that Natalie Crowley and her two children had travelled to Paris on Wednesday morning. The tickets were purchased in person at Cork airport, just before departure. Anna felt her heart sink – Natalie had left the city in a hurry. But why had she left her sister behind? Anna felt sure the gap was firmly closed now between doubt and certainty that Kate Crowley was involved in David Gallagher's shooting. She just couldn't believe it was true – the girl she had known in school was kind and so … normal. But they were children then, Anna reminded herself. And with their involvement with the Gallaghers, Anna knew they would have found themselves in a world of violence and danger. A world where anything was possible.

Anna read the dates of birth of Natalie's twin daughters, Rachel and Rhea. They were just three years old. If Natalie and Kate had only moved to Cork in 2014, then Natalie must have fallen pregnant with the twins almost immediately after meeting David Gallagher. And then her life was bound to a vicious criminal forever. A man who grew increasingly violent towards his partner, who threatened his children. The word *motive* plagued Anna – both Kate and Natalie had plenty of reasons to want David Gallagher dead. But only one of them was still in the city when he was shot.

There was little progress being made on the case – the job book items that were completed had yielded little else of value. There was no sign of Kate Crowley in the city or suburbs near her home. Door-to-door searches had yielded no new information. Tom and Mae Gallagher were putting pressure on the Gardaí to release David Gallagher to them for burial – but the State Pathologist had yet to complete her work. She was waiting on toxicology reports to be finalised, but some results were back that confirmed that David Gallagher had cocaine in his system at the time of his death. The pathologist had indicated that David Gallagher's body showed signs of a violent assault prior to his death, which was consistent with blood and other evidence of a fight at the property. The mystery of what had happened in Kate's house grew deeper.

With a shudder, Anna read that Detective Taylor had been informed by one of her contacts that Tom Gallagher had offered a reward to anyone who delivered Kate to him – and more cash if she was delivered alive.

With a heavy sigh Anna printed out her completed work and added it to the file, then made her way to the incident room. The door was partially open, and voices were raised inside. She recognised them as belonging to Chief Superintendent Janet McCarthy and Elise Taylor.

"You can't be serious!? Two is not enough!"

"I've explained my position and I'm not going over it again, Detective!"

As Anna hovered in the doorway, Janet McCarthy exited the room and stepped around her. Her face dark and brooding, she stormed away from the incident room.

Anna rapped gently on the door.

"What is it?" Elise barked.

Anna closed her eyes briefly; the tension in this building was a physical force, pulsing around everyone like a predator ready to pounce. It was wearing her out.

She stepped into the room and walked towards the detective. "The notes you left on my desk are typed up, I'll leave them here."

Elise didn't acknowledge her presence – she was sitting hunched, scrolling through crime-scene photographs, completely engrossed in the macabre images.

Anna hesitated, momentarily transfixed. She knew she should leave – the detective appeared to be in a foul mood and Anna had plenty of work waiting for her – but she couldn't take her eyes off Elise's screen. David Gallagher was lying in a pool of his own blood, his eyes wide open, staring at nothing in particular. His mouth was slack, his skin ghostly white. A black stain at his neck – dried blood, she presumed – showed where the bullet had struck him.

"*Do you want something?*"

Elise spoke with such venom that Anna was taken aback. Elise ran her fingers through her short blonde bob and looked at her.

"Sorry," she said then, grimacing. "It's a tough case." She looked at the folder of notes. "Thanks for that."

Anna nodded. "Sure, no problem. Listen … I …" she hesitated, unsure whether she should go on.

Elise's contrition was over; she stared at Anna, impatiently waiting, her mouth a thin line.

"I know Kate and Natalie Crowley," Anna said in a rush, "From primary school. I haven't seen them since then. It's just … Kate doesn't seem the type to kill someone. It must surely be self-defence? And the report from the pathologist said David Gallagher suffered a violent assault – she could hardly have done that. There must have been someone else in the house."

Elise's threw her hands up in exasperation.

"Who the hell knows? Witnesses only put two people at the property, Kate and David. There are two sets of fingerprints on the gun – Gallagher's and an unknown other. Those prints are all over the house, so we believe they are Kate Crowley's. All the evidence points to her as the shooter. Her sister had left the country by then. And God knows both Crowley sisters had plenty of reasons to want him dead!"

Elise stood up, picking up her empty coffee cup. She passed Anna her card.

"My mobile number is on there if you think of anything important. But do me a favour – stay out of this. It's a messy case, and just because you once played with the suspect as a child doesn't mean you know her, OK? I appreciate you prioritising the work, but that's where your involvement stays."

Elise's hard stare left Anna in no doubt of what she was saying – butt out.

The roads had thawed by the time Anna left work just after six o'clock, having stayed late to make up the hours lost that morning. Traffic was heavy. She felt exhausted by the time she reached home.

Pulling into her housing estate, she thought of William Ryan's words and began to scan the vehicles parked at the kerbs around her home. Her shoulders sagged in relief when she recognised all the parked vehicles – but, she reminded herself, it was Friday night. Who would be working at this hour?

Pushing open her front door, Anna paused briefly – the house was quiet, and warm. No doors were open to let in the cold November air. Switching on the hall light, Anna reached out and dropped her keys into the key bowl, moved back into place last night. The keys clattered against the spare set she kept there. Anna laughed out loud into the empty hallway – her imagination had obviously been working on overdrive, and she was scaring herself needlessly! No-one had stolen her keys – she needed to relax.

Anna thought of the text she had promised to send William Ryan and quickly typed it, feeling foolish.

Putting a frozen chicken curry in the oven, she uncorked a bottle of red wine and set it on the kitchen counter to breathe while she lit the stove in the living room. A small archway separated the kitchen and living room, and soon the heat from the stove enveloped the space, offering a cosiness to the empty house.

On Friday nights, she loved the ritual of settling on the armchair in front of the stove with an open bottle of wine, to wait for her best friend Vivian's call. She and Vivian had been as close as sisters since childhood. She missed talking to her in person. Vivian had been living in Auckland for months now. A number of years ago she and her birth mother had got in touch, and Vivian had finally decided to visit her in New Zealand and spend some proper time together. Anna had no idea when Vivian planned to return home, and she missed her friend.

As the orange flames danced and Anna sipped her wine, she rolled her shoulders, easing the tension held there. The curry was only halfway through heating. She pulled a book from her stacked bookshelf, hoping to distract herself from the facets of her job that were playing on her mind. She was thorough in her work, always ensuring every detail was collected and documented – now those details danced in her thoughts, jumping from one grim aspect to the other. She soon abandoned the novel, its romantic opening too light to hold her attention. She felt jumpy, alert to every sound.

Putting the book back in its place, she pulled out the private investigator's business card from her back pocket and tapped it against the stem of her wineglass. What could Mr. Lane find that the Gardaí had missed? Probably nothing, she knew. The investigation had been thorough. Two grown adults had crashed their car and disappeared after the fact. But they were her parents – she had to try.

She decided that choosing a record to put on her father's old record player would calm her. Soon the familiar sound of Bach's Cello Suite No. 1 in G Major filled the living room. She leant her head back into the armchair and closed her eyes; her mother's favourite music always brought her to a place of peace.

The beeping of the oven drew her back to the present – she must have dozed off. Arranging her dinner on the coffee table in front of her, she checked the time. It was just coming up to eight o'clock, and probably still too early for Vivian to call. She and Vivian had been as close as sisters since childhood. She missed talking to her in person.

As she blew on a forkful of food, she thought of Kate and Natalie. Where were they? There had been four of them in their girl gang, four best friends: Anna, Kate, Natalie and Vivian. They had been firm friends until primary school was over and Kate and Natalie left for Dublin. Anna and Vivian had remained best friends. Anna hadn't given Kate and Natalie much thought growing up; life had been busy, and at sixteen her whole world had changed. Now she couldn't stop thinking about them. The Gallaghers ... they sounded like monsters. Kate's face was etched in Anna's mind. She imagined the powerlessness she must have felt as David Gallagher had abused her sister. Had she killed him because of it? Was the girl she had known capable of killing anyone? It had to have been self-defence – to Anna it was the only thing that made sense.

Anna jumped and spilled wine on her blouse as she heard a noise at the glass sliding door in the kitchen. She listened – it was a banging sound, over and over, loud enough to penetrate the peace of the music. Setting down her glass, heart pounding, she stood and stepped quickly to her father's record player. She switched it off and stood still by the hearth, listening, barely daring to breathe. There it was again, now a dull, repetitive thud. It must be a tree branch come loose, she tried to convince herself. On shaky steps she moved through the kitchen and, turning the light off, pulled aside the white curtain.

Nothing. No tree branch hitting the glass. Peering out into the darkness, Anna could see nothing else, either. She exhaled the breath she had been holding and felt her shoulders relax. She double-checked the lock and went back to the living room. This time she opted to turn on the TV – Bach might be relaxing, but he did nothing to drown out nocturnal noises, nor quieten her wild imagination.

Alex sat at his kitchen table with Samantha, his hands wrapped around a mug of tea. He had filled his wife in on his conversation with Anna from the night before. Samantha was, for once, not working overtime, and they had a chance to catch up on their week.

Alex sat in worried agitation, fidgeting, his mind racing. Samantha had seen him like this before; especially when it came to the mystery of his parents' disappearance. The ten-year anniversary of the event felt like a milestone approaching. She stood up and held out her hand.

"Bed!" she said. "Adding exhaustion to worry won't help."

Alex took her hand and rose wearily to his feet. He looked utterly drained.

Samantha felt a rush of pity for him. "Let's do something fun tomorrow. I don't have to work this weekend."

Alex pulled her into his arms, finding comfort in her weight against his chest. "Thanks, Sam."

She wrapped her arms around his back, and they stayed in the embrace for a few minutes, then broke apart and moved toward the stairs, to bed.

It was no surprise to Alex that he couldn't sleep. He liked to feel in control of his life. Raking up his parents' disappearance didn't seem like a good idea to him and didn't seem like a way to maintain control. He understood his need for order and routine, and for things to make sense. He had been a very young man, just twenty-five, when he lost both parents and took on full responsibility for his teenage sister. To say it had been difficult was a huge understatement.

He hated to remember that day ten years ago, mostly because of the look on his sister's face when he relayed the telephone call from the Guards. Anna had been sitting on the sofa in the living room, completely absorbed in *Lord of the Flies*, when Alex ended the call and, stumbling, made his way to the armchair beside her.

Initially Anna had been too engrossed in her book to pay any attention to her brother. After a few moments, the silence from him drew her eyes up from the page, and registering his shocked expression she had put her book aside.

"What's wrong, Alex?"

Alex often thought he should have softened the message somehow. She was only sixteen after all. The memory of how he had blurted out the news to Anna often caused him to cringe.

"That was a Detective Molloy from the Garda Station in town. He said Mum and Dad's car was found crashed on the motorway to Dublin. But there's no sign of their bodies."

"Their bodies?" Anna had whispered.

Alex shook his head, clearing his thoughts. "No sign of them at all, I mean. They are not in the car or nearby."

"Well, they must have gone for help!" Anna had said with the sure confidence of a teenager who has yet to see any bad in the world.

"Yeah," Alex had agreed, although he hadn't felt any confidence. "That must be it."

But that wasn't it. The hours rolled into days and the days into weeks, and there was still no sign of their parents. Anna spent her days on the sofa, reading, within arm's reach of their telephone, expecting it to ring at any minute. School was forgotten – there was no way she could be expected to concentrate on her schoolwork, nor Alex on his accountancy exams. At night, Alex heard her sobs from her closed bedroom door across the hall from his. He mostly stood outside, unsure how to help her. Eventually, he realised all she needed was for him to be there, sitting on the bed beside her, his presence reassuring.

When she was asleep, he often went and sat on their parents' bed in their room downstairs, hoping for inspiration. Nothing made sense to him. He knew all the details of the case and had kept them to himself. If none of it made any sense to him, how could he explain it to his younger sister?

Michael and Helen Clarke's BMW had been found crashed on the motorway to Dublin. There were skid marks that indicated the driver had braked hard and fast. There was blood on the dashboard, which DNA analysis had confirmed belonged to both of them. The passenger seatbelt had been cut with what appeared to be a sharp blade, perhaps a penknife. There were no belongings in the car – no handbag, coat, or driver's licence. Which gave Alex hope. Surely, they had escaped the car accident, and had gone out onto the motorway, looking for help? There were some blood spots around the car, but no trail that gave any clue of which direction they might have taken. There were no witnesses to the accident, only the driver that had come on the scene of the crash and called the Gardaí, and he hadn't seen any sign of the occupants of the BMW.

The Gardaí searched every angle of the case. Every hospital in the country was quizzed to find out if any patients had been admitted showing injuries consistent with a car accident. Every outhouse and shed for two hundred kilometres were searched. News bulletins showed the Clarkes' photos nightly. But the pair seemed to have vanished.

Weeks turned into months and, before Alex really had time to catch his breath, months had turned into a year. Detective Molloy stayed in touch, updating Alex on the lack of progress every couple of weeks. After two years he called to the house, said he was retiring, and expressed his deep regret at not solving the mystery. Alex was gracious; he assured the detective that he knew he and his team had done their best. What more could he say?

Anna was not so understanding. Her tears had dried, and her resolve had hardened. She had read enough mystery stories to know that there was *always* an explanation. *Someone* knew where her parents were, and what had happened to them. The Gardaí had just failed to figure it out. She had no answers – instead she had a growing hatred. She had no Bad Guy to blame for the gaping hole in her life – but she had Detective Molloy and his team to blame for incompetence, for what she perceived as disinterest. It didn't make sense to her that her parents couldn't be found; the enduring mystery burdened her at night and prevented sleep. It was all-consuming. The Missing Persons Bureau had encouraged them to do public appeals, which they had, but still nothing changed. The mystery endured.

Somehow, ten years had passed since then. Alex embraced a different life. He had no choice. Anna eventually returned to school; Alex finished his exams and qualified as an accountant. Neighbours helped when they could, the Pearsons in particular, but Alex was always aware that the responsibility for Anna lay with him now. He had accepted their parents were not coming home. And he had thought Anna had too.

The hatred and anger in Anna that had worried Alex began to soften after she returned to her beloved Taekwon-Do. The martial art had been a bond between them and their father. Michael Clarke was a black belt and an advocate of the skillset. His training mate Jason had coached Alex and Anna too, and Michael had often practised manoeuvres and stances with them in their back garden. When Anna returned to the practice she rediscovered a calm way to channel her anger. It became a lifebuoy for her. She trained every day until she had finally reached black-belt level, and then kept training.

Alex and Anna had grown closer in the last ten years than any other set of siblings he knew. It stood to reason – they had been through a shared trauma. Even though she was an adult, he still felt very much responsible for his sister. He knew she would hate that and would tell him there was no need. Anna was capable, a black belt, and well educated. Alex hadn't been surprised when she told him she was going to work as Garda staff – he knew the order and logic of the job would appeal to her. Alex wondered if a part of Anna had hoped working for the Gardaí would lead her to answers.

Alex tossed and turned all night. Sleep proved elusive, as it had so many nights in the last decade. There were things about his childhood that Anna had never been told, or if she had, she had never found them to be unusual. Their English parents had moved around the U.K. throughout Alex's childhood, living in a variety of small towns. They had been a very private family, never making close friendships, never bonding with their neighbours. To Alex, it seemed his parents had deliberately kept themselves aloof, and at a distance. Michael had a variety of jobs, changing with every new town, and Helen kept to herself. Alex was nine years old when Anna was born; the Clarkes had moved to Ireland only the previous year, telling young Alex they wanted to make a fresh start. As a child he hadn't questioned his parents; as an adult, he wondered why?

In Ireland, they had relaxed. Helen had fallen in love with the house at Willow Rise and Michael had beamed as he handed her the keys. Alex remembered the day they moved in with fondness. Helen had been heavily pregnant, and Michael had laughingly attempted to carry her over the threshold, while Alex groaned in embarrassment – looking back, it was one of his happiest childhood memories. His parents had finally joined community groups and attended parent-teacher meetings, had made friends and a real effort to settle in. Michael had met a good friend in Jason Walsh and resumed his Taekwon-Do training. He had set up an accountancy practice in the city. Baby Anna had completed their happiness.

The man that arrived when Michael and Helen disappeared introduced himself as "Bob". Back then, Alex had accepted what the man told him and was most likely in shock at the time. Looking back with the benefit of hindsight, he was suspicious. He had never met the man before, nor heard his mother or father speak of him. Helen had spoken of a sister and her parents who had died many years before he was born. Alex knew his father had been raised in London by his grandmother, and never knew his parents. He had certainly never mentioned a "Bob" to Alex, but the man identified himself as a close friend of his father's, and at the time Alex had believed him.

Bob told Alex and Anna about a trust fund their father had set up in the event anything should happen to him or Helen. Alex had been surprised but accepted it as something his prudent father might do. When five hundred thousand euro was transferred to his account, Alex was astonished. Even more so when he never heard from Bob again. The man had left a business card; Alex had called the number but it had always rung out. He had eventually stopped calling. He had hesitated to throw away the card though – it was in a box in the attic somewhere with old medical receipts and birth certificates.

Now that he was older and a father himself, Alex had many questions. Why take such measures, setting up such a large trust fund in the event of your death? It seemed extreme. His parents had insurance policies that had eventually paid out, but nowhere near the amount of the trust fund. And how did his father even *have* half a million euro to put aside?

Alex had unanswered questions, and not just relating to his parents' disappearance.

As dawn broke, he had to admit a tiny part of him was intrigued – what could the private investigator possibly uncover?

12

Saturday

William Ryan stood with his hands in his pockets and surveyed the house. He had parked a few hundred yards away and had approached the house on foot. It was early on Saturday morning. He planned to knock, hard, on the front door and ask his questions. He didn't have a warrant yet. But that needn't stand in his way.

Gina had been less than thrilled that William was leaving so early. She had plans to go into the city and start her Christmas shopping. She wondered whether he might like to come. William wondered why she stuck out her bottom lip when he refused. Her childish response was the latest in a line of protests that he was working at the weekend, or late at night, and he was growing tired of it. He had explained when they met that he had sought a transfer to a busier Garda station because he loved the job and wanted a more demanding post. And he had explained to Gina over dinner the night before that he had a pressing matter very early in the morning. Lately, William felt that he was always explaining his choices to a woman he had only met a few months ago. She hadn't seemed too upset last night – perhaps she thought her fillet steak and bedside manner would persuade him to abandon his plans. This morning she had hurled the bedside clock at his departing back and told him to go to hell.

The bungalow was set in a crowded estate just outside the city. A small white van was parked in the driveway, a ladder securely attached to the roof. Magnetic business signs decorated the doors of the van: *Dean Harris Security*. The man was unimaginative. And cheap. He had been the cheapest quote available, according to the seven homeowners William had spoken to yesterday.

It had taken William less than an hour to contact the victims of the break-ins yesterday and discover the information he needed. Anna Clarke had made detailed notes, including their phone numbers. The woman was thorough. William had identified himself, and said he was following up. No-one had queried that. He had enquired if they had installed house alarms after the break-in. All had said yes, and that they had done so within a few days.

One by one, all the homeowners had given William the name of the "very nice young man" who had installed the alarms for them. Dean Harris had given them the most reasonable quote, and was "so obliging", able to fit the alarms almost immediately. He even returned a few times over the following days to make sure everything was just as the client wanted. And to scope out the neighbourhood, William was sure. He thought he had enough probable cause to get a search warrant of the house, but he knew that would take time. And he also wanted a DNA sample.

He stood now, near the gate outside the house, with his hands in his trouser pockets, and rocked back and forth on his heels. He had looked up Dean Harris, of course. Harris lived alone, and was clean – no points on his license, no drunk and disorderly arrests as a teenager, not even a parking fine. His DNA was not in the system. Perhaps he was very clean-living. Or perhaps he was a very careful serial sexual predator.

The driveway was unkempt. William passed weeds shrivelling in the winter morning wind as he walked slowly up the short path. The front door to the house was a faded shade of blue, peeling in many places. The house paint wasn't much better. There was no door knocker, nor doorbell for that matter. So, William pulled off his black leather glove and knocked hard on the faded wood. Repeatedly.

It took a few minutes of knocking before a rattling noise at the door indicated Dean Harris was awake and attempting to open a chain at his front door. He yanked open the door.

"What the fuck! Do you know what time it is?"

In a T-shirt, boxer shorts and bare feet, Dean Harris was a few inches shorter than William Ryan, which put him at six foot by William's estimation. His brown hair was receding, and he had a pallor that suited a man accustomed to late nights. There was nothing resembling stubble on his thin cheeks – perhaps he was one of those middle-aged men that had trouble growing a beard, William wondered, as he pushed his fingers back into his leather glove.

William's ice-blue eyes connected with Dean Harris's and gave nothing away. He stayed silent for a beat too long, and saw it had the desired effect. Dean Harris looked around William, left and right, and his voice shook when he spoke again. He was less aggressive now, and adopted a conciliatory tone, perhaps sensing he was in a dangerous situation.

"Do I know you?"

"Not yet," William answered, enjoying the look of sleepy confusion on the man's face. "Let me introduce myself." He pulled his ID from a pocket in his black overcoat and flashed it quickly.

Dean Harris reacted as all guilty men do, in William's experience. His eyes bulged slightly, his shoulders tensed a little higher, and a small breath escaped his lips, captured in the cold air as a chilly puff of guilt. All slight, almost imperceptible movements and responses, all detected by William countless times before. He lived for moments like this.

"Tell me. Do you employ any other personnel?"

"What? What's that?"

"It's a very simple question, Mr. Harris. Anyone else on the payroll in the security-alarm company?"

"What? No. Why?"

"I'm investigating a series of crimes. Your alarm company has been in the vicinity of each of those incidents. It puts you at the scene, so to speak. Do you understand what I'm saying, Mr. Harris?"

Dean Harris did understand. A red blush crept up his neck and enflamed his pale face. When he spoke again, spittle flew into the air in front of him.

"This has nothing to do with me!"

"Wonderful!" William offered a broad smile. "You won't mind giving a DNA sample then. Shall we head down to the station?"

The door slammed in William's face, flecks of blue paint landing on the concrete.

With his hands back in his pockets, William sauntered slowly down the drive. From the corner of his eye he noticed a curtain twitch inside the house, and so he paused a little to inspect a strangled-looking plant halfway down.

William was in a buoyant mood. He loved rattling a suspect. It might not yet be eight o'clock on a Saturday morning, but it was time to go in search of a warrant. Dean Harris was, without doubt, as guilty as sin.

13

Anna realised she was fast becoming a creature of habit. She was only twenty-six years old, but somehow her life had sure and solid routines, and she loved the secure feeling that offered. Her degree in mathematics offered little in helping her to understand what that meant about her personality. She could guess, though, that the order of her life offered a safety that had been forever threatened ten years ago.

Last night she had laughed and gossiped with her old friend Vivian, and on Saturday morning she felt revived for it. There was no party or offer of a night out that could deter Anna from taking Vivian's call. She missed her friend, and sometimes the longing to hug her and catch up in person was overwhelming. But Anna understood; Vivian was getting to know her birth mother and she was happy. So, Anna kept her feelings to herself and soaked up their weekly chats.

On Saturday mornings, Anna followed a routine that a hangover would never permit. She rose at six, often while it was still dark. Every Saturday she drove to the gym in a nearby hotel and pushed her body hard, with Jason as her training companion. Then they headed to the small room off to the side of the gym and trained in Taekwon-Do for at least an hour. Anna was keen to progress her skills further.

By ten o'clock Anna was showered and changed and driving home. She had the boot of her car full of groceries and sipped a latte as she navigated the frosty roads. She felt alive and invigorated, as she did every Saturday morning. And there was a nervous flutter in her stomach that wasn't entirely unpleasant. Her date with Myles was only hours away, and Anna realised she was excited.

Anna drove into Willow Rise and pulled up outside the Pearsons' house. She gazed up at the exterior walls and saw what she had been looking for – a rectangular white box with a blue flashing light. A security alarm. So, her neighbours had had one installed … Anna wondered if they would tell her by whom.

She pulled two bags of groceries from the boot and made her way up the driveway, before ringing the doorbell. She jumped slightly as the Pearsons' cat purred beside her and wound himself between her ankles.

"Hello, Rebus." She bent to stroke his soft fur.

As the front door was opened Anna stood up and smiled. Mrs. Pearson opened the door slightly, allowing only a view of a sliver of her face. Rebus streaked inside.

"Hi there, Mrs. Pearson, it's Anna Clarke."

Anna heard a chain rattle and the door was opened wide. Mrs. Pearson smiled and stepped aside.

"Hello, love. Do come in, it's freezing!"

"I've brought you some groceries. Just a few essentials."

Anna stepped inside, relishing the warmth of the house.

"Ah, you're very kind. There was no need. Bring them through to the kitchen and we'll have a cup of tea."

Anna followed Mrs Pearson through to the kitchen at the back of the house. The house smelled like a home – scones were baking in the oven, and there was a faint smell of lemon and disinfectant – Anna felt a pang of sadness wash away her earlier excitement and tears stung her eyes. Her neighbour's home was laid out exactly like her own, with a small kitchen at the back, adjoining a living room. Her own home was much more eclectic in its style; the Pearsons had more traditional decorative tastes.

Anna smiled to herself as she remembered how kind the Pearsons had been to her and Alex after their parents' disappearance, often dropping over food, and they had taken care of Anna a few times when Alex needed to go away for work. But they had busy lives of their own, with four grown children and some grandchildren. Now that Anna spent her days at work, contact with the Pearsons had been largely reduced to waving as she drove in and out of the estate, and a box of biscuits dropped over at Christmastime.

Mrs. Pearson put the kettle on to boil and Anna settled herself on a wooden kitchen chair, setting the groceries on the floor beside her.

"Tell me how you take your tea, Anna."

"Lots of milk, no sugar please. I hope you both are recovering well. I was sorry to hear about the break-in."

A shadow crossed Mrs. Pearson's face as she busied herself with making and pouring the tea. When she sat down opposite Anna her face betrayed her emotions – she was barely holding it together. Her skin was pale, and she had dark shadows under her eyes.

"It was a terrible ordeal, truth be told. I don't know if Derek will ever get over the shock."

Mrs. Pearson raised her eyes to the ceiling, to the bedroom upstairs.

"He's still asleep now. Never have I known him to sleep

100

in – he's always up and about, doing some job or other, or going to get the newspaper. He's had such a shock, you see. We both have."

Anna sipped her tea and nodded sympathetically. The oven-timer beeped – the scones were ready and Mrs. Pearson rose to tend to them. She placed a plate of them in the middle of the table with some butter and jam, and sat down again.

"Help yourself, love."

"Thank you, they smell delicious." She took a scone and began to butter it. "Were either of you injured at all?"

Anna knew from the report at work that Mr. Pearson had been seriously assaulted. She sensed that Mrs. Pearson needed to talk it all through.

The elderly woman was putting jam on her scone, holding its hot edges gingerly. "Yes, the poor man! One of the fellows that broke in punched him, knocked him to the ground, then kicked him. He has a cracked rib, and the doctor said he needs to take it easy. But he's always been such an active man! It's terrible, just terrible." Her voice wobbled as she spoke. "People have been so kind. And we've had an alarm fitted, by a lovely young man. We should have done it years ago!" She laughed a little. "How that man didn't kill himself up on that ladder all day is beyond me! It took him such a long time to fit it. Luckily he wasn't charging by the hour!"

Anna offered a tight smile and took a bite of her scone. So – the "lovely young man" had taken his time up the ladder, affording himself a view of the neighbouring houses. The scone was moist and perfectly cooked but felt like a lump of cement in her throat.

"That's really something I should look into getting myself. Could you tell me the name of the company you used?"

Mrs. Pearson pursed her lips, trying to recall, eventually blushing with embarrassment.

101

"Gosh, my memory isn't what it used to be! I'll have to fish out his card – I have it here somewhere."

As she rose from her seat a feeble cry from upstairs startled them both. Mrs. Pearson looked to the ceiling, then back at Anna.

"Poor Derek. He'll be needing some breakfast."

Anna rose quickly.

"I'll see myself out. Give Mr. Pearson my best. And you have my number – could you call me with the name of the security company?"

"Of course! And thanks for checking on us."

Anna didn't want to press the issue and intrude any further; the Pearsons were clearly still suffering from their ordeal. But she would have to get the name of that security company! She decided to call again on Monday after work if she had not heard from Mrs. Pearson by then.

When she sat into her car, she found that her hands were shaking. She carefully manoeuvred her car the short distance home and brought her gym gear and groceries inside the house. Once the door was closed, she leant against it, drawing air deep into her lungs. The house was quiet and still. Tears spilled down her cheeks – catching her off-guard. She was disappointed not to have the contact details of the security-alarm company – but that was not why she was upset. In truth, she wasn't sure why she was crying.

Yes, the Pearsons had suffered a terrible attack, and their suffering was obvious. But Anna had known that all along. And yes, she was agitated to see that the Pearsons had had a security alarm installed, but she had suspected that they would.

Anna realised she had felt close to tears ever since she had set foot inside the Pearsons' home. Perhaps it was the smell of a *home* that had made her emotional? Anna's house hadn't smelled like that for years. It wasn't just the baking,

102

and the cleaning products – it was the smell of warmth, and other people. Anna realised she was lonely. She was tired of living alone. And she really missed her parents.

It was a long time since Anna had been inside her attic. In fact, she usually did everything she could to avoid going up there. Her fear of cramped spaces was irrational, she knew that, and not something she could trace back to any childhood trauma. But the fear remained. When Alex had left the house to buy his own home with Samantha, Anna had used some of her trust-fund money to redecorate her home. One of the first things she had done was have a wide, pulldown staircase fitted to the attic, followed by a skylight window. Now, with the sense of space the wider opening and natural light offered, she could just about tolerate being up there.

There weren't many photographs of her parents throughout the house. Today, Anna felt like looking back over old memories. And while she was up there, she reasoned, she could pull out some Christmas decorations. Chloe loved to help with that – decorating the house together would bring some warmth into the place.

Once the groceries were put away, Anna made herself a strong coffee and carried it upstairs and into the attic. The day was bright, though very cold, and sunlight streamed through the skylight window. The wooden attic floor was covered with linoleum, and Anna sat down, breathing deeply. Nausea crept up her throat, but she sat with her legs crossed and her eyes closed, concentrating on her breath until the feeling subsided.

When Anna opened her eyes, the first thing she saw was a box marked "**FAMILY PHOTOS**". Very quickly she realised there really weren't that many photographs of anyone besides her and Alex. Her parents had captured their every waking move when they were babies, and plenty of them sound asleep in a tiny cradle too. After that, as Alex and Anna got older, the photographs seemed confined to occasions. First days at school, holidays to West Cork or trips to Dublin Zoo. Anna usually sat atop her father's shoulders, and it seemed her mother had been the chief photographer – she was in very few photographs.

Anna had never given it much thought until she was about eight or nine, but the realisation had come then that she and Alex had no cousins. She remembered doing a project in school, a type of "family tree", and having the smallest one in the class. She had been very sad that all of her grandparents were dead, and she had no aunts or uncles, and no cousins to play with. She could remember being mocked about her family tree in the yard at breaktime and recalled Kate Crowley putting her arm around her shoulder.

"Natalie and I have only one cousin, and his breath smells like old socks!"

Anna had laughed heartily at that.

"Don't worry about it, Anna – Natalie and me can be your cousins if you like."

The next box Anna found contained clothes. Layers and layers of clothes. Helen Clarke had never liked to throw anything out, it seemed. Anna pulled out an old sweater that used to belong to her father – a round-necked navy-blue wool sweater that he used to wear over a shirt to work. Anna buried her face in it, hoping to inhale something of him, but whatever scent it used to hold had long since worn away. She dug deeper in the box, and gasped as she pulled out her mother's winter coat. It had been her favourite. She'd had it dry-cleaned every winter, and worn it for three months, every day, always reluctant to put it away. It was a thick coat of the brightest, fire-engine red, with four jet-black buttons, and it had hung all the way down to her knees. Anna had loved that coat. In her childhood it had been a symbol of winter – whenever the temperature began to drop as autumn deepened, Michael would venture into the attic for his wife's best winter coat.

As Anna bundled the coat and sweater back into the box, her eyes rested on her mother's cello, propped up in the corner. She moved towards it, touching the strings gently. Helen had never played for them, in Anna's memory, and had said it was a hobby she'd had as a young girl. Anna knew her mother had loved the sound of the instrument, and concerto music was played so often in their home that it felt like a soundtrack to Anna's childhood.

She knelt at the cello for a few minutes, running her hands over the wood, trying to remember everything she could about her parents … how had ten years passed so quickly? Where were they?

Anna shook her head and moved away. Coming up here had been a mistake. This trip down Memory Lane was not doing her any favours. She felt deflated, and even more emotional than she had before. She resolved to find the Christmas decorations quickly and get on with her day.

As she searched, she pulled an old, faded bedsheet aside, and found a box marked *"Anna's School Things"* in red permanent marker. It was her mother's handwriting. Anna smiled. She reached forward and pulled the box towards her, taking things out one at a time. Report cards from her first to her final year in school – she had been a bright and well-behaved student, always excelling in maths. There was a medal she had won with a group of other students for a project on composting, and handwritten letters from her friends on fancy pink and purple paper, the scent they once held long gone. There were notes and letters from Vivian – who always signed her name with a love heart over the i's instead of the usual dots – and Kate and Natalie. The notes were those that had been passed between the girls during class, and for some reason Anna had kept some of them. They detailed trivial irritations over teachers and homework and boys that were being particularly annoying. One set of notes, held together with a yellow paperclip, reminded Anna of a time when Natalie was being bullied by a girl a year ahead of them in school. Anna read through them, smiling at the childish handwriting, at their view of the world.

"You should tell Miss. Just get nasty Beth Willis in trouble – she deserves it!"

"Definitely! We're all here to help you, Natalie!"

"We can sort it. We won't put up with her!"

"Ugh! She's the worst!"

Anna looked over the notes, at the words *we*, underlined. She thought it was Kate who had written that. She and Natalie had always spoken in terms of *we* instead of seeing each other as individuals. They had always had each other's backs – Anna had felt many times that she and Vivian were on the edge of the world the twins shared. Kate and Natalie had been each other's best friend, just as Anna and Vivian had been as close as sisters.

Anna pulled a framed photograph out of the box and a lump formed in her throat. Tears threatened to spill over again, but she was smiling. The four friends were standing together in Anna's back garden, arms around each other's shoulders, all grinning broadly. Anna marvelled at the image of herself, probably fourteen years ago – short with pale hair and big brown eyes. The Crowley twins stood in the middle, with identical bright-green eyes and long, curly red hair. Vivian stood on the far right, taller than the others, her brown hair in a high ponytail. Anna remembered her parents had thrown a barbeque to celebrate the end of primary school and had had the girls all sign the white cardboard surround of a photo frame, with copies given to each girl. Through tears of nostalgia Anna read the words they had written there, their friendship etched onto the card for ever. At the top of the frame, in pink marker and large bubble letters, Kate had written the caption: *Best Friends For Life.*

Anna put the photograph back inside the box and sat still, sipping her now cold coffee, her friends on her mind. Where was Kate now? Anna would do anything to help her. And, thinking of her date with Myles tonight, she realised she might soon get a chance to do just that.

Quickly checking the time on her phone, she hopped up with a start, bumping her head on the ceiling. It was practically lunchtime, and she had a hair appointment! She had been thinking about cutting her hair for a while now. She thought of her school-report cards and her routine life, and the way Frank Doherty had called her a "good girl". She was ready to make a few changes, and what better place to start, she figured, than to update her look. She had worn her hair long for years. Perhaps shorter hair would make her actually look her age.

Quickly locating the boxes of tinsel and festive figurines, and with determination in her step, Anna headed back downstairs.

14

Tom Gallagher hated it when someone in his presence lost their temper. He saw it as the ultimate sign of weakness. It wasn't that he couldn't understand the urge to punch a hole through a wall. It was the loss of control that he disrespected. He cared nothing for men in positions of power who proved their "manliness" by lashing out. That was why he'd had trouble accepting David as a wife-beater. Natalie Crowley might not have been married to David, but she was the mother of his two daughters, of Tom's own grandchildren, and as such deserved David's respect. It made her part of the family and the Gallaghers never mistreated their own. And they never personally got their hands dirty; they hired men to dish out punishment beatings.

Tom had worked hard for years to earn and keep respect. He had a reputation for being brutal when crossed, but he liked to think those he had dealings with thought of him as an honourable man. Tom had always treated Mae like a queen; his own sons had witnessed nothing less. He had stressed to David that if he felt the urge to knock a woman around, there were plenty of hookers on the payroll, plenty of junkies desperate for a fix. But it seemed David just couldn't control himself, and that disappointed his father more than anything.

Tom maintained an office at the back of one of his clubs, the Oracle. The office walls and door were thick, turning the DJ's efforts into a muted din. He had walked through the premises earlier, inspecting the bar and floor staff, and the podium dancers. He believed in being present, in reminding them he was the boss, always around. With one son dead and another missing, he needed to show control now more than ever. He had sampled a whiskey from a new supplier, and pressed the flesh, if you called squeezing the barmaid's bottom that, and he sat now at his rectangular oak desk, in anticipation of good news.

Murray had taken four of his best men and they were positioned in the Mad Hatter. The manager of the club, Nick, was an old friend of Murray's, and he was being more than accommodating. He had promised to stay out of Murray's way, and turn off the CCTV recording system for the night. Nick was poised to point out Kate Crowley as soon as she arrived. Tom had decided to stay out of it – she was familiar with him; they had met at his granddaughters' christening, and on a few other occasions. He didn't want her to get spooked and run again. He expected to have her in his hands before midnight. There was still no sign of John – but Tom felt sure that once he had Kate he could unlock that mystery.

The telephone on his desk rang and he snatched it up. It was too early for his men to be calling him to say they had her in the back of a car. It was Mae.

"Tom!" she whispered urgently.

The hairs on the back of Tom's neck stood on end. This sounded different to a whiskey-fuelled meltdown.

"Please come home. They're here!"

"*Who's there?*" he asked, rising to his feet.

"Two guys, eastern European maybe. They say they have John and they want to speak to you!"

Tom swallowed hard. His hand clenched tight around the handset. *The Meiers.*

"I'm on my way!" Grabbing his coat from the back of his chair, he bellowed to his driver: "*Marco!*"

For the first time in his life, Tom Gallagher felt close to losing control.

15

"What I don't understand is how the fuck they got in!" Marco said.

As Marco sped through the streets of Cork, Tom stared out the window, his anger mounting. He had two men on the entrance to his house for protection. He had high electric gates and the two sentries had sat inside for over ten years. No-one had ever penetrated the security system, nor dared try. He didn't answer Marco. Staring through the window, intently enough to burn a hole in the glass, he concentrated on quelling his anger and staying focused.

As they pulled into the property the double gate was wide open.

Where the hell were the security guys?

Marco drove along the winding driveway slowly. A black Range Rover was parked to the left of the front steps. It appeared to be empty. Marco stopped the car just before the front door, the headlights illuminating the wide flagstones. The steps appeared darker in one area. Tom exited the car and bent down to inspect them. Blood. There was a considerable amount of blood pooled on the porch step. He made a quick decision and held out his hand.

"Pass me your weapon, Marco!"

Marco had been manoeuvring his large frame out of the car. Without question he leant over to the passenger side and removed a handgun, fully loaded, from the glove compartment. He heaved himself out of the door and passed the gun to Tom. Tom tucked it into the back of his trouser belt. The front door was unlocked and slightly ajar. Together they entered the house.

In the wide tiled hallway, by the foot of the staircase, lay the crumpled bodies of the two security guards. Large dark gashes smeared their throats, their blood marking a track from the front door. Tom felt bile rise in his throat, quelled by his mounting fury.

"Take care of this! Get rid of the bodies!" he instructed Marco. "I don't want the Guards here!"

Marco nodded and pulled out his phone. He was a big man, muscular, and one of Tom's most loyal followers. He had seen his boss through many dark days, but these days seemed darker than most. He had cleaned up similar messes for Mr. Gallagher many times. Ely Murray and some of his best men were at the Mad Hatter. But there were others Marco could call to remove the bodies – he had no intention of leaving the boss here without protection.

Mae sat stiffly at the marble dining table. Her back was straight, her hands resting in her lap, her eyes cast down. She looked more sober than she had been in days. Facing her were two men. Although seated, Tom could see their long legs stretched out under the table, their broad shoulders pressed together. They were sallow-skinned and fair-haired. Tom had never met them before, but he assumed he was looking at two of the Meier brothers.

As Tom entered the room, they shifted their gaze from

Mae to him, a half smirk playing on the elder's lips.

"No need to stand," Tom said coolly. "You can make the introductions from there."

The older-looking of the men nodded. His eyes were hooded, the lids heavy. It gave him a sly appearance.

"I am Tobias Meier and you are Tom Gallagher. We've never met of course, although our intermediate has brought us together on many mutual business ventures. I think you'd agree they've been lucrative?" He gestured around the room and widened his hands, to take in the whole house. His accent was thick but his English perfect.

"Here is my brother Karl. He would shake hands but ..."

Karl sneered and held up his hands to display bruised and cut knuckles. The message was not lost on Tom and Mae Gallagher – these were the hands inflicting savage pain on their son.

Mae whimpered and tears began to fall down her cheeks. Tom could smell whiskey as he sat beside her – he put a steadying hand on her knee.

Tom had never felt this level of fury before. He knew he would have to draw on the self-control he had practised all his adult life to get through this. It took all his effort not to pull the gun from his waistband and empty it into their faces.

"Where is John?"

Tobias Meier sighed in mock exasperation. "I have come to the conclusion that even if I remove every one of your son's fingers, he will not tell me where the key is. I actually think he does not know."

In the midst of Tom's rage, two thoughts forced their way into his consciousness: *John was still alive. What key?*

"I gather from the information your son has managed to tell me that the items are perhaps lost. You may repay me for the money and diamonds of course, cover their value like for like, but the key I simply must have. Much less

113

patient men than me need it very urgently. It must be returned."

He spoke lightly, as if he were discussing the weather. He stood up, stretching his back from side to side, and began to move around the room, fingering photographs and ornaments, touching things gently. He stood at least six foot six and looked to be as broad.

Tom eyed him carefully, ready to move if he came too close. Mae kept her eyes on the marble tabletop.

"It's very simple. You give me the key. I give you your son. In one piece. Almost."

He winked at Mae and sat back down.

Tom sat as still as a stone, impassive, but his mind was racing, trying to recall the particulars of this deal. Ainsley, their usual middleman, had set it up. After a spate of robberies in Dublin, which the Meiers orchestrated from Munich, cash and diamonds needed to exit the city fast. David had driven to the capital, received possession of the goods, and was keeping them safe for a few weeks. It was a foolproof strategy that had worked many times. No-one searched the small city of Cork for items taken in the big smoke. After a period of time the items would be collected, the Gallaghers paid their holding fee, and the world kept turning until the next occasion their services were needed. Tom recalled the deal. Ninety thousand euro in cash, bundled in small notes, and four large diamonds. Tom was ignorant as to the true value of diamonds – to him they were expensive trinkets he occasionally bought for Mae. David had spoken animatedly about the four stones, perfectly oval and flawless, stolen from a jeweller at gunpoint in O'Connell Street, Dublin. They were worth tens of thousands each, apparently. The Gallaghers were happy to charge an extortionate fee for hiding them, and happier still to hand them back. Except they couldn't. The bag David had stored the items in was missing. Tom Gallagher had only one suspect. Kate Crowley. Natalie was too timid, too beaten down, had no spark left in her. But Kate, she was a sassy one, never leaving well enough alone.

This "key" Meier spoke about was news to Tom. David had never mentioned it. But how was he to gain information on it without alerting Tobias Meier that he wasn't fully clued in, fully in control of the dealings of his own business? Tom cursed David – what had he got the family into?

"As I'm sure you're aware, David is dead. He was murdered a few days ago. We are working on bringing his killer to justice. That same killer robbed him when she shot him. When we find her, we will have your key. Certainly, we will reimburse you for what you've lost right now. A Gallagher never reneges on a contract. We agreed to hold cash and four diamonds. I can compensate you for those. You can estimate the value of the diamonds."

Tobias Meier nodded, looking more serious than before.

"As for this key, we can cover the value of that too. Plus ten per cent for the time you've wasted. And then I expect you will return my son without further harm." Tom reasoned the key must surely be to a house or a building of some sort. He could afford to pay out. He wouldn't lose another son.

"I think you misunderstand." Tobias spoke softly, aware now that Gallagher had no idea what he was talking about. "The key is not replaceable – it cannot be covered by money. It is a computer key, you see – perhaps you call it a USB stick? Your son acquired some very interesting information that is worth a lot of money, information that very important people have paid a lot of money to secure. It is my job to return it to them. My life depends on it." He smirked. "And so does your son's!"

Mae attempted to stifle a sob. Tom gripped her hand tight under the table.

"Our dealings have been profitable. You have been very useful to us, and always honest. And I am a reasonable man. I'm willing to offer you a little time. I strongly suggest you find this thief, Mr Gallagher. Shall we say within twenty-four hours? Time really is pressing on. I will keep Mrs. Gallagher here company while you show Karl to your safe and pay some of your debts."

Mae looked at Tom, terrified. Tom had no choice but to follow orders. He hadn't taken orders from anyone in years. It enraged him, threatening to erode his normally cool composure. A tiny vein bulged and pulsed in his neck, but he kept his anger in check as he rose and walked into the hall. He kept his face expressionless and waited for Karl Meier to follow him. He visualised himself pulling the gun out and blowing Karl's face apart before running to the dining room to shoot Tobias in the back of the head. But he abandoned the fantasy and maintained his composure. The Meier gang was large, and his son remained at their mercy. Tom knew that if the brothers didn't return to whatever rock they had crawled out from under, his son would be executed.

Tom kept his wall safe hidden behind a family portrait in the study. Avoiding looking at his sons painted there, he lifted the frame from the wall and entered the combination. Karl pushed him roughly aside, took a folded-up shopping bag from his pocket, and filled it indiscriminately, taking every bundle of notes the safe contained. Once satisfied, he returned to the dining room. Tom followed, wondering how it had come to this.

Karl nodded once to Tobias and the elder brother stood up to go.

"Twenty-four hours. We will be in touch."

"Give me your word!" Mae spoke from her seat.

Her voice startled the three men who all turned in her direction. She looked wretched, her face shiny with tears, but strength emanated from her eyes. "Do not harm my son until then. Give us time – leave him be!"

Tobias studied her face for a long moment.

"For now," he answered quietly, and they were gone.

After he heard the front door close, Tom Gallagher turned to the dining-room wall, and punched a hole straight through it.

16

On Saturday night Myles was waiting by the fountain on the Grand Parade when Anna arrived. He looked dapper, in jeans and a blazer, his wild dark hair straightened and gelled back off his face. He smiled warmly at Anna and pulled her into a hug as she reached his side. Anna was caught off guard by the physical contact and laughed despite the tension she felt about the evening ahead.

"Hey!" Myles said. "You look great. I love your hair!"

Anna touched the ends of it lightly. It felt so short – she wasn't sure she had done the right thing. Her hair rested on her shoulders now, cut into flattering layers that framed her face. The hairdresser had assured her she'd get used to it, and Anna was sure she was right. It just felt so short!

"And I love yours!" Anna said, gesturing to his.

Myles adjusted his glasses, grinning broadly.

Anna wore a black wrap dress, leggings and a short leather jacket. She also wore knee-high boots, to keep her legs warm as much as to dress up the outfit. A large red scarf was wound around her neck and shoulders. The streets were beginning to freeze. She rubbed her hands together, wishing she'd thought to bring gloves.

Myles reached out and linked arms with her. "This is your city – lead the way!"

Anna took a deep breath and smiled. "The Mad Hatter's not too far from here."

"Thank God for that, it's freezing!"

Anna felt at ease as she moved away from the fountain in the direction of the Mad Hatter. Myles had a calming effect on her. As they walked through the busy streets and Myles chatted about his day, Anna realised that she was enjoying his company. He was fun and easy-going, and the pangs of loneliness she had felt earlier faded away. She was still having difficulty placing his accent – Dublin, Wicklow maybe? – but enjoyed the warmth of a body pressed close to hers.

Cork city was thronged with shoppers heading to the multistorey car parks or revellers starting their night on the town, and the couple moved quickly between them to the club.

Anna had been thinking about Kate all day, hoping she would turn up that night and that she'd get a chance to speak to her and warn her. Tom Gallagher had put a price on her head: thirty thousand euro dead, fifty thousand alive. Anna didn't need to delve deep into the dark side of her imagination to picture what he would do to Kate if he found her.

By the time they reached the Mad Hatter, they were freezing and spent the first few minutes inside rubbing their hands together and trying to blow some heat into them. The club was already busy. The bar area was crammed with bodies jostling to be served. Saber were setting up in one corner of the venue; it looked like they had a while to go yet before being ready to play. Anna chose a booth with a high leather sofa, a semicircle around a shiny tall table. It afforded them a view of the door and the bar area. It was a great vantage point to keep an eye out for Kate.

The clientele of the Mad Hatter appeared to Anna to be young professionals letting loose. There was plenty of money on show. She observed the crowd from her seat while Myles went to get the drinks. Designer handbags and shoes, trays of shots, expensively applied hair extensions – these were people with cash in their pockets, determined to spend it. She wondered if there would be lines of cocaine snorted in the toilets later like the many she had been offered, and declined, in college – was that still a thing? While she adored the buzz and excitement of Cork city by day, it was a long time since Anna had been in the city on a Saturday night, and she felt woefully out of touch.

As she scanned the venue she couldn't see anyone she recognised from work – none of the Gardaí or detectives, nor anyone she knew from the drug squad. She knew they were here though – Elise Taylor would have made sure of it.

Myles returned with two long-neck bottles of beer and passed one to Anna. It was ice-cold. "Cheers!" he said as they clinked bottles.

"So where are you from?" Anna asked. "Your accent is confusing me!"

Myles smiled as he shrugged off his coat.

"I was born in Dublin. My mother is Greek, and we spent some time there when I was a child, then some time in America. So, I guess it's a mixture of everywhere!"

Anna sipped her beer and savoured its freshness.

"So how did you get into the Guards then?" Myles asked, leaning closer to Anna as he spoke.

The Mad Hatter was surely at full capacity now; couples and groups stood in clusters and swarms at the bar. The band started playing Snow Patrol covers.

"I finished a post-graduate diploma and sat the civil service exams. I got stationed first in the Revenue offices, then I applied for a transfer to the Garda staff and the rest is history." She didn't add that she had hoped to find information on her parents' disappearance, somehow, in that new role. It had been with great disappointment she realised the only files she could access were the ones she had typed up herself. Still, she enjoyed the work. It was a busy post, where she rarely had a clear desk, but she had learned that that was the nature of the job. The order of the role suited her – the logical compilation of facts to solve a crime.

"What did you do your courses in?"

"I have a degree in mathematics and a post-grad in statistical analysis."

Myles looked stunned.

Anna laughed at his expression – she had seen it before. It wasn't everyone had chosen her educational path.

"What drew you to mathematics?"

"I've been told I have a logical mind." Anna shrugged. "And I like facts. They are 'ordered', you know? Mathematics is either factually accurate, or it didn't happen. There's no wriggle room, no mysteries."

Myles nodded. He could appreciate that.

"And statistical analysis?"

Anna shrugged and smiled. "I just find the logic and analysis of facts interesting."

Myles looked into her eyes appraisingly. "Pretty *and* smart – a killer combination!"

"Very corny!" Anna groaned and Myles had the grace to look sheepish.

Anna was embarrassed by the compliment but couldn't help smiling. It was ages since she had been on a date, and she had to admit she was enjoying herself. She took a long drink of her beer.

"And what about you?" she said, attempting to redirect the conversation.

Myles laughed. "Now that would be telling!"

Anna sipped her beer again and studied him.

"Why so shy? How did you end up working in the Special Detective Unit?"

Myles looked like he was considering his words.

"I was caught doing something a little … outside the rules."

Anna's eyebrows shot up – she was intrigued.

"I came to the attention of the Gardaí for the wrong reasons. They could tell I'm a good boy though!" Myles put his hand on his heart and adopted a puppy-dog-eyes expression. "It was decided my skills could be put to better use. I was … shall we say … encouraged into the force."

Anna leant in closer to hear him – the band seemed to have grown louder.

"Were you a hacker? Did you get caught hacking into government files?" she teased.

Myles smiled and he sipped his beer. "I'm saying no more!"

"You've got to tell me!"

Anna couldn't believe Myles would leave her hanging like this, giving her only half the story. He continued to shake his head, smiling.

"OK, fine! You're off the hook, for now."

The beers were gone, and Anna stood up, indicating she was going to the bar.

It was then she saw her. As the music pulsed around her, and as she moved through the crowd to the long wooden bar, she kept her eyes on the woman. Hunched over a drink at a corner table, she was alone, with her back to the wall, gripping a glass of dark liquid, staring into it. Her hair was short, roughly cut, and dark. Her body language screamed tension. Her shoulders were hunched over, and she sat on the very edge of the seat, as if ready to spring up and run. She looked up, her eyes scanning the crowd. Her face was pale and tired, but her eyes were the bright green Anna remembered. It was the faint ring of darker skin at her hairline that convinced her – hair dye. This was Kate Crowley. She was trying to disguise her appearance, and she was in trouble.

The crowd was heavy and swaying to the music from the band. Anna struggled to keep Kate in sight as she pushed her way forward.

Suddenly Kate stood up, picked up her coat and began to move, heading towards the back of the club. She kept her head down, pushing through the dancers, and made her way into the ladies' toilets.

Kate was relieved to find the small space empty. She needed some time in the peace and quiet to steady her nerves. She stood at the sink, staring at her reflection. How was it possible to look so terrified? She was taken aback by her gaunt and pale appearance. She felt that she stood out a mile from the glamorous crowd – still wearing her jeans and blue jumper from Wednesday. She couldn't believe she was still in this city! If she hadn't stupidly left her passport behind, she would already be in France, instead of waiting for Nick in this packed club.

What she knew for certain was that she was running out of options, and she was beginning to doubt she would get out of Cork alive. Her nerves were rattled as she waited for Nick – the loud music, the crowd – it was too much. She hadn't eaten properly in days and she felt weak and cold. She pulled on her coat, checking that her scarf and hat were safely tucked into its pockets.

Suddenly, the door opened and a man stood in its frame, taking up the whole space. He was huge. Dressed in black, he

123

was what she knew was referred to as "muscle". He smiled coldly, accentuating a scar that ran from his lip to his ear.

"Kate, I presume?" He stepped towards her. "Tom Gallagher wants a word."

Terror paralysed her. She stood rooted to the tiled floor.

Then a young woman appeared behind him.

Kate registered her blonde hair, her black dress, saw her mouth open and form a familiar word:

"Kate!"

The man turned to face the blonde woman.

She locked eyes with him.

"Private business in here – *get out!*" he snarled.

He reached to grab her by the hair, perhaps to throw her outside the door. Whatever his intentions, they didn't materialise.

As he reached out she swiftly stepped to the side and palm-blocked his arm, before punching him hard in the kidneys. His shock registered as she kicked out viciously, connecting with the front of his knee. He fell backward with a groan, and his head jerked to the side, hitting one of the white porcelain sinks. He fell to the floor, unconscious.

Kate watched it all as though it were a slow-motion movie, her mouth hanging open.

The woman held out her hand.

"Kate, we don't have much time – we have to get you out of here!"

She gestured for Kate to step over the man.

But Kate couldn't move. Everything was still in slow motion.

Standing at the door, Anna looked to her right and saw two men walking along the corridor leading to the toilets. They were dressed much the same as the man lying unconscious on the floor, with grim expressions marring their faces.

She darted back into the ladies', slamming the door

behind her, feeling around the handle for a lock. "Damn!" she muttered, not finding one.

Adrenaline pumped through her veins. The man on the ground was stirring and soon it would be three against one.

Small windows opened outward in each toilet cubicle. She pushed Kate towards one of them.

"You have to climb out, do you understand? Our friend here," she jerked her thumb in the direction of the man stirring on the floor, "has two friends on their way in!"

Kate just stared at her open-mouthed. Anna knew she had no choice – she slapped Kate sharply on the cheek. The slap was effective – Kate's eyes regained focus and she darted forward.

The window was small, but just big enough to squeeze through. Kate wriggled her way through it, Anna following. As she exited Anna saw the man rise from the bathroom floor and heard him roar out in anger. She jumped to the ground, her heart pounding. The concrete was hard and the heels on her boots thin – a jolt of pain shot up her legs and into her lower back.

Both women stayed low to the ground.

"Thanks!" Kate whispered, breathing hard. She looked at her rescuer in confusion. "Anna?"

Anna nodded. "We need to get out of here. I can get you to a safe place – come with me, *please!*"

Kate hadn't seen Anna Clarke in years. She had survived this long by relying on her instincts and by staying alone. *How did Anna know about the Gallaghers?*

They were in an alley at the side of the club. There were bins and empty beer kegs lining the walls.

Anna wished she had her phone to call the Gardaí, but it was back at the table with Myles.

Abruptly Kate stood up and jogged toward the entrance of the alley, intent on getting out of there.

125

"*Wait!*" Anna called, struggling to her feet.

Suddenly a man turned into the alley from the entrance of the street. It was one of Gallagher's men. Kate was only feet away from him, and he grinned in satisfaction.

Everything happened so quickly then.

The man reached for Kate, but she twisted to the left, pivoted on her left foot and spun, her right leg dead straight, kicking the guy in the face with such force he crumpled in a heap on the ground. She stepped over him and, without a backward glance, ran into the dark.

Anna dropped to the ground behind a large bin, out of sight.

What the hell was that?

Anna recognised a skilled defensive kick when she saw one. Kate had just delivered a powerful blow and knocked a man out.

Alarm bells rang loud in Anna's head. What exactly was going on? Her theory that Kate must have shot David Gallagher in self-defence was looking less likely – with such skills she could have knocked him out! Why did she have to kill him? Anna thought of the pathologist's report, that Gallagher had suffered a vicious assault. Was Kate capable of such things?

Anna stood up and ran out of the alley, past the man now regaining consciousness on the ground. She needed to get back to Myles and their date. And she needed to speak with Elise Taylor.

17

Elise Taylor sipped her fourth coffee of the night at her work desk. This was not how Elise had wanted to spend a Saturday night. She was exhausted – sleep had been impossible since the shooting.

She checked her mobile phone for the umpteenth time – no message. She was growing increasingly restless as she waited for word from the undercover drug crew from the Mad Hatter. The undercover detectives Connors and Moore were pros at this. Their professional façade was easily eroded by a few days' unshaved stubble and the right clothes; they could easily blend into the nightclub. But they were all Janet McCarthy would sanction. Elise felt sour about that – this bloody political conference was taking over everything, pushing all other cases to the bottom of the "urgent" pile. The Chief Superintendent would deny it, but the fact that it was a serious criminal who was dead was contributing to her apathy, Elise was sure of it.

She remembered her heated exchange with Janet McCarthy yesterday lunchtime.

"David Gallagher will still be dead when the political conference is over," Janet had said.

"But our only suspect might have fled the city by then, maybe even the country!"

"There are many people who had reason to shoot Gallagher. I agree it looks bad for the Crowley girl, it being in her house. But for all we know she's dead too!"

"That's why I need more bodies in the Mad Hatter Saturday night – if whoever is looking to buy a passport *isn't* her, then fair enough. But, if it is, she can give us some answers. And we should try to bring in the seller too."

"I'm sorry, Detective, I really am. Connors and Moore are all you're getting."

Elise would have gone to the club herself but for her fear of spooking Kate. They had met many times in the last two years. Kate had reported David Gallagher's abuse of her sister to Elise on numerous occasions. Elise remembered her as tearful and angry, disgusted at what her sister was suffering – but murderous? Elise didn't think so. Vengeful? She certainly had motive enough to kill the man, especially after Gallagher had threatened her nieces.

Elise screwed up a sheet of paper into a ball and threw it at the bin, her frustration mounting. She checked her mobile again – still no message from the undercovers.

She pulled her notes toward her and reread the pieces of this puzzle one more time. Kate Crowley was seen by a neighbour at the scene. She was the current tenant at the property where Gallagher's body was found. Her prints were on the gun. But it was clear she had fled and leaving a packed suitcase and passport behind certainly didn't paint the scene of a premeditated murder. If she was a victim of an assault, and his shooting was done in self-defence, then why didn't she act like a victim and wait for the Gardaí? Why did she act guilty and run?

128

Where was she?

Elise needed answers. She needed to find Kate Crowley.

Suddenly the door to her open-plan floor opened and she was momentarily startled. She half rose from her seat, then her heart rate returned to normal when she recognised Anna Clarke from the clerical crew downstairs, and a detective from Dublin with her.

Anna looked flushed, her nose and cheeks red from the cold.

"Detective Taylor, I'm glad you're here! I was hoping to find you, or at least get your number. I left your card on my desk yesterday."

"What is it?" Elise's sharp tone betrayed her frustration.

Anna and Myles had stopped in front of her; both seemed out of breath.

"What happened?"

"We were in the Mad Hatter and –"

"*What?* Why were you there?" Why was this girl meddling in the case, just because she had known the suspect? "I told you not to get involved!"

Anna reddened.

"We went to watch a band," her companion explained, his hand resting on Anna's back. His brown eyes observed Elise, his tone a warning to take it easy. She ignored him.

"*And?*" She glared at Anna.

"And I met Kate Crowley in the bathroom. One of Gallagher's guys, I think, followed her in. We had to jump out the window, and there was another guy in the alleyway – he went to grab her and –"

"Jesus Christ! Are you sure it was her?"

"Positive!"

"And the guy in the alley?"

"She knocked him out."

"*What?*"

129

"She kicked him in the face – it was definitely a kickboxing manoeuvre or something like that …"

Anna trailed off as she observed Elise's red face, anger pulsing in her eyes.

"What the hell is going on here? If she can knock a man out, what possible reason does she have to shoot him?"

"Exactly!" Myles said. "We thought you should know."

Elise glared at Anna again. Taking a deep breath, she fought an inner battle to calm down.

"This could explain some of David's injuries. The pathologist said it looked like he had been in a fight." Elise rubbed a hand over her face. "So, Kate's gone from the club? I'll need to call in Connors and Moore."

She turned narrowed eyes on Anna.

"I want your statement as soon as possible! And don't mess any further with my investigation!" She paused, her eyes softening. "You could get hurt."

A young uniformed Garda put his head around the partition to her office cubicle.

Anna was glad of the interruption.

"Detective, did you hear? Two dead bodies found in the back of a car, near the Peace Park."

Elise's eyes widened, and the blood drained from her face.

"Christ!" She pinched the bridge of her nose with her thumb and finger, exhaling deeply.

"What happened?"

The Garda rocked back and forth on his feet with nervous excitement. "Hard to say just yet. A car was stopped and searched at one of the checkpoints set in place for the conference. The driver was acting suspiciously. There were two dead bodies in the boot of the car. Apparently it looks like two of Gallagher's guys."

Without another word, Elise grabbed her jacket and rushed to the stairwell.

18

Natalie Crowley was restless and lonely. She realised she had been chain-smoking for an hour now and pushed the cigarette packet away in disgust. She refilled her glass of wine instead. Kate had called her and told her everything – David was dead.

Natalie had cried for over an hour after she put the twins to bed, barely managing to control her grief until then. David had attacked Kate and he was dead. Shot in the neck. Natalie wondered if there had been much blood and if he had been scared in his final moments. She wondered what he had looked like. She didn't love David anymore, she knew that. He wasn't a good father, and he was a lousy partner. Still, she grieved for him. David. The father of her children, the man she had been obsessed with for almost four years.

Once her tears had dried, she felt only agitation. She needed her sister.

The hotel apartment in Chartres was sparsely furnished. Natalie had taken a booking for two weeks, hoping Kate would join them long before then. They had the basics, but it was hardly the home comforts her girls were used to. There were two bedrooms, one tiny bathroom, and an open-plan living area. It was a far cry from the luxury four-bedroomed house she had shared with David. Even when she had occasionally taken the twins and fled to Kate's modest three-bed semi, it had been a lot nicer than this. But the hotel offered anonymity, sanctuary. It would be a safe haven until Kate joined them. Natalie was still thanking God that the flight to Paris had had three seats to spare at the last minute. Chartres was familiar to her; it was the place the Crowleys had spent two weeks on many summers in her childhood. It had been as good a base as any – an hour on the train from Paris.

Now Natalie had nothing to do but wait. And hide.

But she didn't want to hide alone. She needed Kate, had always needed Kate, and never more so than now. The small apartment felt too big without her.

Natalie had spent the last few days taking the girls to the park or to the market, walking the streets, teaching them French phrases, smiling as they tried to pronounce the unfamiliar words. The nights were always the same. Once she had Rachel and Rhea settled, she would sit on the small armchair drinking cheap wine and smoking, waiting for the telephone to ring. Kate had told her to invest in a new mobile phone the day before she left Ireland – so Natalie had done that, then switched off her old mobile phone and thrown it into a public waste bin outside Cork airport.

Kate was clever that way – she was certain the Gallaghers had a Garda on their side and didn't want to take any chances. David and his brother John had always known when Kate had approached the Gardaí over Natalie's mistreatment at David's hands, often before she had even reached home. She was convinced the Gallaghers were being tipped off rather than properly investigated.

So, she had made Natalie promise to get rid of her mobile, just in case it could be traced and her whereabouts passed to the Gallaghers. Now only Kate knew her phone number – they were alone in the world. They had been alone before, but always alone *together*. Natalie didn't like this feeling.

Natalie and Kate had literally done everything together their whole lives. In school and college, they were always side by side. Through their parents' divorce they had been a constant support to one another. From their red hair and green eyes, to their opinions and interests, they were almost always completely identical. They even shared a hatred of their mother's new husband and had grieved together over the death of their father – they had never wanted to be apart. They were two women joined as one.

Until Natalie met David Gallagher. For the first time, someone was coming between the twins. Of course, they each had had boyfriends before, some of whom the other twin hadn't got along with. But David was different. Natalie fell in love quickly and completely. David was daring and confident. Natalie had been mesmerised by his charm and charisma. He had access to the best clubs in Cork, bought her generous gifts, and showered her with compliments. He hated for them to be apart and was never happy when she was with her sister. At the time, she had been flattered by his jealousy. She took it as a sign of how much he loved her. If she was honest with herself, she felt lucky this handsome, successful charmer had noticed her at all.

Until David convinced her to move in with him, he used to call her up to twenty times a day. Kate was furious with him and with her sister – she told Natalie that David was trying to check up on her, to control her. But David told her he was just making sure she was OK, and she believed him.

Before long, she left the house she shared with Kate and moved in with him. It was the first time the twins had ever lived apart. Kate had been crushed. Not because Natalie was moving in with a man so soon, but because she was moving in with *him*.

But despite the growing tension and division between the sisters, it was Kate's house Natalie fled to the first night David attacked her.

Natalie had grown increasing isolated over the following months. At first, David convinced her she didn't need to work, and she quit her job as a linguist and part-time teacher. Then she discovered she was pregnant early in the relationship – she was shocked, but David's delight soothed her fears. Soon, though, he began to physically abuse her. It started with squeezing her arm too tight or pushing her over. It quickly progressed to punching, kicking, and squeezing her throat so tight she would see black spots dance in front of her eyes.

She sensed her sister's disgust that she didn't leave David. But she couldn't. He had eroded every bit of her confidence, quickly, imperceptibly. When David swore each time would be the last that he hit her, she always believed him. Even when she caught David cheating on her, she stayed. And he swore he would change for their children. He was so excited to be a father. He spoke of marriage, and Natalie had never felt happier. She wanted to put the bad times behind them.

On some level, Natalie knew David was a monster. Kate went to great efforts to point out his failings to her – every time the Gallaghers were mentioned disparagingly in a newspaper article, she would save it for Natalie. But the articles only made suggestions about the Gallaghers' activities, never outright accusing the family of criminality. Journalists knew better than that. Every time there was trouble on a night out, Kate made sure Natalie knew about it and examined the facts.

"Drugs being dealt in David's club! Natalie, read this article."

"It's only speculation!"

"For God's sake, wise up!"

"Well, it's hardly David's fault! He's a businessman – these things happen! What's he supposed to do? Police every single person in every one of his clubs?"

"He's a low life, Natalie! He and his brother are thugs. You hear the stories about them, you see the way men eye them when we go out. They are dangerous men!"

Natalie had shut her ears and her mind to facts she knew to be true.

Kate, on the other hand, seemed to grow even stronger in her resolve to break them up. The relationship between the twins became strained, but never fractured.

When her twin daughters were born Natalie felt a shift in David and his family. The Gallaghers had always been ambivalent towards her. She knew they viewed her as just another woman on David's arm, even when she was living with him. But with the birth of their grandchildren Natalie found Tom and Mae Gallagher to be claustrophobic. They were always interfering, and she could never do anything right. David never stopped his ill-treatment of her. And he was an ambivalent father. He made no secret of the fact he had wanted sons – daughters were a disappointment to him – he disregarded his children while his parents more than made up for it in harassing her about their upbringing. David resented the neediness of the babies, the crying and sleepless nights. And he made it perfectly clear what he expected of Natalie, regardless of how tired she was. He soon grew bored of Natalie and the twins and took to bringing women home after a night out at a club in the city.

Natalie was trapped in a living hell and Kate was her only supporter.

One night, after Natalie suffered a particularly vicious beating, Kate went to the Gardaí. She had filed many reports, but this time she threatened to go over their heads if nothing was done about it. On her way home, she was attacked. She gave as good as she got, but she was left shaken and bleeding. The message was clear – keep your mouth shut.

And still Natalie didn't leave him.

Looking back now, Natalie wondered who she was then. A woman in love, a woman desperate to make a family, a woman exhausted from single-handedly raising her twins.

Once, Natalie *did* threaten to leave David. He had been more abusive than usual and bringing women to the house. Natalie felt like less than nothing. In a heated argument she threatened to take the girls and leave for good. How David sought to punish her still sent a chill down Natalie's spine. On a night she still could not bear to think about, David had come to the house, and taken the girls. David had driven with their daughters to the Cork docks, parked, and telephoned her, threatening to drive off the quay.

When the Gardaí brought her children home to her, unharmed, Natalie had made up her mind. It was as though gears and levers had shifted into place, leaving her questioning who she had been for four years. Suddenly, her mind was clear. She was leaving. She knew now that she would, that she would have to find a way.

Kate had begged her for years. Now that Natalie was finally listening, she never said "I told you so"; she just remained a solid support. And then, an opportunity presented itself, and Kate knew just what to do.

Natalie pushed herself up from the armchair and moved to the twins' room. She stood in the door frame, no longer able

136

to sit and wallow in the memories of the last few years of her life. Her daughters slept in a double bed, back to back. There were no curtains on the window, and the moon sliced through the darkness to illuminate the twins. Their curly auburn hair was messy on the pillows, their mouths slightly open, their small arms wrapped around identical blue teddy bears. The teddies' eyes sparkled in the sliver of light, twinkling at her. Natalie looked at her future; it made her feel at peace to watch her daughters breathe.

Her ringing mobile phone drew her back to the living room; she snatched it up from the coffee table.

"Kate!"

"Are you all OK?"

"Yes – are you? Where are you?"

Kate sighed. "Still in Cork. It's dangerous here. Gallagher is searching for me."

Natalie stifled a sob. "Why can't you just get out of there?"

"Natalie, it won't be for long more. Just hold it together for a few more days. I love you. I'll see you soon. Are they safe?"

Natalie looked over her shoulder towards the bedroom. "Yes, always in sight, I told you."

After Kate ended the call, Natalie burst into loud sobs. She couldn't take much more of this. With shaking hands, she reached for the cigarette packet and lit another.

19

Sunday

Sunday morning dawned bright and cold. Anna set the shower to cool and felt herself come alive under the chilly blast of the water. Her lower back ached, probably from the jump from the Mad Hatter's bathroom window.

As she dried her hair a text from Myles drew her attention: **I'm going surfing!!! Join me.**

Anna glanced out her bedroom window, at the white frost-covered grass, and shuddered. Myles Henderson was mad!

No way! I'd freeze to death!

Dinner then. I'm not taking no for an answer!

Anna smiled. Their date had ended very abruptly. After their brief – and extremely tense – conversation with Elise Taylor, Myles had hailed a taxi, paid the driver, and kissed Anna quickly on the cheek. As dates went, it had been extremely adventurous, and completely unexpected. Myles had been on Anna's mind as she drifted off to sleep. His firm hand on the small of her back as they spoke with Elise, his soft kiss as he said goodnight. Anna realised there was no way she was refusing a dinner date.

I'll be in town later – I'll meet you in the seafood restaurant next door to your hotel at 6. If you're not a block of ice by then!

Myles responded with a selfie of himself giving a thumbs-up, the cold waves rolling onto the shore behind him on Garrettstown beach. Anna grinned. She really liked this guy.

Over breakfast, Anna looked again at the business card from Kristian Lane. She had a three o'clock coffee meeting with him in the city. She knew she'd have to tell him everything she could remember, and she wondered what files he would have access to, if any. Anna knew Alex had some documentation about the investigation, and she wondered if Kristian Lane could apply to access old Garda files. The butterflies that danced in her stomach could be from excitement or dread. She was prepared for anything the private investigator might find. She had told herself that anyway.

She brewed fresh coffee and sat at her kitchen table. She had lit the stove in the living room already, and the heat was invading the whole downstairs of her house. She pulled her laptop towards her and looked up the morning news headlines.

TWO BODIES FOUND IN CITY CENTRE CAR SEARCH was the first item of breaking news.

Anna read quickly. Two males thought to be in their late forties or early fifties had died violent deaths. Their bodies were discovered in the boot of a car after Gardaí detained and searched a vehicle in the city centre. The report went on to speculate that the victims were killed elsewhere. Anna knew *this* particular piece of information would have been assumed due to lack of blood where they were found. Gardaí were appealing to the public for information.

She sat back and thought of DS Taylor, wondering if she

139

was at the crime scene this morning. She had been irate last night. Anna felt a twinge of guilt – maybe she should follow Elise's advice and not get involved in Kate's predicament. It didn't feel like advice though, it felt like an instruction, and it irritated her. Going to a club was hardly inserting herself into the investigation, although she did admit to herself she had hoped to speak to Kate.

Anna had saved the detective's mobile number into her phone – she had wasted time last night returning to the station to look for it. If she *did* run into Kate again, she wanted to be able to call DS Taylor immediately.

She realised she herself had had a lucky escape last night. She felt thankful that her father's enthusiasm for Taekwon-Do had rubbed off on her.

She thought of Kate, wondering what was going through her mind this morning. Things did not look good for her old school friend – a man had been shot dead in her house, after which she had fled and was hiding out somewhere. She had dyed and cut off her hair in an attempt to go undetected. Her sister had taken her children and left the country. Anna had been so sure of Kate's innocence, and that the shooting had been self-defence. But last night she had seen with her own eyes that Kate was extremely capable of defending herself – without a gun. All of those facts added up to a woman with secrets, a woman desperate to evade both the Gallaghers and the Gardaí.

Anna sat forward again, fingers poised over the laptop keys.

It was time to do some investigative work of her own.

20

Detective Superintendent Doherty was keenly aware it was four days to the conference; Janet McCarthy was apoplectic about the discovery of two dead bodies in the boot of a car. William Ryan was bothering him about some sexual assaults, the Gallaghers wanted their son out of the city morgue, there were suspected German criminals running about, and now this. Doherty was sure he would need to get his blood-pressure medication refilled before the end of the day. He observed the gathering crowd of onlookers near the park – journalists and civilians with their cameras out. Doherty moaned to himself. Elise Taylor had better have this under control.

Elise had expected to be joined by her colleague William Ryan at the crime scene, but she stood alone near the entrance of the park, behind the parked car. Apparently, William was trying to get a warrant to follow up a lead on the serial sexual-assault cases. Elise was unhappy to let him take the initiative on that; she was next in line to take over the investigation on those cases, but she couldn't be in two places at once. William was newly transferred in, and Elise didn't think he had enough experience to wrap things up. But she had bigger problems. She could clean up that mess when she was done here.

Elise had been in discussion with a member of the forensic team regarding the expected arrival time of the pathologist, and now stopped to watch Doherty approach, his face bright red, his eyebrows almost joined together. Elise sighed. She had few answers, and that wouldn't be what Doherty wanted to hear. She felt a migraine forming at her temples.

"Taylor," Doherty said by way of greeting.

"Superintendent Doherty."

He observed the bodies lying in situ in the boot. The Garda Technical Bureau team were in the process of finalising the preliminary examination before the bodies were moved.

"Fill me in," Doherty ordered, shaking a tablet into his palm before hurtling it into his mouth and chewing fiercely. He bent over and inspected the bodies briefly. A large, dark gash in one man's neck made his stomach turn; he stepped back quickly.

Elise's voice betrayed her exhaustion.

"The deceased are Seán and Bill Addams, cousins and both known employees of Tom Gallagher. We've met these two guys before – they worked security at the entrance to Gallagher's property. Cause of death appears to be knife wounds to the throat – the bodies were transferred to the boot after. Both are carrying their wallets, which appear untouched, so we have no reason to suspect a robbery. We need to talk to Gallagher, and the victims' friends and family. I want to find out if they were into anything more dodgy than usual."

"And the driver and passenger?"

"They both have records, minor stuff. They are in custody and refusing to answer any questions."

"Surprise, surprise." Doherty rubbed his jaw in thought. He surveyed the scene. "Could this have anything to do with David Gallagher's death?"

"It's possible, certainly. The Gallaghers are having a bad week."

"That's an understatement. We know the Meier gang are in Cork. Do you think this is an inter-gang war?"

"Possibly, sir, and don't forget John Gallagher is missing."

"That's not our problem until someone reports it. Bloody hell! Janet McCarthy is going to have a fit. We have the Taoiseach's security team breathing down her neck, not to mention multiple European state offices looking for detailed security plans. We cannot have this hanging over the conference. Get this wrapped up, Taylor. I want an update by lunchtime!"

Doherty stormed back to his car, his trench coat flapping at his calves. Elise gritted her teeth. She'd been awake for twenty-five hours now, and it looked like sleep wouldn't come until she could convince Doherty, and Janet McCarthy for that matter, that the streets were safe. Doherty was a tough man to please – now that pressure was mounting on his shoulders, Elise knew dealing with him would become even more difficult.

Elise knew finding Kate Crowley was crucial to restoring normality around here. It seemed that in shooting David Gallagher she had unleased a river of bloodshed into the city, and it was falling to Elise to stem the flow.

Balling her hands in fury, she turned back to the gruesome crime scene.

21

When Mae Gallagher opened her eyes, she was momentarily paralysed with fear. She had no idea where she was. A clock on the wall read one o'clock, and she guessed from the light outside that it was one o'clock in the afternoon, not the middle of the night. She was lying in a double bed, covered in a heavy, flowered duvet. She clutched it to her chin as she took in her surroundings. An oak bedside locker and matching wardrobe, a chaise lounge under the window … recognition pulled at the edge of her consciousness and she sat up.

Yes, she knew where she was now; a black-and-white photograph on top of the bedside locker, of two young girls digging sandcastles on the beach, confirmed it. Mae was at her sister Christina's house.

So, Tom had got rid of her. Shipped his wife with her whiskey and her vials of Xanax off to her sister's house, the better to have her out of the way.

Mae could have felt offended in that moment, but she knew her husband. In many ways, he was a very predictable man.

Removing his fragile wife from the house could only mean one thing – Tom Gallagher was preparing for war. It was better to remove any innocent bystanders than risk them getting hurt. Mae smiled as she lay back against the pillows. She wouldn't fancy being in those German boys' shoes right now. Nor Kate Crowley's either. Tom was about to right some wrongs, and Mae felt positively giddy with anticipation.

22

Anna had a Facebook account, but only to keep in touch with her friends from college or to see whatever photos Vivian posted online. She barely used it. And if she was honest with herself, when she did use it, it was mainly to search for her parents' names, just to see what came up. Not that she imagined they had set up social-media accounts if they were living somewhere with full amnesia.

Sitting at her kitchen table, Anna entered Kate Crowley's name and got a handful of results, but none of them the Kate Crowley she was looking for. She tried searching with the forename Catherine and got the same result. Spelling Catherine with both a K and a C yielded nothing. Kate Crowley did not have a Facebook account.

She chewed her bottom lip, thinking. She needed to widen the search. She keyed in Natalie's name, but again, there were a handful of Natalie Crowleys with Facebook profiles but none of them were the one Anna was hoping to find. She included Twitter and Instagram in her search, as much as was possible not having either account herself. Another dead end.

Now what? She had already exhausted Google and LinkedIn, both yielding only professional details relating to Kate's work as a graphic designer.

Anna tapped her pen against the notebook; she hadn't expected her search to crash out so quickly. She leant forward as an idea struck her. Trying to remember the notes she had typed up, to recall the date the twins moved to Cork … 2014. They had graduated that year and had returned to Cork after finishing college.

Anna began to type, concentrating on the colleges in Dublin … Trinity College, Dublin City University, University College Dublin, Dublin Institute of Technology… searching for posts with the caption "Class of 2014" or graduation photographs.

This time she got results. Profile after profile flashed on the screen, responding to her instructions, and she rejected one after the other, until one grabbed her attention and caused her breath to still.

It was the Facebook profile page of a woman named Pauline Forde. She currently worked in AIB Bank in Dublin and had recently celebrated her birthday in Temple Bar. But it was her profile uploads from 2014 that had drawn Anna's attention.

She read out loud into her small, empty kitchen: "*So sad to say goodbye to my BFFs. UCD's been a blast, but the 6 musketeers are no more. Luv you, guys!!!*"

Anna clicked on the photograph underneath and it enlarged, showing a smiling group of six graduates in long gowns, most of them holding on to their caps to stop the wind carrying them off. It looked to be a blustery day; their gowns were captured by the photograph in various states of disarray, long hair whipping around their grinning faces. There was Pauline, centre stage, flanked by her BFFs, as she had put it.

Anna touched the one face that seemed familiar: a

young woman standing to the far left of the group. She was smiling broadly, her arm linked with the woman beside her.

Kate Crowley.

Or Natalie, Anna realised. The women were identical twins after all. Anna sat back in her chair, adrenaline pulsing in her veins. She wondered which twin was featured in the photograph, looking carefree and happy with her friends. Her fingers flying, Anna began to search Pauline Forde's profile page.

Pauline Forde had been close to both Crowley sisters in college, and it was easy to piece together a profile of their friendship from Pauline's Facebook page. The banker kept her security setting at Public, allowing access to whomever wanted it. She didn't appear to be on Instagram or any other public platform, but Facebook gave Anna more than she had hoped for.

Both Kate and Natalie Crowley had led an active social life in college. They were involved in a drama club, and Natalie in a French cooking club. In their earlier college years, they socialised more frequently judging from the copious number of bleary-eyed photographs the sisters were tagged in, in a variety of clubs and bars in Dublin.

As time passed, as the group of friends grew older and their course work more intense, the photographs changed to those of study groups in coffee shops or the college library. There appeared to have been few nights out, but Pauline had documented what little there were on her profile page. She was a supportive friend. A woman named Jules had her twenty-first birthday extensively covered, another named Hannah got first-class honours in her degree, celebrated with steak and champagne, the photographs uploaded for all to see. They seemed like a tight bunch of friends. Looking at the photographs, Anna felt a pang of longing to see Vivian again.

148

It was the celebratory photographs and accompanying text that documented Kate Crowley's extra-curricular achievement in her third year of college that left Anna stunned.

"So proud of you babe, you did it!!!!! Retained your title, Inter-College Champion whoop whoop!"

Underneath a photograph of Kate, dressed in a black martial arts pants and belted top, being presented with a trophy, were the words '**Inter-College All-Ireland Kickboxing Championship**'. Kate beamed at the photographer as she accepted the small trophy and shook hands with what presumably was the judge.

Anna sat back into the wooden chair, absorbing this new information. It confirmed what she had realised the night before: Kate Crowley was skilled in self-defence. She had kicked one of Gallagher's men so hard he was knocked out.

So why then had she shot David Gallagher, when she could quite plausibly have incapacitated him instead?

Anna rubbed her temples, thinking. Elise Taylor would have to be shown this. The shooting had happened only a few days ago, and no doubt Elise had her team working on getting background detail on Kate. Anna knew this information had never been mentioned in the case notes.

Anna looked again at the group graduation photo of Kate and her friends. They looked so ... hopeful about the future. With a pang of sadness Anna thought her old friends had no idea what was coming in *their* future – namely, David Gallagher.

Taking the name of each girl tagged in the photograph, Anna searched online for as much information as she could. All of Kate Crowley's old college friends either lived in mainland Europe or Australia, according to Facebook. Only Pauline Forde was still in Ireland, in Dublin. After graduation Jules had emigrated to Sydney, and Hannah

149

was utilising her degree working in a large chain of jewellers operating out of Antwerp. A quick search of Crowleys living in the area also came up short; it appeared they were a small family.

Anna closed her laptop with a firm thud. Her belief that Kate was innocent was truly shaken – Kate Crowley, wherever she was, had a lot of explaining to do.

23

Kate buttoned up her coat and wound her scarf around her neck. Jamming her hat down over her ears, she left her hotel and kept her head down. The wind stung her face and drew tears from her eyes. She walked hurriedly.

At lunchtime on Sunday the streets were quiet. The footpaths were littered with the usual debris from a vibrant city's Saturday night offerings. Today, though, council workers were out in force. Sweeping and power-washing away the beer cans, discarded chip packets and vomit puddles, soon they would have erased any evidence of the debauchery of the night before. Others were erecting crowd-control barriers lining the city's main streets. The city was readying itself for the political conference. Kate had read about it in the newspaper over the last few weeks. She imagined all the city's business owners sprucing their premises up in anticipation of a visit from any of the VIPs the conference would attract.

She bought a coffee and a ham sandwich from a street vendor near the city library, grateful they were open even on a Sunday. She eyed the newspapers on a stand nearby as she waited for her coffee. Her heart raced as David Gallagher's face looked back at her from the front page. The letters of the words in the caption above his face swam in a dizzying blur, refusing to focus. But David's killing was relegated to only the top corner of the front page – there had been two bodies found in the boot of a car in the city the night before. She shuddered as she read the headline.

"Here you go, love!" The ageing male barista leant over the counter and handed her a steaming, extra-large cardboard coffee cup. "Terrible business these killings!"

"Yes." She kept her eyes down. She longed to walk away but didn't want to draw attention to herself by being rude. She took one step back, the man still talking.

"What's going on at all? A shooting last week, and now two men turn up dead in the boot of a car!" He shook his head. "Rumour is they were working for Tom Gallagher, the fella that owns the nightclubs and bars. Terrible business his son being shot last week. Shocking!"

She gripped her coffee tightly, the lid almost popping off. Tom Gallagher's men, dead! Her mouth had gone completely dry and her legs began to shake. Drawing in a deep breath of cold air, she pushed her legs forward, one after the other, and walked hurriedly away.

"*Love! Your change!*" the barista called after her, but she didn't stop. She knew this was the work of the Germans. No one else would take on the Gallaghers in their own city. The timing was too coincidental; it had to be them.

Fear wrapped her heart in its cold fist. If Tom Gallagher knew anything about what had gone on in the last week between her and David Gallagher, he would kill her. His men had found her last night. Going to the Mad Hatter had been so reckless. She had to leave this city forever, one way or another. She pressed on, the cold air burning her lungs, her legs pounding the city streets.

24

"If there's a reason you're at my front door on a Sunday, it had better be fucking good!"

Tom Gallagher was clearly unimpressed to see Elise.

She stood with her hands behind her back. He had answered the front door himself, a very unlikely scenario. Elise had left word at the station that she was headed here, as a precaution. She was glad of it. Tom looked a mess.

"I'm surprised not to have heard from you. If my son was shot dead I'd be banging down the door to the Garda station until they found the killer. But you've been strangely quiet on that front. Being kept busy?"

Tom glared hatred at Elise.

"Aren't you going to invite me in?" she asked.

Gallagher was dressed but it looked like yesterday's clothes – crumpled, with a wet stain on his shirt. His eyes were red-rimmed, and his hair stood on end, as though he had run his hands through it many times. He didn't answer or invite Elise inside, just stood in the frame of the front door to his large Tudor-style home, arms bunched into fists at his sides.

"I see your usual security men have been replaced. Feeling unwell, were they?" Elise pressed on, hoping to draw out a response.

Gallagher continued his silent stare; he had been too well coached by his legal team to ever give anything away.

"Do you want something, detective?"

"The fact is," Elise continued, "we have identified two victims of a violent crime to be the two men you normally employ in that post. They were found dead late last night. You may have heard about it on the morning news bulletin on the radio?"

Gallagher shrugged, remaining silent.

"Are you concerned at all that they haven't turned up for work?"

Gallagher was beginning to unnerve Elise now. He looked fraught, every pore in his body radiating aggression; he was practically baring his teeth. He looked like a man unravelling at the edges. Elise regretted not asking another detective to join her for this visit.

"I see you've been power-washing." Elise rubbed the stone steps on the porch with the toe of her shoe, over a faded dark patch on the grey flagstones.

Gallagher slammed the front door in her face. Elise heard him bellow in rage from inside the hallway. She felt sure she had found the site of the murder. She would leave asking a judge to issue a warrant on a Sunday to Chief Superintendent McCarthy.

25

Marco was in the doghouse. He knew he brought brawn and loyalty to Tom Gallagher, but not much else. The boss had been good to him over the years and had forgiven Marco's stupidity on more than one occasion. To show his appreciation, to make up for his own personal failings, Marco would do the unimaginable for his boss if he told him to. But that was the thing – Marco needed to be *told* what to do. He just didn't have much between the ears, as his long-dead mother used to say.

When he had told the two men to remove the bodies, he should have given clear instructions. He should have been explicit. But he had assumed they were professionals, that they knew how to have the bodies dumped in the river or at sea, weighed down and never to be seen again – with their wallets removed to prevent indentification. Above all, that they knew not to drive through the city centre! But he had been too preoccupied with protecting the boss from the Meiers; he had wanted the bodies removed quickly. And the only two men he could get in a hurry turned out to be thicker than himself. Amateurs. Ran right into a checkpoint. Marco's oversight had brought heat to Mr. Gallagher, attention he loathed, and a detective to the door. Mr. Gallagher had been understanding. He was always patient with Marco. And he had given him a chance to make amends. A new plan, with clear instructions, which Marco was determined to follow to the letter. He couldn't let Mr. Gallagher down.

Alan Ainsley, the Englishman, lived over one hundred and twenty kilometres away in Waterford with his wife. He was old enough to be Marco's father; was probably in his sixties. He wore large glasses that slipped down his nose, needing to be pushed up constantly – the movement irritated Marco. He had met the Englishman a number of times and had never enjoyed his company. Everything about the man grated on Marco – his accent, his laugh, and his stupid glasses. He was an associate of Mr. Gallagher, a middleman as Marco understood it.

When Marco knocked on the door that Sunday afternoon and said he must join him on a drive to Cork, Alan had been packing a large suitcase. He had been reluctant to accompany Marco, said he was taking a holiday with the missus, but Marco insisted. Mr. Gallagher was waiting.

On the drive back to Cork the Englishman repeatedly wanted to know what this was all about. He was nervous, Marco could tell. Maybe he had seen the news, heard about the dead bodies in the car, or that David was dead, and John was missing. Maybe he knew the Meiers were in town. Marco enjoyed letting him squirm. The truth was Marco had no idea why Mr. Gallagher wanted to speak to the Englishman. So, he didn't bother to answer the man, just kept the radio volume turned up loud to hear the match results and enjoyed the drive.

If Alan Ainsley thought it strange that Tom was conducting business from home, he kept it to himself. The house was

156

full of people – all Gallagher's men, all sitting in various places – the hall, kitchen, living room – every available seat was taken. They were eating, or reading notes, or watching TV. Alan had been here before, and never seen Gallagher's street army inside the house. He knew Gallagher liked to conduct much of his work from his offices at the back of his clubs, to keep Mae removed from his business dealings. There was no sign of Mae, come to think of it. The realisation made him nervous. He wondered what she would make of all these muscle men lounging around her home, their heavy boots resting on her floral upholstery, leaving crumbs on her furniture and abandoned drinks on her coffee tables.

Alan waited in Gallagher's office, with Marco standing behind him in the corner. Alan had given up making small talk. He was perspiring heavily, mopping his brow and neck. His glasses kept slipping down his nose from the sweat, even more than usual. It took all of Marco's self-control not to knock them off his face.

After ten minutes Gallagher appeared, Murray at his side. Gallagher moved past Alan and sat down, facing the Englishman, the table between them. Murray stood just inside the door, and Marco exited, like faithful guard dogs with a practised routine. Alan had never heard Murray speak – he had no idea if he was local or not. The scar on his face and the look in the man's eyes chilled Alan's blood.

The air in the room was cold, made colder when Tom entered. He was freshly showered, his hair slicked back, his shirt sleeves rolled up. But his eyes set Alan's nerves on edge – they were red-rimmed and manic; he looked mad, yet … focused. It was the look of a very dangerous man with nothing to lose.

Alan swallowed nervously and noted Gallagher hadn't shook his hand as he had entered. Gallagher was a man you could rely on for gentlemanly manners. Clearly, not today.

Alan had a fair idea of what was going on, and he was terrified now. Seeing Gallagher had confirmed it – Alan was in deep trouble.

"Do you know why you're here?" Tom began, his voice soft, his eyes probing the man sitting opposite him.

"What's the meaning of this, Tom? Jean and I have a flight to catch in the morning, and you just order me up here? Let me tell you –"

"You're here because you helped my son to arrange a deal with the Meiers behind my back. Now they are in town, torturing John until I return what David was planning to sell them. Which I know nothing about."

Tom threw a small, blackened item at Alan, who caught it and quickly recoiled, tossing it onto the table between them.

"*That is my son's finger,*" Tom said, fire in his eyes and his voice like ice. "You had a role in this, and you are going to bring it to an end!"

Alan sat still, fighting the urge to retch into his lap. Tom silently glared at him, waiting for him to speak. Alan had been around long enough to know there was no point bluffing a man like Tom Gallagher. He cleared his throat, willing his heart rate to return to normal so he could stay composed and controlled. He knew the game was up – he was stuck between Tom Gallagher and the Meier brothers, and needed, somehow, to wriggle out.

"Alright, Tom, I won't lie to you. David was keen to do something for himself, on his own. He knew you planned to leave the business to John and he wanted to impress you. He knew he was making a mess of things in the clubs. He had messed up with Natalie and the twins and was taking too many drugs. He knew he was disappointing you and he wanted to put things right. He saw an opportunity to sell information for a ton of money, and he approached me. Of course I found a buyer – there's always a market for information." He spread his hands wide, willing Gallagher to understand. "Believe me, Tom, I was trying to help him!"

Tom was quiet as he digested Alan's words. It sounded plausible – David had been in a bad place in the months before his death but had a renewed spark about him in the few weeks before that fateful night. Tom and Mae had spoken about his turnaround, had hoped David was putting the bad times behind him. As much as Tom loved his son, and could understand him wanting to impress him, he was furious that David had shut him out. He refused to let David's mistake cost John his life.

"Do you know where the Meiers are hiding out?"

"No, Tom, I swear!"

"But you can contact them?"

Alan swallowed hard; he really did not want to be in the middle of this. But what choice did he have?

"Yes, I can contact them."

"Then do it. I'm not waiting for them to get back in touch with me. We do this on *my* terms. Suggest a meet-up tonight at the Oracle. Ten o'clock. Tell Meier I have the USB stick, or key as he called it, with the information he's looking for. Tell him to bring my son to the side entrance, and once we have John on the premises, I will toss him the key. He can even use my office computer to verify it and satisfy himself. A nice public place, no more harm to anyone. Job done. Then we cut all ties. No more dealings with them, understood?"

"Do you have it? The key?"

Tom didn't answer, just stared with undisguised hatred at the Englishman. "Make the call."

Tobias Meier was sick of County Cork. It was truly the most boring place he had ever set foot in. The farmhouse they were staying in had been uninhabited for a while before they made it their base. It was freezing both day and night and had no internet access. They barely had coverage on their phones. The area was too remote, apparently. The Meiers were accustomed to freezing temperatures and bad weather. But the lack of technology was hindering their operation.

Tobias's three younger brothers were restless; they longed for beers and clubs, and for women. But the town was Gallagher's, and Tobias knew they could not venture into the centre of it to enjoy its spoils; they would certainly draw attention to themselves. Acquiring the memory key was far more important than beer and women – there would be plenty of both when they had got what they came here for.

For far too long they had searched for the information David Gallagher had sold them. They had a buyer who had agreed to pay more money than Tobias had ever dreamt of earning. Alan Ainsley had given them a sample of the intelligence David had found, and Tobias had had no trouble finding an interested party. Tobias had set the game in motion. A game he was beginning to regret playing. David Gallagher had got himself killed and upset the whole operation. Tobias's buyer was impatient now. A man of his nature demonstrating his impatience was not something Tobias wanted to experience. The man had already paid fifty per cent of the fee and wanted what was his. Tobias wanted the other fifty per cent and to be done with this wretched city.

They had driven by the house of Kate Crowley several times. A steady stream of people in various uniforms were stationed there – the white forensic jumpsuit, the uniform of the beat cop, the slick suit of the detective. There was no way inside. No matter. What they needed was not there – Tobias had intelligence in many places, enough to know the memory key was not at that property. Intelligence enough to know Tom Gallagher was moving the earth itself to find

Kate Crowley, and the memory key, if she possessed it. All Tobias had to do was threaten John's life and mutilate the man to keep the pressure on his father.

John Gallagher had been moaning all day; Tobias was surprised he was still alive really. His blood had long ago dried on the carpet floor, and he shivered with cold as he lay there, curled into a ball.

A text message interrupted Tobias's thoughts – he had coverage where he stood in the living room at the window. The message was from Ainsley, the Englishman. The intermediate. His role was much like Tobias's own, in many respects.

Tobias quickly read the message. Gallagher had the memory key and wanted to set up a trade. Tobias's eyes narrowed in suspicion. How quickly Gallagher had found the key, when only yesterday he hadn't known it existed! Perhaps he had found the girl, the one who had shot David Gallagher.

Tobias would proceed with the meeting, and if Gallagher was bluffing he would lose another son.

26

"Janet McCarthy sends her apologies – she is in a briefing meeting regarding the political conference," said Frank Doherty.

"What's new?" came a voice from the back of the room.

A withering glare from Frank silenced the Garda responsible.

"Fill us in and be quick about it, Taylor. Time is of the essence, as the saying goes."

Elise stood to address the room, feeling exhaustion wash over her in waves. It was a physical force weighing her limbs and clouding the space inside her head. She had been on her feet for close to thirty hours. Her hands shook a little as she passed out typed summary notes to the assembled detectives and Gardaí in the Cork station's meeting room. She physically couldn't drink any more coffee. She felt herself sway a little on her feet but dared not sit down. She had to show she was in command of this situation, to Doherty and everyone else.

David Gallagher's eyes bored into her from the large

photograph tacked to the noticeboard at the front of the room. His shooting was still unsolved. Kate Crowley's picture was in place beside him, still missing. Still the prime suspect.

Superintendent Doherty stood at the front of the room, his trench coat in situ despite the warmth blasting from the electric heaters arranged around the room. He stared at Elise, making it clear he was a busy man and she had better get on with it. His wife was *not* happy he was working on a Sunday. If Doherty was miserable, so must everyone else be.

Elise cleared her throat and glanced at the notes in her hand, to better gather her thoughts and put them into some semblance of order.

"We have two males, Seán and Bill Addams, both known associates of Tom Gallagher. Both men were killed from knife wounds to the throat; preliminary reports from the pathologist state that both victims had their jugular veins severed, and the men were attacked from behind by a right-handed individual or individuals. We are looking at the possibility that there were two attackers, owing to various factors. We believe the men were killed at an unknown location due to the lack of blood at the scene. There would have been extensive bleeding, but there was scarcely any blood found in the car."

"So, we are still searching for the crime scene?" The question came from the back of the room. William Ryan.

Elise met his eyes with some level of hostility.

"Thank you for that interjection, detective," she answered coldly. She was so tired; she wanted to get through this without any interruptions. "And to answer your question, yes, we are still searching for the crime scene. The bodies were moved to the boot after the fact. There was a Garda checkpoint in the city that night, and the driver of the vehicle was acting suspiciously, attempting a U-turn. He and the passenger haven't said a word since their arrest. I may have made a breakthrough on the site of the murders. I visited Tom Gallagher at his residence this morning. He seemed like a man who couldn't care less about the fact that his two security guys didn't turn up for work – he had replaced them of course. He was quite dishevelled."

"Word on the street says John Gallagher is missing," a young Garda from the back of the room interrupted. "I imagine the Gallaghers are pretty pissed off."

Elise eyed the Garda coldly. More interruptions.

"Yes, I imagine they are. I told Gallagher of the discovery of the bodies and he barely batted an eyelid. There was staining on the steps to his front porch, and there was evidence of cleaning there. Power-washing, I'd say. I quizzed him about it, and he slammed the door in my face." Elise turned to Doherty. "Superintendent, I'd like to get a warrant to search the property, to take samples from the flagstones in front of the house. It's highly probable the men were killed there. If anything, it gives us an opportunity to look around. Two of Gallagher's men are dead – it's a logical step to search the property where they were scheduled to be at the time of their deaths. I'd also like to bring Gallagher in for questioning."

Superintendent Doherty chewed on a blood-pressure tablet as he spoke. "There's no way Judge Corden will give us a warrant based on a man washing his flagstones on a Sunday morning. You've been warned where Gallagher is concerned – if it's not airtight, we don't move."

"With all due respect, sir –"

Doherty turned puce as he barked, "*Forget it, Taylor!* Unless you have cold hard evidence, Gallagher is not to be touched. That comes from upstairs – we have our orders!"

Yes, Elise seethed, and you have your retirement to think about.

She knew Gallagher and his legal team had caused

headaches every time he had been questioned in connection with one of his many crimes, but Gallagher had laid low for a while after each interrogation and, in Elise's opinion, it was worth the rap on the knuckles, so to speak.

William Ryan spoke again from the back of the room. His long frame was draped casually over a desk, and he played with a toothpick as he spoke. He had a cocky demeanour. Elise had heard he'd had a breakthrough, a solid line of investigation in the recent spate of sexual assaults in Cork. The fact annoyed her.

"John Gallagher is missing, going on five days now, apparently." Ryan looked directly at Elise as he spoke. "And even more concerning is the arrival of the Meier family into the city. They have been under surveillance for years. They are careful – they've rarely put a foot wrong. What would have drawn them to Cork?" He folded his hands in his lap, rolling the toothpick around with his tongue.

Superintendent Doherty nearly choked on his blood-pressure pills. "What's your point, Ryan?"

"I'm not making any point. I imagine Detective Sergeant Taylor is exploring the angle that these two gangs may have fallen out – maybe there's a grudge war going on. I doubt Gallagher killed his own men. I read his file. From what I understand, he runs a tight ship, and it's a long time since he's had a man step out of line."

William gestured to the images of David Gallagher at the front of the room.

"The Gallagher family are certainly having a bad week."

Elise was seething. What was this jumped-up newcomer playing at, butting into her investigation? In front of a room full of her colleagues, and Doherty staring at her the whole time.

She struggled to keep the animosity from her voice as she said, "We are of course looking at every angle. To recap for those of you not included in the investigation into the shooting of David Gallagher, four members of what we believe are a criminal gang from Munich arrived into Cork a number of days ago. We are most definitely concerned that there's a link to his killing. Our investigation informs us they rented a Ford Galaxy and drove southwest. The rental was returned after twenty-four hours. After that they disappeared. We have no evidence they are still in Cork, but we are looking at all possibilities. I'm waiting on further intel from our counterparts in Germany but, as far as we can ascertain, they've kept their heads down."

"Could they pose a terror threat for the conference?" As usual, Doherty was singularly focused on the upcoming political conference.

"We don't think so. It's thought they move in different circles, drugs and the like, money laundering, women, that sort of thing. Terrorism doesn't appear to be their speciality."

"Maybe they are on holidays, eh?" a uniformed Garda sitting near the back of the room suggested sarcastically, smiling. There was muttering and low laughter from colleagues clustered around him.

William Ryan turned and glared at the man, who blushed and folded his arms across his chest.

Superintendent Doherty was beginning to perspire under his trench coat. He pulled a handkerchief from his pocket and began to mop the back of his neck.

"Find out if they're in the city and what they want. We cannot have some type of gang war in Cork, not this week. The conference is happening in a few days, people! I want this wrapped up, Taylor – pull in whoever you need to but get answers. There'll be no warrant to search Gallagher's property, but I'll see if I can do anything about at least talking to the man, purely because he was the Addams' employer." He rubbed the top of his bald head with the now damp handkerchief. "Any update on the whereabouts of the suspect in the shooting?"

"No." Elise was still seething over events the night before. "Our undercovers missed her at the club, but we do believe it was Kate Crowley attempting to buy fake documents. We're looking into getting the CCTV from the venue."

"Bloody hell, it's hot in here!" Doherty moaned, pulling at his shirt collar. "Why can't we find this girl! There are very few bodies to spare with the conference on Thursday. I cannot stress the seriousness of this enough – there will be too many government ministers in this city in a few days, including our own top people, for anything to go wrong. We *will* have a peaceful conference – all of our jobs depend on it. Taylor, find out all you can on these Germans – find out where they are staying, what they are doing here – I want to know what they eat for breakfast. Pull in every available man. This needs to get wrapped up. Got it? And pull in all your eyes and ears around the city to find the Crowley girl."

Elise nodded wearily. Her lack of enthusiasm went unnoticed by Doherty.

"Janet McCarthy has a press conference at three, so I want a full report on everything in an hour, everything you have." He paused and stared around the room. "Is there anything else?" His expression made it very clear there had better be nothing else to blight his mood any further.

William Ryan cleared his throat and raised his finger. "We've made significant progress on the case of the sexual assaults occurring in the city and county over the last few years. I'm confident of an arrest soon. I'm waiting on a warrant to come through."

"Good," Doherty answered. "I expect the report is on my desk."

Doherty pulled open the conference-room door and stormed out, trench coat flapping.

Elise gathered up her papers as her colleagues filed out. There were some half-hearted offers of help after hours, but she didn't raise her head or acknowledge anyone. She had always made an island of herself here at the Lee Street Station – her achievements were her own, she wasn't concerned about pulling in favours. Once she was back at her desk, she would decide who she was dragging into this case, and it wouldn't be "after hours" either. This needed everyone's full attention. The clock was ticking on the arrival of VIPs into the city. The killing spree associated with the Gallagher family needed to be resolved and filed away.

William Ryan approached her. "You look tired, detective. I'd be more than happy to pitch in with the murder cases and finding the Meier boys."

"Sure," Elise said, pulling on her suit jacket. "I could use a good man on this one."

William missed the sarcasm in her tone or ignored it – Elise didn't care. There was no point antagonising the man, she thought, it was better to have him in her camp than not.

They walked out together.

27

Anna gripped the steering wheel with whitened knuckles as tears of rage pooled in her eyes. Just as she had parked her car in the city, ready to meet the private investigator as arranged, he had cancelled. And not with a telephone call either, just a pathetic text! He couldn't make it today, sent sincere apologies, and asked to reschedule.

She stayed in her car, breathing calmly, until her tears had dried and her heart rate returned to its normal beat. What was she hoping for anyway? That Kristian Lane would find her parents living in a little cottage somewhere? With no memory of the children they had left behind, but alive and well? It was a fantasy she had played out many times – in her mind, it was the only explanation that made sense. Her parents would never leave them. But no sign of their bodies had ever been found! It was infuriating!

Anna had grown weary of this mystery. It shrouded her heart and she was tired of carrying its weight. Maybe Alex was right – perhaps it was time to move forward, to accept the past.

But now she had three hours to kill until it was time to meet Myles.

She texted him. **Hi! Could we meet at 5pm instead?**

She decided to head in to work and make her statement about what had happened with Kate Crowley, as DS Taylor wanted. Then she could easily pass time around the shops, maybe make a start on some Christmas shopping. Her mobile beeped as Myles' message of confirmation came through.

Meet me at the briefing centre, third floor. I'm catching up on some work.

Anna admired Myles' work ethic. She knew where the briefing centre, as Myles called it, was – in a new development of offices in the city centre near the docks. It was a short walk from the main shopping promenade.

Making her statement to the detective on duty took less than an hour, and soon Anna was in the heart of the city, jostled along by the shoppers and festive spirit. The city streets were gleaming, the debris from a typical Saturday night washed away. She wondered about the influx of people into Cork for the conference – heads of state with security guards and staff for each dignitary. They would find the city looking its best, the Christmas lights already adorning every building. Her breath formed a halo in front of her as she walked through the streets. It was almost the end of November and the temperature was firmly below zero. The shoppers that moved around her were indistinguishable in their winter coats and scarves, their arms laden down with bags, their cheeks ruddy from the wind. Anna wondered about Kate – would she recognise her if she saw her now, mingling with the crowd? The pantomime had begun its winter season in the Cork Opera House. Anna smiled at the children, wrapped up in bundles of layers against the cold, as they moved excitedly in that direction. She made a mental note to buy tickets for herself and Chloe, thinking that her niece was probably old enough now to enjoy *Aladdin* on the stage and stay up past her usual bedtime.

As she browsed the perfume section of the city's biggest department store her mobile phone rang in her bag – Lauren. Anna smiled as she answered. Her exuberant friend was just the tonic she needed after the disappointment of the private investigator cancelling their meeting.

"Hello! I've been waiting for your call! How was last night?"

"Sorry, Lauren, I completely forgot!" Anna thought of the online searches for Kate Crowley and realised she had been so consumed by it she had completely forgotten to call her friend. "Last night was … very eventful. I can't really go into it here, I'm shopping, but loads happened – I'll tell you about it at work tomorrow. Myles was a complete gentleman – I'm meeting him for dinner tonight actually."

Grinning, Anna pulled the phone away from her ear as Lauren squealed in excitement. After they agreed to meet in Victus for coffee before work the following morning, Anna said goodbye, and brought the perfume she was holding to the checkout. It would be a perfect Christmas gift for her friend – there was no time like the present to get started on her shopping.

Just before five o'clock she made her way to the briefing centre building. It was dark now, but the Christmas lights overhead lit the way for her. She walked briskly to the office block by the docks and stopped outside. She looked up at a chrome-and-glass building. This was the place. She pushed through the revolving door and stepped inside. The interior was bright and spacious, with a bank of lifts directly opposite the entrance, and an information desk to the left. Men and women, dressed in suits and carrying files and

171

briefcases, walked to and fro, in and out of lifts. It was a busy place, despite the fact that it was a Sunday evening.

She headed towards the lifts. She noticed they were attended. A suited and pimply young man asked her which floor she was going to, and she was there in seconds. As she stepped from the lift, he bid her a pleasant evening and was whisked away again.

Her feet sank into plush cream carpet. She was standing in a spacious, square hall, with several doors off three of the walls. A lime sofa lined the fourth wall and she sat, unsure what to do next. There was no receptionist, nor any signage indicating a company name. The walls were bare. She marvelled at the luxurious décor and surroundings. Compared to the Lee Street station, the briefing centre was plush.

Before she had a chance to pull out her mobile phone to call Myles, he appeared in front of her, smiling warmly.

"Anna, I'm so glad you came!"

She stood up and was immediately engulfed in a massive hug. She smiled into Myles' chest.

"You're freezing! Come on in, I'm almost finished." He turned and disappeared inside a room off one of the doors.

Anna followed, stepping inside a conference room that was dominated by a large oval table with twelve black leather chairs. On the wall at the back of the room a projector screen was mounted. Along the left-hand wall a number of computers were stationed at smaller tables, screens full of text and other information. A small coffee station stood in the corner.

She walked to where Myles leant over the screen at a table at the back of the room, shutting down various applications.

"How did the surfing go?" she asked, looking around her.

"Great! Amazing actually. I could have stayed out all day."

Her eyes spotted the slight indentation in the wall by the door.

"Ugh! I hate these storage cupboards! We have them too – stealth storage, Lauren calls them. They give me the creeps!"

Myles laughed. He pulled on a thick black jacket and wound a scarf around his neck.

"Stealth storage – I like it!" He grinned at Anna as he linked her arm.

They walked outside, Myles switching off the lights and locking the door after them.

Myles took Anna's gloved hand as they made their way outside. She felt him shiver with the cold beside her as they walked quickly. He made easy conversation about his morning surfing in Garrettstown. He seemed thrilled with it, despite the cold. His hair was still sleek, damp from a shower earlier; Anna imagined it would be a mess of curls again once it was dry.

"I see you've been shopping," he said as they reached the seafood restaurant. "I hope you didn't spend too much on my Christmas present?"

Anna laughed as they entered.

It was hot inside the restaurant, and they peeled their coats and scarves off and hung them on a coat-stand. Soon, they were seated at the back, Anna's shopping bags under the table between their feet. A waitress arrived with their menus.

Anna glanced at Myles and smiled – his brown eyes were serious behind his glasses as he perused his options. She marvelled at how at ease she felt in his company.

"*Er*, I should have said earlier but I'm not a fan of seafood to be honest." Myles' brow was furrowed in concentration. "My Greek mother threatened to disown me, but unless it's a fish finger or something coated in batter and ready for the oven, I usually steer clear."

173

"I thought you love the sea!"

"Just the surfing part!" Myles said with a grin.

Anna laughed. "OK." She quickly read through the menu. "They have steak and chicken – you're safe!"

"With chips on the side?"

"Sure."

"Done!"

Having decided on seafood chowder, Anna sat back and looked around the restaurant. It was busy and adorned with Christmas decorations already. A large tree stood in one corner, decorated all in white – it was beautiful. The din of the restaurant swelled around them like a warm embrace – and she allowed herself to relax – her earlier anger and irritation at the sudden cancellation of her meeting with the private investigator forgotten.

After they had ordered, Myles reached across the table and grasped her hands in his.

"You're still freezing!"

She blushed a little; she felt like an idiot, smiling so much.

"You were telling me last night how you joined the Guards," she prompted, with a wicked grin.

He snorted with laughter. "I knew you'd ask me that!" He met her eyes briefly before pulling his hands back and concentrating on the silver cutlery in front of him. "Fair enough. I'll tell you. No secrets. But don't judge me, OK?"

Wide-eyed, Anna crossed her heart with her little finger.

"I'm a bit of a prodigy, you see." Myles looked up again and winked, prompting an eye-roll from Anna in response. He burst out laughing. "Seriously! This is me being modest. I built my own functioning computer when I was ten years old. I skipped a year in school and ended up in college at sixteen. I've a Master's degree in computer science and a PhD in Software Design. Can't talk to women, though, but I can decode software all day long. I swear, what I gained in

IT skills I completely lost in social skills. My brothers joke that one day I'll just build myself a robot girlfriend and we'll ride off into the sunset together and decode algorithms for the rest of our lives."

Anna burst out laughing. Myles seemed pleased to have entertained her.

"I got a job in Dublin City College, lecturing in a range of computer subjects. I liked it. I didn't think I'd have the neck for standing in front of people all day, talking, but hey, it worked out. Until I messed up."

"So, what did you do wrong?"

"I had my suspicions that one of my students was dealing."

"Drugs?"

"Yeah. And I was right. He'd show up to class, always on his phone, always disrespectful, drawing attention to himself for the wrong reasons. He would have covert conversations in the corridors, quiet words with people, moving off whenever someone approached. On more than one occasion I saw notes, money I mean, pushed into his hand by some of the other students, who quite frankly were looking worse for wear. Their grades were slipping, they started missing class. I just had a feeling he was dealing drugs – but I had no real evidence. I took it to my supervisor, but what could they do? They certainly weren't prepared to act on my suspicions." He pushed and pulled his napkin into various shapes, looking sombre. "I'm not exactly proud of this. I hacked into his mobile phone. In class he was always using it. He used the college WIFI – his phone was wide open if you knew what you were doing. I accessed his texts and it confirmed everything. He was dealing cocaine. I passed the information to my superiors and to the Guards, but I was naive. I had breached my contract and was dismissed. It was his first offense. He received only a four-year sentence and will probably be out

175

in half that! I lost my job. It was a disaster!"

Anna exhaled loudly. "Wow, that's rough!"

"Yep. But somehow my name ended up on the desk of someone … shall we say, important? And here I am."

He had finished his story and sat back.

The waitress brought their drinks and some bread in a basket. Anna felt sorry for Myles. In trying to do the right thing he had lost his whole career.

She changed tack. "So, you have brothers?"

"Four of them!" He brightened again. "As I said, my mother's Greek – she's from a very large family. She was blessed with five sons!"

"Lucky her." She sipped her sparkling water. She was enjoying the conversation and the laughter was a welcome relief.

"What about you? Do you have family?"

"Yes, a brother, Alex. He's married – he has a little girl."

"Are ye close?"

"Very. He took care of me after my parents –" Anna abruptly stopped. She didn't know what to say next.

Myles sat still, waiting.

She hated talking about this subject. She looked at Myles; his brown eyes were kind behind his thick glasses. She took a deep breath and decided to fill him in on her greatest sadness.

"My parents were great. My dad was an accountant. My mum loved music, anything orchestral. They were heading to Dublin for the weekend to attend a performance by the RTÉ Concert Orchestra. Alex was twenty-five at the time, and I was sixteen, so there was no problem leaving us at home. Anyway," she sighed and looked down, brushing imaginary crumbs from her jeans, "they crashed on the motorway. The weather was bad; it was winter. When their car was found, the doors were open, but my parents were missing. Their personal things were all gone too – wallet and purse, that sort of thing. I like to think they both banged their heads and are living somewhere with their memories wiped and someday they'll realise Alex and I are still waiting for them to come home."

Anna laughed, but it sounded forced, even to her.

Myles reached across the table and squeezed her hands, his eyes warm and full of sorrow. "Do you and Alex have any other family?"

She shook her head, "None. My parents were from England. After their accident a man got in touch, to say he was an old friend of my dad's. I had never met him. Other than that, we have no link to their past."

They sat in silence for a few minutes.

The waitress brought their meals. Neither Myles nor Anna paid her any attention.

"The detectives said they had explored every angle. The case was referred to the Missing Persons Bureau, but there were never any leads. The file is still open, but …" She shrugged helplessly.

"What were their names?" Myles asked.

She appreciated his interest. "Helen and Michael. They were great."

Silence descended on them again, Myles staring at Anna, and Anna staring into the bubbling water in her glass.

Eventually he broke the stillness. "You seem relatively normal."

Anna laughed aloud and wiped her eyes. She couldn't believe she was laughing while talking about this.

Myles squeezed her hand. "I'm sorry this happened to you. Thank you for telling me. And I'm glad to have met you."

Anna smiled at him. "Me too."

28

Betsy felt good. Real good. Better than she had felt in a long time. It was Sunday night, her shift at the Mad Hatter was over, and she didn't have to set foot in the place until lunchtime on Wednesday. She was going to let her hair down and party, hard.

Her apartment was small but very clean, and real nice. It was hers and she loved it. Loved to clean it, keep it sparkling, loved to push open the tiny windows and let the air in to swirl around inside the small space and freshen it up. She never smoked inside, always heading downstairs to the front entrance of the building, and God help anyone who dared to light up indoors. Because she finally had no-one to answer to, she had decorated the apartment just the way she wanted to – her bedroom was a pale lavender, with fairy lights strung around the mirror, and pink cushions scattered on the bed. She had put up wall stickers here and there, each with an inspirational quote – *You are Worthy! Dream Big! You Got This!* She had saved hard for the small leather two-seater, cream to match the cupboards in her kitchenette. The TV had been a cast-off, but perfectly adequate for her quiz shows and Netflix. She piggy-backed on her sister's Netflix account – Elise was generous that way.

Elise Taylor was Betsy's older sister. They were close in many respects, and strangers in other ways. It was probably impossible to have a normal relationship when you consider how their lives had started out. Elise was a good older sister though – she had saved Betsy many times. Saved, as in, helped her get clean, helped her kick out the latest lowlife she couldn't remember inviting to move in, helped her to find work when she couldn't get a reference. It was Elise who had got Betsy the interview in the Mad Hatter, said the manager owed her a favour. Everyone owed Elise favours in this city. Betsy felt protected being her younger sister.

Elise and Elizabeth – they had always been teased about their mother's lack of imagination when it came to choosing their names. They were two peas in a pod; at least that's what people used to say when they were running around the flats together as kids. Life was hard on the girls back then, but Elise always had a way of making things bearable. Whenever their mother had a new man around, or was too high to get out of bed, or was throwing a party that seemed to never end, Elise always made sure they were fed, were warm, were safe. Betsy would do anything for Elise. She wasn't surprised Elise was a detective – she liked to boss people around, and she knew the way criminals thought – she had grown up around enough of them.

Tonight, Betsy was meeting a new man. Excitement coursed through her as she spritzed herself with perfume and added a final layer of lipstick. She appraised herself in front of the mirror. She might be in her forties, but she still had the body of a woman much younger. Her highlights were freshly done, and her false eyelashes were perfectly applied. She felt gorgeous.

Betsy caught the bus into the city, wishing she had more

than a flimsy jacket on over her dress. But her dress was low-cut and sexy, and she wanted to make a good impression on Steve. He owned a hotel, the Kingsman, just a little two-star place off the main city thoroughfare, but still – a businessman! Elise would never believe her. They were meeting at the hotel reception, and he had promised her a night out in town, a fancy restaurant and a club after, then back to his place. He lived at the hotel, he had explained, it was more economical that way. Betsy could see herself running a small hotel like Steve's, decorating each bedroom to her own feminine taste, welcoming the guests at reception … as the bus rolled into town she was lost in the fantasy of a better life.

Once she reached the city she walked as briskly as her stilettos would allow to the hotel. It was so central, perfect to head back to after the club. The streets were quiet now – most people were probably at home by the fire, relaxing before their return to work in the morning.

Steve was waiting for her at reception, leaning over the counter to give orders to a young, acne-scarred lad who was obviously taking the nightshift at reception. Steve was a big guy, sexy in a "Grant Mitchell" type of way, bald and broad and tattooed. He grinned at Betsy as she walked in, his eyes roaming over her, clearly liking what he saw.

"Hey, babe!" he drawled, putting his arm around her and pulling her into him, resting his hand on her bottom and giving it a squeeze. He looked at the teenager behind the counter. "What do you think, Neil, isn't she something?"

The kid just shrugged.

"You ready to party, sweetheart?" Steve said.

"Sure!" Betsy answered sweetly, looking all around her. She took in the reception area, the small coffee station, the plastic potted plants in the corner, the "out of order" sign taped on the lift door. Oh yes, she thought, she could spruce this place up alright, bring it up a star rating or two, make a fortune. She could give up waiting tables in the Mad Hatter. She smiled up at Steve, keen to play her cards right tonight.

The hotel door opened and brought a blast of cold air inside. A young woman walked in, her shoulders hunched inside a heavy coat, a woollen hat pushed low over her short hair. She kept her head down, her hands in her pockets, and moved towards the stairs, clearly aware the lift was out of order. Memory pulled at Betsy's mind – where had she seen her before? The woman was a guest here, heading upstairs to her room. Maybe she was a tourist, and Betsy had seen her about town – maybe she had stopped by the Mad Hatter for lunch or drinks.

That's it! Betsy thought with a start. It was the woman Elise was looking for, the one who had sought to buy a passport from Nick. She was a guest here at the hotel.

Betsy reached into her bag to find her phone and call her sister, but it appeared her date had other ideas. He pulled a tiny plastic bag from inside his jeans pocket and dangled it in front of her face. It contained several round white pills. He didn't seem to care that his teenage receptionist could see and hear them.

"Look what I got for us, babe!" He put his hand on Betsy's elbow and steered her towards the door. "Let's go have some real fun!"

Betsy pulled her hand back out of her handbag, almost forgetting about the woman, about Elise. Momentarily she hated herself for the fact that she was practically salivating at the sight of the drugs. But she pushed the thought aside – it was one night, hardly "falling off the wagon"'. And the woman would still be at the hotel in the morning. Where was she going to go at this time of night, in this weather?

Giggling, Betsy linked her arm through Steve's and cuddled closer to him as they stepped outside into the cold November night.

181

29

Tobias Meier was in a brooding mood. He sensed a trap. It was eleven o'clock – Tom Gallagher had suggested a ten o'clock meet, but let the man wait! The icy roads had been no match for the Range Rover he had acquired; they had sped easily into the city, John Gallagher stuffed into the boot. The streets were deserted. It was Sunday after all – people had jobs to go to in the morning, and children to drive to school. His brother Leon had parked the Range Rover near the fountain in the city, a vantage point that offered a view of the streets and the neon sign for the Oracle club up ahead. Its blue light flashed irritatingly, blinking on and off, on and off. His brothers Karl and Stefan were sitting in the back, eager and excited to meet the Gallagher band of men.

Tobias felt uncomfortable with this whole arrangement. The Range Rover was warm, but he felt chilled to the bone. He counted eight cars parked immediately outside the club – strange that the venue was so busy when the streets into the city had been so quiet. Gallagher clearly had deployed all his men to the club, to outnumber the

Germans. They had robbed him after all, completely emptied his safe. Not to mention the man might be harbouring a grudge for the mutilation of his son.

Tobias worried that his own desperation to retrieve the memory key was causing him to lose his edge – were they walking into a trap? A man didn't get to his stature in life by being easily fooled. Tobias had never been outwitted, and tonight wasn't going to be the first time.

He had fought his way to this position in life. It had come to him the hard way. There were bodies stacked up behind him, in his past, people he'd had to move out of his way. Sometimes, at night, he dreamt of their faces, how their skin had sagged, and their muscles had twitched in the final moments between life and death. At night, he felt vulnerable, freaked out by the dead. By day he was in charge again, a man not to be crossed, nor to be defied.

There were few people he feared in this world left alive. One of them was a man he could not move out of the way – the pool ran too deep. Removing that man would send a ripple effect Tobias could not contain. A wave of Dutch mobsters descending on him and his brothers was not something he could deal with.

So, the memory key had to be found. Tobias didn't care what Tom Gallagher did to find it. All he cared about was the payment the Dutchman offered and keeping his head on his shoulders.

He felt a grudging admiration for Tom Gallagher. He had established a fine business for himself and, like himself, had fought off all competition. Tom Gallagher had earned respect. Tobias especially liked Gallagher's wife. She was aging well. She was exactly his type of woman – well kept, strong and sensible. Tobias remembered his visit to her home – he had encountered her strength then. Yes, she was just his type.

He felt like drawing out tonight a little longer. He would take a gamble, and if he was wrong and ultimately late to their meeting, so be it. Tom Gallagher wasn't exactly in a position to complain.

"Turn around!" he ordered, and Leon started the engine. "We will wait for Gallagher at his house instead. Keep Mama Gallagher company."

He heard some feeble cries for help from the boot and a soft banging, as if the man was attempting to kick out with his feet. Tobias smiled at John's folly – he was wasting his energy – although he had to admire the man; he had endured much this last week and still had fight in him. Despite being bound at the hands and feet and gagged, he was still managing to make enough noise to penetrate Tobias's thoughts. He turned up the radio.

He felt so cold but he was used to the cold, its familiarity somewhat easing his sense of foreboding. He desired nothing but to end this mess, to deliver the memory key and collect the money. He longed to return to less complicated things, like guns and drugs.

After less than fifteen minutes they pulled into Gallagher's property. He saw the gates were open and unattended – perhaps Gallagher still hadn't replaced his security men? He most likely had all his men stationed at the Oracle, the better to ambush the Meiers. Tobias grinned smugly to himself – let Gallagher come home to find his wife being entertained while he was out on a wasted errand.

They drove up to the front door. The few parked cars in the driveway were empty; the house was in complete darkness save for a light on upstairs.

"Stay here," Tobias ordered Leon. "Karl, Stefan, you come with me."

The younger Meier brothers climbed out of the back seat and followed their elder to the door. It was locked. Tobias had brought a hammer from the tools they had used on John Gallagher, and he used it to work on the lock until it gave way. They moved quickly inside. The tiled hall in front of them was in darkness but the headlights from their vehicle lit up the entrance from behind. Tobias looked up to the light on upstairs and, smirking, motioned to his brothers to follow him up.

As he stepped away from them towards the staircase, he heard an almost imperceptible noise and became aware of swift movement from both the left and right sides of the hall.

It was as if the walls had come to life.

His brothers suddenly began to gag, clutching at their throats as they fell forward. Tobias watched in utter disbelief as two shadowy figures stepped away from his brothers who were now lying twitching on the floor.

The figures swiftly moved outside to the Range Rover, taking Leon completely by surprise. He barely struggled. Tobias looked away as his brother was dragged to the ground.

Tobias closed his eyes.

"Two for two," a voice said softly from the back of the hall.

Tobias whipped his head around and saw Tom Gallagher step from the shadows.

"Your driver makes it three to me, but then, who's counting?"

Gallagher moved slowly forward until he stood inches from Tobias. In the lights from the driveway illuminating the space, Tobias saw Gallagher's eyes burn with hatred.

He had underestimated the man. The cold hand of fear tightened around his heart.

"Marco?" Gallagher called softly, looking past Tobias into the driveway.

Tobias turned and saw several men lifting John

Gallagher from the boot of the Range Rover and carrying him to one of the parked cars.

A heavyset man replied, "*Got him, boss!*" before climbing into the driver's seat and speeding away.

Four men entered the hallway and roughly dragged Karl and Stefan Meier from the house into the driveway. Leon lay outside on the ground, clearly dead. Tobias felt like he was watching them in slow motion, like they were moving under water. Somewhere deep in his subconscious he realised he was in shock.

He turned to look at Tom Gallagher. The man was rolling up both sleeves of a black shirt. He grinned, and in the half-light he looked like a maniac.

"Looks like it's just you and me," he said.

30

Dean Harris had got used to scaling high walls over the last few years; the concrete wall and the high metal gate that enclosed Anna's house posed no problem for him. Opening the lock on the sliding back door was even easier – he had the right tools and it gave way quickly. He pushed the door shut; it was stiff and heavy. She kept the house neat and tidy and he liked that. He moved quietly through each room, a curious spectator in her most private place, touching things here and there. He ran his gloved fingers over the keys of her laptop on the kitchen table, over the covers of her books on the bookshelf.

On the back of the sofa a scarf was thrown, casually discarded. He lifted it and buried his face into it, inhaling her deeply. It gave him a thrill to know she would arrive home soon, not knowing he was in her home, not knowing his plans for her. He had been watching her for days now, observing her coming and going. He could wait no longer. The detective – William, was it? – had been curious and intimidating. But Dean was confident the Gardaí had nothing on him. He was far too excited to be worried and he had put too much work into this to abandon things because a detective was sniffing around.

He had watched this house while she'd been at work. He had ample view by day, but she worked late, and he'd had to come back at night to be sure she would be alone. He knew that she slept in the bedroom on the right side of the stairs. Last night he had watched from the street outside as the light went on and then off. She would surely arrive home soon. She had been late last night, and he had almost frozen to death. In the end, he had abandoned his plan. Dean guessed the woman would be home earlier tonight, having work in the morning. He knew from past experiences that assumptions like this might not come true, but he felt sure she would be home soon, and the thought thrilled him. Here, in this game he had created, he felt powerful and in control.

Dean began to move through the house toward the stairs, his bag held loosely in his arm. He wanted to explore her bedroom – he could hardly contain his excitement. She was small, probably just over five foot five, compared to his six foot. It would be no contest, and anticipation pulsed in his veins.

When Anna pushed her front door open, she knew she wasn't imagining it. Someone had been in her house. The house felt colder somehow, as if a door had been left open. She thought of her sliding back door again. Turning on the lights as she moved, she made her way toward the kitchen, pausing in the living room to pick her scarf up from the bookshelf – it had been on the back of the sofa, she was sure of it.

Shit, she thought, what the hell is going on?

As she stood in the middle of the living room, a cold

breeze from outside tickled her skin. Turning, she walked through the archway to the kitchen and realised her sliding door was very slightly ajar, the night air penetrating her house. Holding her scarf and barely breathing, she tensed as a floorboard creaked upstairs.

Anna had lived alone for six years, and never in all that time had a floorboard creaked upstairs. She knew houses made noises – settling sounds, as her mother used to say – but that sound coming from her upstairs landing was entirely unfamiliar.

She had always been a logical person. She had a keen ability to analyse a situation. Standing in her kitchen, her heart pounding loudly in her ears, she quickly and calmly weighed up her situation. There was an intruder in her house – upstairs – and she was in danger. There was a distinct probability it was the attacker she had feared could target her over the last few days.

Despite being capable in self-defence, or probably because of the skills she had learned, she had no impulse to go upstairs and challenge the intruder. Logically, it didn't make sense. She had known he would come, sooner or later, whoever *he* was. But she had no idea how big he was, or what weapons he might be carrying.

She needed to get outside the house as quickly as possible. She thought of the back garden. It was enclosed by high walls, walls she wouldn't be able to scale. Her metal side gate was locked, and she would have to locate the key in a kitchen drawer, making noise and taking time. She would be trapped in the back of her house. The front door was a better option.

Moving quickly through the kitchen, Anna dared not breathe. Suddenly, a noise again. The stairs creaked and groaned. He was coming downstairs.

With her heart pounding, she ducked behind the living-room door. She had no choice but to wait. There was no way out and the intruder would reach the bottom of the stairs before she could reach and open the front door. The stairs creaked ominously as he made his way down. She was surprised to feel anger surging inside her. She moved her body into position, an automatic, learned response to an imminent threat.

She watched and waited for the shadow to darken the crack between the door frame and the door. She dared not breathe, but she was ready.

Fortitude, Anna! A memory, her father's voice, came to her. Self-Control, Indomitable Spirit – Anna chanted the tenets of Taekwon-Do in her head, a calming mantra as she waited.

It happened exactly as Anna knew it would. He stepped into the room, his confidence betraying him, causing him to disregard the shadow that shouldn't be lurking in his peripheral. When he turned towards her his shock registered in the perfectly formed O of his mouth and his wide eyes. Dean Harris never had time to react.

Anna stepped forward confidently. Three high kicks in quick succession and he was down, unconscious. For now. Anna stepped over him and quickly left the house. She doubted the Pearsons were awake at this late hour but she ran to their front door. She would wait for the Gardaí there.

31

Monday

Monday morning dawned bright and dry. Dean Harris was warm, cosy even, in his hospital bed. He could tell it was freezing outside but he didn't care – his hospital room was kept at a nice nineteen degrees. He'd had to eat his liquid breakfast through a straw, but his doctor said he should be able to go home today – he would heal quickly. His jaw hadn't been quite broken, just a hairline fracture, and Dean was feeling more like himself already.

He knew he had his nurse to thank for that, a beautiful Welsh girl with huge blue eyes and hair a deep shade of brown. His favourite colour. She was kind to him. While some of the others on the night shift had been rough with the needles, seeming to relish taking blood samples so as to jab into him, Grace was gentle and caring. She chatted non-stop while she fussed over him this morning, and she smiled warmly every time she set foot in the room.

There was gossip about him – Dean had heard whispers at the foot of his bed when the nurses thought he was asleep, but his Grace never took part in any of it.

"They caught him in a woman's house, after breaking in!"

"I heard she almost broke his jaw!"

"Good for her!"

"Did you hear they found a type of 'sexual-assault kit' on him last night, condoms and everything. I bet he's the guy, the rapist. I hope they throw the book at him!"

Dean had pretended to be sleeping, the better to hear what was being said about him, the better to understand what the Guards actually had on him. He was beginning to worry. He had been meticulous about forensics, but there was always the possibility he had left something behind. He was a fan of true crime documentaries, often watching them late into the night. He loved *CSI*, *Criminal Minds*, *The Shield* – those shows were ingenious in his opinion. They were a source of so much information it was astounding they were even allowed on TV. Thanks to those programmes Dean knew that even the tiniest fibre could be his undoing. But he knew how virtually impossible it was to leave a crime scene completely untainted. So, Dean had made sure to never give the Gardaí any reason to have his DNA on file.

Things had gone a bit wrong with his recent attempted conquest. He realised he had been foolish there – his latest crush was obviously some kind of a nutjob. And violent, too, very unladylike.

Dean was more than happy to forget about her and begin his courtship of Grace, the beautiful nurse, as soon as he could speak more coherently again and get himself off any charges the Guards came up with. He had caught Grace's scent many times as she had tended to him this morning – Chance by Chanel, he reckoned. He could only imagine how she would taste ...

In the meantime, he deserved a rest. He had been so stressed lately trying to keep his secret. And his jaw ached, despite all the medication he was on. He would lie back in his soft bed, in the warm hospital room, and enjoy Grace's gentle touch. Closing his eyes against the bright morning sunlight, he rested his head on the pillow, waiting to hear her cheerful voice.

The door opened and footsteps approached the bed. Many footsteps. Dean opened his eyes and looked into the clear blue eyes of a tall dark-haired man dressed in a grey suit and long dark wool coat. The man smiled at Dean as he pulled I.D. from inside his pocket – *William Ryan, Detective Sergeant*. His was the victorious smile of a cat who has cornered the mouse.

"We meet again!"

Dean remained silent, aware his hands were trembling as he gripped the thin bedsheet.

"Dean Harris, I am arresting you on suspicion of …"

Dean felt faint. A loud buzzing sound rang loud inside his head, drowning out the rest of what the detective had to say.

No! No! No! he groaned inwardly.

"You are not obliged to say anything unless you wish to do so," William Ryan grinned at the irony of his words as he took in Dean's swollen jaw, *"but anything you say will be taken down in writing and may be given in evidence."*

Dean could no longer hear the man; the buzzing sound inside his head was back, making it impossible to hear anything except the sound of his own shallow breathing. He became aware of others standing in the room, staring at him – his doctor and two other Gardaí. And his beautiful Grace, her hands clasped together, her eyes downcast. He met the detective's eyes and a weariness settled over him. He knew the game was up. William Ryan had the cocky look of Horatio Caine from *CSI Miami*.

"Get dressed," the detective ordered. "The doctor here says you're good to go. You're being discharged this morning into Garda custody." He rubbed his hands together. "Nice and warm in here. Cold in the cells, mind you!"

32

On Monday morning Elise woke from a deep sleep to the incessant buzzing of her mobile phone. It vibrated on the wooden surface of her bedside locker, adding a dullness to the shrill of her ringtone. She winced as she sat up.

Her Sunday had been far from a day of rest. Hours had rolled into one another as she had met the pathologist and forensics team, and spoken to witnesses, attempting to make some sense of the finding of the Addams cousins dead in a car boot.

There was no reason to suspect Gallagher of killing his own men, apart from the staining on the flagstones at his front door. That in itself, she knew, amounted to speculation at best. As far as Elise was aware, Gallagher's men had never stepped out of line. He ran a tight ship and seemed to instil loyalty. There were few who would cross him – she was certain of that. The man driving the car and his passenger were still tight-lipped. They wouldn't say a word.

It seemed to Elise that chaos had followed the Meiers

into the city. She wondered if they had anything to do with the killing. And with the shooting of David Gallagher, for which Kate Crowley was still the main suspect.

Chief Superintendent McCarthy had far too much on her mind to bother about that aspect of the investigation, try as Elise might to get her to see the connection and assign resources. She had put it all into her report – surely the Chief Super would accept there was a connection between the shooting of David Gallagher, the murder of the Addams cousins and the arrival of the Meiers into Ireland? The woman was utterly preoccupied with the political conference later in the week – right now, she didn't want complications – all she wanted was for the murders to be solved as quickly and simply as possible, so her PR spin could reassure any jumpy security personnel that the city was safe.

The whole thing was proving impossible.

Elise had been lightheaded with tiredness by the time she finally reached her apartment last night, yet unable to fall asleep. A double shot of whiskey had helped. She had sat in her armchair for an hour, savouring the heat of the whiskey, swirling it in the tall glass as her thoughts swam. Images from the crime scene were etched in her memory, every line and angle, every colour. The white of David Gallagher's face, the dark brown of the fleshy gunshot wound in his neck.

Elise had gripped her glass tight – how she hated Cork city! She wanted so badly to quit, to leave it all behind. People ran off to deserted tropical islands all the time, didn't they? But it didn't have to be a luxury getaway – anywhere would do! To leave the city with its dark shroud of filth and crime, lies and memories behind, was Elise's idea of heaven.

She thought of Betsy, her younger sister. She was a

grown woman now and Elise had long ago vacated the "mother" role she had been thrust into. But still she couldn't quite quell the maternal instinct towards her sister. Betsy had made a mess of her adult life so far, and she always expected Elise to row in and put the pieces back together. Drugs and pimps had had control over Betsy for many years. Elise had pulled her back from the brink of her own destruction so many times, made criminal charges disappear, strong-armed men from her flat ... but she never blamed Betsy. Their childhood had been difficult. Elise had always risen to the challenge of their mother's addiction; she had learned to be strong enough for Betsy to lean on her. A long time ago she had realised that Betsy was the only reason she was still in this city.

When Elise had announced to her mother and sister she was joining the Guards, they had laughed. And her friends had been worse, accusing her of being a traitor. But she knew she was smarter than all of them, and not afraid to search for a way out. She wanted better for herself than the life her mother expected was good enough.

She studied hard and rose through the ranks; now she was a respected detective. Yet daily she still struggled. She felt the weight of other peoples' desperate attempts to escape, to climb to the top. Daily she waded through blood and vomit and pools of desperation, and she'd had enough.

Now, as the light on her mobile phone almost blinded her, she regretted the decision to stay up brooding and drinking whiskey. Her alarm clock told her it was just after six o'clock. She'd had just four hours' sleep in almost two days.

"For God's sake!" she muttered wearily as she answered the call.

"*Taylor!*"

It was Doherty, and he sounded hyper. "We've had a

report of a burnt-out vehicle on Monastery Road, near Douglas. There are four bodies inside. Get on it! It might be those Germans finally turning up!"

Elise was stunned. She rubbed sleep from her eyes and fought the urge to retch.

She was unable to mutter more than "Yes, sir."

This situation just kept getting worse. She pushed herself out of bed as Doherty ended the call. She badly needed a shower and food. It would delay her arrival at the scene, but she stepped under the warm water of the shower anyway, praying this nightmare would end soon.

33

Betsy sat on the edge of the hotel bed and lit a cigarette. It felt good to light a cigarette indoors for once. It was freezing in the hotel, and even worse outside. This wasn't the luxury city hideaway Steve had made it out to be.

Steve had run out of cash by the end of the night, so they'd had to walk back to the hotel instead of getting a warm cab. Although the hotel had a pretty central location, the temperature outside was sub-zero, and her date wasn't gentleman enough to offer his jacket. Betsy had been frozen to the point of shaking, and her feet ached by the time they reached the tiny bedroom.

At least she hadn't had to sleep with him – Steve had passed out on the bed and was snoring so loudly Betsy was sure the whole floor could hear him.

It had been a heavy night. She had to admit she'd enjoyed herself. It was a long time since the music and disco lights had blended together in a drug-induced euphoric state for her – she had missed it. Missed the confidence of feeling that everyone she spoke to hung on her every word, that each song was her *absolute favourite,* that she could dance forever. Betsy had missed the pure, raw abandonment she felt with pills.

She didn't miss the come-down though, the nauseous panic that washed over her every few minutes, the paranoia, the tiny sounds that scratched from the walls. She knew it would pass, and that the cigarette would steady her nerves. Luckily, the hotel wasn't the type of place to prohibit smoking, not that she cared.

She rubbed her tired feet, one after the other, as she took a deep drag on her cigarette.

They had taken the pills in the Oracle club as soon as they had arrived. After that there had been dancing and lots and lots of drinks. The night was a blur of sweating and laughing with strangers, men she had never met before, but who had seemed so interested in talking to her … Betsy loved the self-assurance drugs gave her. Maybe she could be one of those casual drug-takers, in control of it now that she was older? Not let the highs and lows destroy her life. And not need her sister to bail her out so often, sometimes literally.

Elise! She had been meaning to call her all night.

The morning sunlight cast a harsh glare through the thin curtains as Betsy fumbled around the floor for her handbag. She wasn't worried about waking Steve. She didn't think she'd see him again, businessman or not.

Finding her mobile phone, she sat back down on the bed and dialled.

Elise answered on the first ring. Always so efficient.

"Betsy, I really don't have time."

"Well, don't answer the phone then!"

"What do you want?"

Elise sounded as if she was moving quickly, rushing around her apartment. She sipped and swallowed a drink loudly and munched on something, the sound amplified through the mobile phone.

Nausea clawed at Betsy's insides.

"I've found a new man!"

"Great."

More moving, lots of rustling in the background.

"You'd like him, he owns a hotel in the city centre."

"*Mmm.*"

"His name's Steve."

"Betsy, I really have to go. I'm in the middle of a murder case."

"OK, OK – it's just that girl you were looking for? She's staying at Steve's hotel. I thought you'd like to know."

Betsy smiled at the silence that descended, getting a kick out of shocking her sister into stillness.

"*You're sure it's her?*"

"One hundred per cent!"

Betsy could hear the excitement in Elise's voice. "Give me the address!"

"Well, I'm not sure what street it's on – we had a heavy night if you know what I mean, but it's in town."

"*Tell me the name!*" Elise screamed into the phone, her rage carrying over the airwaves.

Betsy was silent for a moment, in shock at Elise's change in demeanour.

"Jeez, Elise, keep your hair on!" she managed to say with a shaky laugh. She felt as though ice water had been poured over her – this wasn't how it was supposed to go.

"It's the Kingsman, in the city," she said, and Elise immediately hung up.

Betsy sat and stared at her mobile phone as though it had stung her. Tears sprang into her eyes and she made no attempt to quell them – she let them spill down her cheeks with her smudged mascara. Screw you, Elise, she thought.

She was always trying to impress her sister, and nothing was ever good enough. Well, she would show her!

Sobbing, she selected the number from her contact list and pressed dial.

"What?" the man groaned, clearly woken by the call.

Betsy calmed her sobs and spoke as clearly as she could.

"Nick, it's Betsy. Do you remember the girl in the Mad Hatter that was looking for a passport? How much is it worth to you to know where she is?"

34

Lauren frowned as she approached her desk – no Anna. She had stood her up in Victus and her mobile had gone to voicemail. Now she wasn't at her desk. What was going on? Lauren hadn't minded eating her breakfast bagel alone, and the coffee in Victus was amazing, but she was worried. Anna was reliable. She didn't usually forget things and she would never not turn up without sending a message to cancel.

The central telephone line was ringing as she sat down. She answered.

"This is Detective Sergeant Elise Taylor. I've tried Janet McCarthy and William Ryan's lines, and no one is answering. Where is everyone?"

Lauren adjusted her glasses and grimaced. The detective sounded irate. That woman was growing more and more tense – although, now that she thought about it, all the detectives in the station were on edge. She couldn't wait until the political conference was over and things could settle down around here.

"Most of the detectives are in a meeting in the briefing

centre with the Special Detective Unit," she answered. She knew the meeting was scheduled for this morning – she had arranged it. Elise had received an email invitation to attend as well.

"Right." Elise paused, thinking. "You'll have to interrupt the meeting. I've had a tip-off that the main suspect in the David Gallagher killing has been spotted in the Kingsman Hotel. Get some detectives over there now!"

Elise's tone didn't invite discussion on the matter. She hung up before Lauren could say another word.

Lauren sat at her desk, momentarily stunned. What should she do? The meeting in the conference centre across town was of top priority; the political conference was in a matter of days. But, still, she knew Elise was right – she would have to get someone's attention and organise officers to go to the hotel.

Lauren jumped as her mobile rang. She grabbed it – Anna!

"Lauren, I'm so sorry I didn't meet you for breakfast. You'll never guess what happened here last night!"

"Anna! Thank God you rang, I was worried about you. And you sound OK! But, I'm afraid I have to ring you back. Elise Taylor just hung up on me. She sounds as mad as hell – what's new there? – I have to get some officers to go to the Kingsman Hotel. Apparently the main suspect for the David Gallagher shooting was spotted there. I'm so sorry! I have to ring you back."

Anna sat in stunned silence at her kitchen table, her mobile phone in her hand. So, Kate had been found. Now she would be arrested, and probably charged with murder.

Anna drummed her fingers on the wooden table … Elise had told her not to get involved. But Kate had been one of her best friends … could she really just sit here and wait to hear what had happened? A tiny voice inside warned her to stay where she was but she wondered whether, after all she had witnessed and experienced in the last few days, she should ignore the impending arrest of her old friend. But what exactly could she do? The safest place for Kate was in Garda custody – she could tell her side of the story; whatever that was.

William Ryan had told Anna to rest after her ordeal. She decided she could respond to any text messages later in the day, after she had caught up on some sleep. Now that Dean Harris had been arrested, she felt she could relax. The night had been long, and mostly spent answering questions from Detective Sergeant Ryan. Alex had accompanied her, and Anna was grateful to him, but also glad to be alone now. Alex was sometimes overbearing in his determination to keep her safe. He had been extremely stressed about the fact her house had been broken into.

She held onto the bannister as she made her way wearily to bed. She drew the curtains, shutting out the daylight. Before she switched off her bedside lamp, she pulled the framed photo of her parents out of her locker drawer. They were posing at a neighbour's barbeque, smiling broadly, arms around each other's waists. She stared at their faces for a moment before putting it quickly back in its place. It never helped her to dwell too long on their faces. In a few weeks, it would be ten years since their disappearance. She and Alex never marked the day in any way – they had no graves to go to, no memorial place to visit.

With a lump in her throat, she quickly shut the drawer and pulled the duvet over her head.

She fell into a deep sleep.

35

Tom Gallagher knew he should feel exhausted, but he didn't. He wasn't an eloquent man but, if he had to guess, he would describe himself as feeling invigorated. Joyous, even. Victorious, certainly.

As Monday morning dawned bright and cold, Tom was sitting at the hospital bedside of his son. John was alive and would recover in time. He had a long road ahead of him. But he was young, and his father had considerable resources, so he was lucky.

Marco had taken the responsibility of getting John to A&E as seriously as life and death. He had stayed at the hospital until Tom turned up there himself, not wanting to leave John alone. It had suited Tom to give Marco this mission; Marco felt important, and still part of the team despite his mismanagement of the disposal of the bodies of the security guards. Tom could recognise unwavering loyalty when he saw it, and he valued that as much as any attribute in a man. But some tasks needed a man who was more than just loyal. Thus, Tom had needed Marco out of the way for the other significant task, the more important job of disposing of the Germans. That needed a man who wouldn't panic under any circumstances. Murray, his second in command since John had disappeared, had proved himself again to be both capable and resourceful, precise to the letter. And, vitally, calm under pressure. The Germans were out of the picture. Retribution was served. The Gallagher hallway was a bloodbath, but that was a problem easily solved.

Tom had known Tobias Meier wouldn't turn up at the Oracle. He had stationed Alan Ainsley there with a handful of men to maintain the ruse, but he knew the German would seek out his own arrangement that night. Tom had positioned enough cars in the quiet road to plant the seed of doubt; he had learned to read a man, and Tobias was as predictable as any man Tom had dealt with on his way to the top. There would be no comeback for him on this one. The Meiers were well and truly ash by now. There would be no fingerprints, no forensics to speak of; Murray had made sure of it. The heat from a diesel fire left very little behind.

Of course, Tom had never had the memory key, the USB stick or whatever it was called. He had no interest in it, and no time to find Kate Crowley. This was a big city, and she was but one lowlife, with many places to hide. The hunt was still on though – this changed nothing. If anything, Tom wanted her now more than ever. She had caused so much suffering to his family, to his wife and sons. She had to pay, and she was top of the list of people he needed to take care of. Just ahead of Alan Ainsley.

Alan Ainsley had proven himself to be the slippery snake Tom had always suspected he was. Tom preferred there to be as few links in a chain as possible, but Alan had skills and contacts, and the ability to open up a whole world of business.

When the Meiers had shown up at Gallagher's mansion Murray had called in reinforcements – all the men stationed at the Oracle were called to return to the house immediately. Alan took the opportunity to flee. He simply disappeared. As soon as Murray had the time Tom planned to send him up to Alan's house, to have a nice cosy chat with the man himself, or indeed his wife. Tom didn't really expect either of them to be there. No matter. Let the Englishman have his holiday. Tom Gallagher was a man who held a grudge; it helped him sleep. He always drifted into happy slumber after mentally plotting revenge on whoever had slighted him. Alan Ainsley could join Kate and all the others Tom had yet to tick off the list of vengeance served.

Tom stroked his son's hand. Surgeons had repaired what they could of the nerves and tendons in what remained of his finger and dealt with some internal bleeding. John had many broken bones: his left wrist, a cheekbone, and four ribs. His doctor was a bit too jumpy for Tom's liking. Tom had spun a story about a serious car crash, but he could tell the man didn't believe him. Tom didn't care; all that mattered to him was that his son was alive, and away from the Meiers.

With his mobile phone he took a photograph of John in the hospital bed, sleeping and looking peaceful against the white sheets. He looked serene in the photograph. Tom decided he would text the photograph to Mae later that day. Murray was overseeing the cleaning of the hallway at the house – replacing the front door, repainting the walls and swapping the tiles, removing all trace of Tobias Meier's blood and flesh. Murray had a contact in the trade, a man Tom had approved a few years earlier. The man had been trying to set up a legitimate painting and decorating business with his sons after they were made redundant in the recession. Tom respected that, even more so that the man was including his sons in his business. But the man was being targeted by some upstart wannabes who thought they could charge protection money. In Tom's own city! The man brought the problem to Murray's attention in the pub one night, and Tom had given Murray permission to go full force to deal with it. The man owed them, and he was repaying his debt this morning in the hallway of the Gallagher mansion.

Tom wouldn't let Mae return until all evidence of what had happened the night before was removed. But she would want to know her son was safe, so he would call her and text the photograph as soon as he thought she'd be awake.

He rubbed at his knuckles, red and raw. If Mae noticed them, he knew she would never ask. And if she smelled fresh paint or noticed a slight difference in the hall tiles, he knew she would never mention it. She was the perfect wife.

Tom's right shoulder felt stiff, his back a little tight – nothing that couldn't be remedied with a massage at the golf club later on. His mobile phone beeped in his pocket and he pulled it out: a text message from Murray. The manager at the Mad Hatter had a possible location for Kate Crowley. Tom gave the go-ahead to send a handful of men to bring her in. And they had better get it right this time – at the club she had proved difficult and had a friend on side too. Tom was disgusted his men had been bested by two women. They wouldn't make that mistake again. He would find Kate Crowley today – Mae deserved to put some of her demons to rest. What better way than to present her with the bitch that had shot her youngest son?

"Dad?"

Tom's attention went straight to his son in the hospital bed beside him. It took all his strength not to cry. He hadn't known when John would wake, or if he would have any damage from the beating. The doctor had said time would tell a lot. Tom swelled with pride as he watched his first-born open his eyes and look around the room. He looked beaten and battered, but lucid.

"Where are they?" he rasped. He tried to sit up but quickly gave in, panting from the exertion. Tom stroked John's hand and spoke reassuringly. "Long gone, son. Taken care of."

John met his father's eyes. He understood what that meant. He felt weak with relief.

"The bag? The money and diamonds?"

Tom's eyes hardened again. He had promised Mae she could have Kate Crowley when they found her. But he realised he would want her to himself for a little while first.

"All in hand, John. Kate Crowley will be in the house by the end of the day."

"There's something else. David sold them something . . ." John's voice trailed off. Speaking was difficult for him.

"Everything is sorted, son. It's all under control."

"David! Where?" John rasped weakly.

His father's face betrayed his sorrow. The Meiers had been a distraction; soon Tom would have a funeral to plan.

A small part of Tom wondered about who the buyer was for this memory key Tobias Meier had been so anxious to find. Tobias had mentioned his 'employer'. Tom realised whoever he was, Tobias was afraid of him. A man like Tobias Meier wouldn't risk travelling halfway across Europe to retrieve something unless he was under tremendous pressure.

Still, the Meiers were dealt with now, their bones turned to ash and floating away on the cold November wind.

A pretty nurse with a nametag reading '**Grace**' walked in and smiled at Tom as she picked up John's chart, checking his vital signs. Tom smiled back – this was shaping up to be a great day.

36

Elise stood with her hands on her hips and surveyed the scene in front of her. Monastery Road was shut to all civilian traffic. Firefighters had put out the blaze an hour ago, battling against its intensity for what felt like a long time. The burnt-out shell of a large vehicle remained at the verge of the road, surrounded by members of the Garda Technical Bureau. A huge plume of dense black smoke could be seen for miles, and the acrid smell of molten metal, rubber and flesh was pungent in the air.

Elise had no proof that this vehicle was the one being used by the Meier brothers. But whatever remained of the chassis number or any other identifying markers on the vehicle would soon be found. Her gut told her this was them. There was evidence of four adult bodies inside, all of which would be removed from the scene shortly. They were charred beyond recognition, impossible to tell if they were male or female. Elise had vomited onto the grass verge after she had inspected them – whiskey, coffee and toast all purged onto the frosty grass. This was the grisliest crime scene she had ever attended.

Elise's thoughts were whirring, like gears clicking into place. She reviewed the facts in a mental check-list – the four Meier brothers had arrived into Ireland, David Gallagher had been shot, John Gallagher had disappeared, two of Tom Gallagher's security crew had been murdered, and now a vehicle had been found burnt-out with four adult bodies inside. Logic told Elise this looked like a gang war of epic proportions. She dreaded what Doherty would make of it all, just days away from the political conference.

Her phone buzzed in her pocket – William Ryan. She rolled her eyes as she answered the call.

"Ryan, what can I do for you?"

"Taylor, I hear you are up to your eyes in burning metal," Ryan answered

Elise stayed silent, hoping he'd soon get to the point of the call.

Ryan cleared his throat and continued. "I thought you'd like to know I arrested a man named Dean Harris this morning in connection with the sexual assaults these past three years."

So, William Ryan was calling to gloat. She and her colleagues had failed to solve the cases. Now, the new guy, just transferred, had cracked them. She said nothing, just paced the ground and stayed on the line, silently waiting for the call to run its course.

"Anyway," Ryan continued, sensing her agitation, "I thought this piece of information might be pertinent to your current case. I arrested Dean Harris in the University Hospital this morning. On the way in I passed Tom Gallagher getting himself a coffee at a vending machine in the hall."

Elise stopped pacing and squinted into the morning sun. This was potentially interesting.

"Go on."

211

"I made some enquiries." Ryan sounded smug again, knowing he had her full attention. "It seems Tom Gallagher's son John was brought in overnight. He had emergency surgery for some very nasty injuries. Gallagher claimed it was a car crash, but the doctor on duty isn't buying it – he is thinking about referring it to the Gardaí. He told me, off the record of course, that the injuries look consistent with torture."

Words failed Elise but her thoughts raced in a frantic attempt to slot this piece of information into the puzzle. What the hell was going on? Cork city had descended into the setting for a criminal gang movie. What was Doherty going to say? The man would surely have a heart attack. Elise's own heart was hammering so loudly she could hear it.

Stuttering, her stomach lurching again, she thanked Ryan for the information and ended the call. She could barely breathe. Instinct told her that Gallagher was responsible for the burnt-out vehicle here and the murder of the four people inside it. He had taken revenge for the killing of his two men and rescued his son. Elise recalled the information bulletin that had landed on her desk about the Meiers yesterday – the eldest brother, Tobias, often brokered deals with bigger criminal gangs from Russia and other eastern states, and that could spell trouble. With the Meiers dead, where did that leave things now?

Detective Superintendent Doherty was storming towards Elise, his trench coat flapping. He held two takeaway coffee cups and he handed one to her. This was a first. Elise nodded her thanks.

"Where do we stand?" Doherty asked, his tone betraying his nervous agitation.

"Well, sir, let me put it this way – Janet McCarthy is going to have a stroke."

37

Kate had had enough. It was Monday now. David had come to her house on Wednesday afternoon, and now he lay in the hospital morgue, she imagined. She was hiding in a crappy excuse of a hotel, with the Gallaghers tracking her, and was no closer to leaving the city.

Her plan to buy a passport had failed – she should have realised that Tom Gallagher would be searching for her throughout the city and she should never have attempted it.

But she didn't know what else to do. She had only learned about Nick and his fake documents from David Gallagher's notebook – she wasn't a criminal like him, she had no contacts in the underworld, as it was known. But she did have money. That would surely help her achieve her goal. She was ready to move on.

But how?

Hunger had forced her out of the hotel early that morning. The Kingsman didn't supply their guests with tea or coffee; there wasn't even a packet of sugar in her room to keep her energy up. She was wearing the same clothes since

Wednesday, aside from the new coat, scarf and hat, and mostly grabbing takeaway food whenever she left the hotel. She was tired, she felt dirty, and she missed her sister with a physical yearning.

Wrapped in her winter coat and scarf, her hat pushed down to cover as much of her face as possible, she had returned to the greasy spoon café. She was prepared for the cold but not for the ice that had formed on the footpaths. More than once she lost her footing as she moved along the streets, glad of her thick gloves to help break potential falls against the hard concrete.

Inside the café her hands shook as she ate. She didn't remove her coat or lift her eyes as she devoured her food and sipped the hot coffee. She momentarily forgot her fear. Her mind was blank, her tension quieted, for almost fifteen minutes as she sated her appetite.

But it was time to go back to the hotel. Now, with a stomach full of food and coffee, she hoped to be better able to plan. She needed the internet. If she'd had her mobile phone she could better search ways to leave Ireland without a passport but that had been left behind too, somewhere in her house. She had decided days ago that acquiring a new one would be too difficult. She was on the run from the Gardaí – for all she knew, there would be pictures of her face on newspapers, as there had been of David. And if she wasn't recognised, there would still be conversations with a salesperson eager to sign her up for the best monthly package, and she felt just too weary for the whole thing. Risking eating in cafés was one thing; engaging in conversation with salespeople, possibly having her photograph and details logged onto their system when she was on the run from the Gardaí, was completely reckless.

She thought of Anna – in the alley behind the Mad Hatter she had wanted to help. In almost a week, aside

214

from Natalie, Anna Clarke was the only person who had spoken kindly to her. They had been best friends, the four of them. She felt a stab of loneliness.

She turned the corner and faced the hotel. The Kingsman was narrow and reached eight floors tall. It was at the end of a row of businesses, adjoining a cocktail bar on one side, and had a narrow alleyway on the other. Its front façade had seen better days; pale yellow paint was mottled with mildew, and the S was missing from the name-sign, rusted nails protruding from the wall where it had once hung. It looked cheap, and easily overlooked; as good a place to hide as any.

The lobby was tiny, even smaller than her room upstairs. It was freezing inside; one half of the front door was propped open with a pot plant, allowing in the arctic chill. White tiled floors were stained with dirt, plastic plants were strewn here and there, and stained blue curtains on small windows were pulled back to let in the morning light. She noticed tiny holes in them; the curtains had either been feasted on by moths or burned with cigarettes. She eyed a young man at the reception desk, no more than a teenager. She hadn't seen him here before but then she had been keeping her head lowered, the better to stay out of view. He was pale under the acne that marred his young face, and probably tired from the night shift. He looked bored and extremely cold.

She approached the reception desk.

"Hi!" she said brightly, flashing him a friendly smile.

The teenager looked up at her and blushed bright red. Bingo! His teenage hormones would be his undoing.

"How are you this morning?" She saw no nametag, so abandoned the hope of addressing him by name. "Boy, it's freezing out there!"

Neil felt hot under the collar. He was so tired. His Uncle

Steve had partied all night, falling into the lobby with his date – Betty, was it? – at about four o'clock in the morning. Steve had promised Neil he could clock off at dawn, but he was still sitting here waiting for his cover to show up. The cops had been here, quizzing him about some woman with wild red hair … they said she might have changed her hair. Neil had college to go to! But here was a very pretty lady with big green eyes smiling at him, and he began to feel better already. She looked freezing. He made a show of hitting lots of keys at the computer in front of him, to look busy and important.

"How can I help you, Miss …?"

"Forde," she answered quickly. "Pauline Forde, in Room 224."

Neil smiled.

"It's just I've lost my mobile phone." She grimaced and sighed for extra dramatic effect.

"And I really need to search online for something. Is there any chance I could use the computer?"

Neil typed again and looked up with a broad smile. He wasn't supposed to allow guests behind the counter, but he wasn't supposed to be still sitting here either. Steve owed him. Knowing his uncle, Neil knew he could be passed out until noon.

"No problem – I can set you up here if you like?"

Kate's heart leapt but she kept her face frozen into the bright smile the kid seemed to like so much. She couldn't believe it had worked. She beamed at him and he blushed again.

She moved around the desk as Neil stood up and moved aside. As she sat down, she could see out the door she had just come in.

She froze, her jaw dropping open in shock.

Outside on the street, stepping from a car that had

216

mounted the kerb, were two tall, well-built men. Dressed in black pants and thick padded jackets, with tight shaved haircuts, they were identical clones of each other, except for one striking feature on the man exiting the driver-side. He had a scar that ran from his lip to his ear. Her pulse pounded in her ears. She had seen that man before, in the toilets of the Mad Hatter. Gallagher's men. And they were walking toward the hotel door.

Her mind raced. She visualised every inch of the hotel that she was aware of. No fire exit or back entrance came to mind.

"I left something upstairs – I'll be right back!"

Neil looked perplexed as she sprang from the chair and bolted toward the staircase.

She mounted it quickly to the second floor, taking two steps at a time.

Pushing the key into her bedroom door she darted inside and shut it quietly behind her, leaning against it, breathing heavily. The cramped room felt like a trap. Her hands shook as she brought them to her head, pressing her fingers into her temples to quell her panicked thoughts. She leant heavily against the door, her legs threatening to give way.

The double bed was just two feet from the door, and she moved towards it, steadying her breath as she sat down. She couldn't believe Gallagher's men were downstairs. They always seemed to be one step behind her. She thought of the kid at reception – he would cave easily under their questioning and tell the men everything they wanted to know.

Oh my God, oh my God, they found me, I can't believe it! I've been so careful!

She blinked tears away and looked around the room. She had to get out of here. She needed to stop panicking and leave – fast!

She stepped away from the bed and grabbed the small

red satchel. It was bulging, almost too full to close. She dared not open the bedroom door – she stood facing it, her eye pressed to the peephole, her bag over her shoulder. She heard the rush of heavy footsteps come down the hall, saw movement pass her door, and heard the door to Room 222, beside hers, open.

They had the wrong room!

Either the kid downstairs had given them the wrong number on purpose, or he had made a mistake – either way, her breath steadied as she waited, listening.

The door had opened easily; it didn't sound like the lock had been forced – the kid must have been strong-armed into giving them a room key. She could hear her own ragged breathing but tried to concentrate on the sounds coming from the room next door. It sounded like the bedroom was being ripped apart, the bed flipped, and the wardrobe toppled. It didn't take the men more than half a minute to establish the room was empty. She heard one of the men speaking, then a pause, before speaking again – he was on the phone to somebody, most likely reporting that she wasn't there.

She needed to decide what to do. She had no doubt that it was Gallagher's men that were in the room next door, and probably more were driving the city streets, on the lookout. If she stayed in this room until the men gave up searching, how long would she have to wait until the streets were safe? There was no option but to sit tight until the men gave up the search. She could hardly phone the Gardaí.

She groaned – she should have left the city, one way or another, a long time ago!

Within seconds, her plan to sit tight was abandoned. The handle of the door began to lower – someone was trying to open it. She sat on the bed, momentarily frozen in fear. A loud thud as one of the men attempted to shoulder in the door roused her into action. Springing up from the bed she darted to the window – there was enough space for her to climb through. She wouldn't have to jump to the ground this time – a set of metal fire-escape stairs curled around the outside of the building, and they were within reaching distance of the window.

Grabbing her things, she pushed the window open and climbed out. She was light on her feet and quickly descended the metal stairs, jumping a short distance to land in the alley within seconds. Luckily the alley was empty – the last thing she wanted was to have to take on Gallagher's thugs in this narrow space, even with her award-winning kick-boxing skills.

She hurried own the alley. Her eyes darted from left to right, searching the street outside for any sign that she was observed. She saw the dark car parked on the kerb, thankfully empty.

Stepping out into the main street again, she slowed to a normal pace, anxious not to draw attention to herself. She wound her scarf around the lower half of her face and pulled the woollen hat as low down as she could. Between the intense cold and her fear that she would be seen, she felt there was fire burning in her lungs.

The ice on the footpaths had thawed somewhat, and she moved quickly. She walked towards Parnell Place, a place she remembered from her childhood as the main city bus station. She stepped inside, her red satchel secured over her shoulder, and looked up at the screens advertising routes and bus times. There were buses leaving for a variety of destinations across the country within a few hours. That felt too long for her – where would she hide? Gallagher had found her twice – he could do it again!

A different route caught her eye – heading south to the start of the Wild Atlantic Way. Nostalgia pulled at her; the route would take her home, home to the place they had lived before her parents' marriage disintegrated and everything changed. She knew her family home was long ago sold – but the memories made her smile for a moment. Then the longing for her sister intensified and she felt so burdened she thought she would pass out. The bus station interior began to spin, and she sat down on the cold tiles.

She *had* to get out of here! Who could she possibly turn to?

Hope sparked inside her. Anna's house had been near hers. Did she still live there? Her old friend had tried to help her in the Mad Hatter on Saturday night – would she help her still?

Pushing to her feet, she approached the ticket booth with renewed energy. She had a plan, and nothing to lose.

38

The bus journey to Kinsale was long and tedious. The driver took every backroad possible, it seemed to her. He parked for fifteen minutes at Cork Airport, checking his watch intermittently, steadfastly refusing to leave until the allocated time. No-one got onto the bus there, or on most of the stops. It was mid-afternoon when they set out, and by the time they left the airport, darkness was beginning to set in.

The bus was almost empty. She sat near the back, the red satchel on her lap, her hat jammed down over her ears. The adrenaline rush from events at the hotel had depleted and suddenly she felt exhausted. Her eyelids drooped, but she fought to stay awake. Whenever she felt herself drifting towards sleep she thought of the Gallaghers, and the man with the scar running from his lip to his ear, and how close he had come to finding her again. Someone had tipped them off, twice now. Someone knew her movements. She had been so careful, but someone was watching her. Fear crept over her – Cork was too dangerous for her now.

There was plenty of cash in her bag – Gallagher's cash –

and she had hoped to stay in a nicer hotel to lie low until she figured out how to leave the country. But all the nice hotels in the city were booked up. She had read the details of the political conference in the newspaper – she assumed the fancier hotels were reserved for VIPs. Which right now, she was not. She was a fugitive.

The bus journey from the city was uneventful. From the seat she had observed the other passengers and the road whenever possible. The passengers were not a threat to her, she was sure of that. Although she was tired, where the Gallaghers were concerned she was always alert.

She felt too tired and her head too fuzzy to form any more thoughts or to make any sense of the situation. Her body sagged against the seat. She was heading for home, and she rested her head against the glass of the window, soaking in the familiar route.

She recognised almost everything that flitted by as the bus passed. She smiled a little at the sights. It amazed her that after all this time she still remembered this remote part of Cork. She had lived near the city for three years. She wondered now why she had never sought to reconnect with her schoolfriend Anna, or to return to the town where she had grown up. She had Natalie of course, and very quickly Natalie had David Gallagher, and then the twins – Kate's life had felt too full to rekindle old friendships or step back in time. She had been too focused on surviving the present.

She wondered whether Anna still lived in her family home – she had heard through mutual friends about Anna's parents' disappearance and had followed the story on the news for a while. Shortly after that had happened, Kate's own father had died, and her mother had announced her intention to remarry. There had never seemed a good time to call Anna. Now, as the bus stopped in the centre of Kinsale, she planned to call in person.

She had thought she was cold on the bus but, as she alighted, she realised she had been positively cosy. It was so cold at the side of the road that her cheeks stung and her eyes watered. Tiny drifts of snow fell softly, coating the ground in a pristine white.

The centre of Kinsale had not changed much. In the summer, it was always a bustling tourist hub, the smell of the sea and fish and chips among its memorable characteristics. She smiled despite herself as she remembered days spent here with her parents and Natalie; the funfair, a walk through the narrow streets, then chips for tea and a cone for dessert if the twins were well behaved. Which they always were.

She noticed the sign across the road for the Oceanic Hotel. It was open, and advertising vacancies. If Anna wasn't home, or had sold her parents' house, she would return here and take a room for the night. Regret washed over her – she should have come home as soon as possible, away from the Gallaghers, who seemed to have cast an inescapable net across their territory.

Maybe it would be from where she started that she could escape.

Shouldering the red bag, she turned her back on the street and walked uphill, away from the centre of the little town. Her coat and scarf were heavy, her hat warm, and she was surprised the snow didn't bother her more. Her mind was strangely blank – she had no idea what she would say to Anna, and no energy left to think this through. She would just turn up, and what would be would be. She was done thinking and planning – things just had not worked out the way she imagined they would. Perhaps she would have better luck by winging it.

After ten minutes of trudging uphill in the snow, she saw it. A large, oval-shaped stone, with the words '*Willow*

Rise' chiselled into it. This was it. She had been here to this estate many times, on sleepovers with Natalie and Vivian. She remembered Anna's parents, Michael and Helen, and her crush on Anna's older brother Alex … it was a lifetime ago. She was momentarily scared that Anna wouldn't welcome her here – but then she remembered how Anna had helped her in the Mad Hatter, and she remembered her words as they had hidden in the alleyway: "*I can get you to a safe place – come with me, please!*"

She walked into the estate and quickly found the right house – she had no doubt. After all these years, the door was still red. The paint was faded now. A tiny wooden birdhouse, hand-painted by Anna when they were about ten years old – all the kids had made them in Mr. Browne's class – hung from a tree branch in her front garden. The sight of it hanging there suddenly brought tears to Kate's eyes. In the house they had sold after her parents' separation, her and Natalie's birdhouses had been left behind. She blinked away her tears and her hand shook as she extended her gloved finger and rang the doorbell.

39

Anna's mobile phone had started vibrating on her bedside locker at three o'clock in the afternoon. The noise woke her, and she had barely been off the phone since. Lauren had finally heard why Anna was out that day – Anna knew it wouldn't take long for the news to reach her ears – and was horrified.

"God, your theory was right, but what a way to find out!"

Anna had agreed she'd have preferred to have been wrong on this one. She quizzed Lauren on whether Kate had been found at the location Elise had called in, but Lauren said no. The Gardaí that had called there spoke to the young man at reception, who said he hadn't seen any woman matching that description, long hair or otherwise. Anna sighed as she listened. So, the mystery continued.

Almost as soon as Anna and Lauren ended their call, Alex rang. He sounded weary – knowing him as she did, Anna would wager he hadn't been able to catch up on sleep, worrying about her.

"Anna – I wanted to call you earlier, but I didn't want to wake you! How are you feeling?"

"Good, much better."

"The arrest is already in the online news. I've read all the coverage on it. God, I'd love to get my hands on him!" He sounded choked with emotion.

"Don't worry, Alex, I'm fine. Sure, he never stood a chance! Dad and Jason taught me well!"

Anna attempted to laugh, to lighten the tone of the conversation. Secretly, she had never felt relief like it. She realised she had been anticipating what had happened for a few days; it had felt like walking around waiting for a monster to pounce from the shadows. Now that it was over, she felt lighter. She knew she would have to give evidence in court, but the thought of that didn't bother her. If it meant the guy being locked up and justice being served, she would happily do what was needed. She was so glad the nightmare of the last few days was over.

Alex was full of concern, but Anna managed to persuade him not to call over. All she wanted to do was curl up on her sofa in front of a blazing stove and watch the *X-Factor* repeat.

Myles texted, apologising for not visiting; he said he was really busy at work, with the conference only days away. He was in the briefing centre with Janet McCarthy and a few other detectives. He promised to phone later.

Downstairs, she busied herself with lighting the stove in the living room. The house was quiet, and it slightly unnerved her. She rolled her neck from side to side, flexing her back and shoulders. She had missed another gym session this morning, too busy giving evidence and answering questions, and it rankled her. She looked forward to life returning to normal soon.

It was dark now, and she drew the curtains, shutting out the world, ready to retreat to the sofa. Snow was falling lightly, and Anna thought of Christmas and her niece

Chloe. It was a time she looked forward to. She eyed the boxes of decorations in the hall – she'd invite Chloe over soon to get started.

Her stomach rumbled, reminding her that she had slept most of the day, and not eaten much before that. She moved into the adjoining kitchen and pulled out a pizza from the freezer. Once it was heating in the oven she prepared a salad, finding comfort in the mundane tasks.

Switching on the radio, she selected Lyric FM. It wasn't Bach, her mother's favourite, but the music was soothing and calming. The process of moving around her kitchen and checking the cooking food soothed her nerves. While the pizza cooked, she read a report of Harris's arrest online on her laptop – she was surprised it had made the papers already. She also read the mayor's statement on the city's preparations for the political conference.

The finding of two dead bodies in a car boot and the shooting of David Gallagher no longer dominated the headlines. Those stories were pushed to the second page by more grisly news – four bodies had been discovered in a burnt-out car just outside the city. Anna's eyes widened as she read the article. She thought of Chief Superintendent Janet McCarthy, and all the detectives in the station, trying to maintain law and order in the run-up to the political conference.

She settled on the sofa, her pizza and salad in front of her on the coffee table. She poured herself a glass of wine and had just taken her first sip when the doorbell rang. Rolling her eyes, she rose wearily and went to the door, preparing to scold Alex for calling around to check on her.

But it wasn't Alex. It was a woman, bundled in winter clothes. A red satchel was hung over her shoulder, her lips were slightly blue and her skin so pale it was almost translucent. But it was her eyes, her bright-green eyes that watered in the freezing wind, that almost stopped Anna's heart.

"*Kate!*"

Her childhood friend smiled hesitantly.

"Anna – please, can I come in?"

Anna stood in shocked silence for a few moments. So, here she was, her old best friend, one of the closest she had ever had. She had so many wonderful memories with Kate at the heart of them. So much had happened in their lives since they had parted ways.

And now Kate was standing on Anna's doorstep.

It was only when Anna noticed Kate's lips quiver from the cold that she regained her thoughts and her manners. She stepped back and held open the door.

"Of course! Come in!"

Leading the way into the living room, Anna gestured to the sofa and Kate sat down. Slowly she peeled off her coat and scarf, then finally her hat, revealing her short, dark hair. Anna studied her, looking for the resemblance to the child she had known. She had high cheekbones and pale smooth skin; Anna had no doubt but that she was a beautiful woman when she wasn't on the run from a murderous gangster. The red satchel caught Anna's eye – Kate clutched it to her as though it were a lifeline.

Anna remembered the night Kate had drop-kicked a much larger man in the alleyway outside the Mad Hatter. She momentarily wondered if she should be on her guard, then quickly brushed aside her concern. This was her old friend, and she had come to her for help.

It occurred to Anna that she should really phone Elise Taylor – there was, after all, a murder suspect warming her hands at the stove. She debated calling the detective over and back in her mind, before quickly deciding against it. Instinct told her Kate needed help, and Anna wasn't in the mood to be barked at by Elise – the woman was perpetually angry lately.

Seeing Kate now, Anna was sure she was innocent – that

what had happened was self-defence. What mattered was that she was safe, off the streets, and somewhere Gallagher's men wouldn't know to look. What harm would it do if she stayed here in the warmth and safety of her home for a few hours?

Anna decided she would speak to her about turning herself in, and convince her it was the best option, her *only* option. Once she had explained her side of the story, Anna had no doubt she would be a free woman. David Gallagher was a violent criminal; anyone could see Kate would have had no choice.

Anna would call Elise Taylor, but first she would allow her friend some time to rest. She couldn't imagine the terror the woman had been living under these past few days, fearful that Gallagher's men were around every corner. She thought back to the images of the crime scene DS Taylor had been looking at on her computer at work – the violence in the house that night had been horrifying. Poor Kate had been ambushed there by Gallagher – Anna was sure of it.

She had been through so much. She must have passionately hated David Gallagher because of how he had abused her sister. But just because she had motive to kill didn't mean she had intended to do it.

Kate was perched on the edge of the sofa and looked up at Anna, her green eyes scared.

"I hope you don't mind that I came here. I didn't have anywhere else to go."

Anna sat down beside her old friend and placed her hand over hers. "Of course not! I'm so glad you're safe!"

Kate's eyes shone with tears, and she quickly hugged Anna, before wiping her eyes with a shaking hand. "Thank you! You've no idea how much this means to me!"

She sounded relieved. She sat back into the sofa, her body sagging.

"Do you want some food?" Anna asked.

She shook her head. Anna gestured to the wine bottle open on the coffee table, but she shook her head again and smiled softy.

"Maybe just a coffee."

Anna busied herself in the kitchen, leaving Kate to sit near the stove. Her mobile phone rested on the countertop. She glanced at it. She would call DS Taylor very soon.

She brought two coffees to the living-room coffee table. Kate watched her carefully, a warm comforter around her shoulders. Once Anna had sat down opposite her, they eyed each other warily, neither sure how to begin the conversation.

It was Kate who broke the silence.

"Again, I'm sorry to just turn up like this."

"Don't worry. We always said we'd be there for each other, remember?"

Kate nodded, her bottom lip trembling, tears beginning to fall down her cheeks. She sat still, her shoulders stiff against the back of the sofa. Her skin was ghostly pale. She had dark shadows under her eyes and her lips were cracked at the corners.

"I'm sorry to hear your dad passed away."

"Thank you. And I'm sorry about your parents ... I heard it on the news."

Anna nodded and looked away. Silence stretched between them again.

Kate sipped her coffee, her hands wrapped around the mug, savouring its warmth.

Anna picked at a slice of pizza, not really hungry anymore. She wondered if she should tell Kate that she knew the shooting case inside out. Normally, she would never discuss the details of a case with anyone, but the main suspect in a shooting had never been sitting in her living room drinking coffee before! Anna reasoned that if she wanted Kate to turn herself in, she would have to gain her trust and share what she knew.

"You should know I work in the Lee Street Garda Station, Kate. I'm clerical staff. I know all about the shooting. I know you're on the run."

Kate's green eyes flashed into focus and met Anna's.

"The Gardaí are searching for you. Detective Sergeant Elise Taylor is heading up the investigation."

"What does she have to do with this?" Kate asked quietly, her voice cracking.

"Well, as I said, she is leading the investigation into the death of David Gallagher. And by the way … er … Tom Gallagher has put a price on your head."

Kate's eyes widened in alarm.

Anna continued. "Thirty thousand euro dead, fifty thousand to bring you in alive." She paused before adding, "Sorry to be so blunt about it. It's just that your best option is to turn yourself in to the Gardaí. It's really the safest thing."

Kate put her mug on the coffee table and her head in her hands. Christ! Gallagher had put a bounty on finding her. No wonder his men had been everywhere she went. She knew he was watching her house, and she was convinced Tom Gallagher had a source in the Garda station, so he would know she wasn't in custody. He wanted to kill her; she knew that. He wanted to avenge David's death.

Anna gestured towards the coffee and the pizza, cut into slices. "You should drink. And eat."

She did what she was told. It was the easiest thing she had done in almost a week. Her hands shook as she picked up the mug. She began to eat the pizza and drink the coffee, keeping her eyes downcast. Anna was right; she felt better as she consumed the hot food.

She was very much aware now that she had few choices.

Anna was Garda staff. She was encouraging her to turn herself in. She had put Anna in a terrible position and Anna was unlikely to help her in the way she had hoped. But she had to trust Anna – she had welcomed her into her home after all and was offering food and shelter. There was no sign of a threat, or that she had phoned the Gardaí. She told herself she had to relax. She felt better the more she ate, and the coffee was helping to revive her. She eyed her old friend as they ate – Anna really hadn't changed that much. Her brown eyes were still almost too big for her face, her hair still a light blonde, but shorter now, not long down her back like when they were kids.

"How did you know where I was?" she asked. "In the Mad Hatter, I mean."

"Elise Taylor got a tip-off – from a source, I guess. She said one of her street informers told her you had been in the Mad Hatter, looking to buy a passport. She sent Gardaí to your hotel today too – I don't know how she knew about that."

Kate was horrified. The Gardaí knew she was at the hotel too? How? When she had scarcely left the place? She shuddered at the mention of the Mad Hatter. She realised how foolish she had been to go there, running around the city thinking she was invisible. She had made so many mistakes. But she needed a passport or some other way out of Ireland.

"I take it you're trying to leave the city?" Anna asked.

Kate nodded as she chewed more pizza. "The country! I want to be with Natalie and the girls. They're in France waiting for me. They're depending on me. But, you see, the night I fled my house I left my passport behind – it was with my suitcase."

"I know, Kate, I know. But please turn yourself in! You'll be treated well, and they'll believe that it was self-defence! How could they not?"

232

Kate's green eyes met Anna's.

"It was self-defence, wasn't it?" Anna asked nervously.

Kate nodded quickly. "Of course!"

It was so long since she'd had a conversation like this with anyone, and it was exhausting her. But she felt at ease here; it was as though the years had melted away. There was an easy flow to their conversation, the way there always had been. She felt comfortable, despite the topic of conversation. She felt *safe*. She could explain to Anna, make her understand.

"I don't want to go to the Guards. I've always felt Tom Gallagher has a man on the inside, in the Garda station. And I don't like Detective Taylor."

"You know her?"

"I reported David's abuse to her a few times, and to other detectives as well, but I'm familiar with her. She always seemed interested and wanted all the details, but she never did anything."

Anna nodded sympathetically. "You know there was little she could do if Natalie didn't press charges?"

"I know! But David Gallagher was an animal who treated my sister like a piece of dirt! Every time I reported him to the Guards for beating her up, he knew about it, he knew every detail. Detective Taylor was kind initially, but I think Natalie annoyed her – maybe she considered Natalie was wasting her time, always refusing to file a report against David. I'd swear he had someone on the inside. Tom Gallagher has the Guards in his pocket and David seemed to be particularly well-informed. I had to run after David was shot. Gallagher has a niece in Limerick prison – if I get sent there, I'll be dead within days. And if I don't get sent there, it's just a matter of time before I get handed over to the Gallaghers. I can't imagine what John would do to me." She shuddered at the thought of David's older brother. David had always been violent and unpredictable, but John was … different. John had a feral side to him that instinct had always warned her to avoid.

"John is missing as far as I know," Anna said. "Detective Taylor was concerned about the possible involvement of a German gang that flew into the city last week. John's been missing for a few days now – it was in the report."

Anna watched Kate carefully as she spoke and saw the enormity of her words settle on her friend's face. Kate's green eyes grew huge, and the little colour that had come into her face now drained away. This was a story that ran deep, and again Anna found herself questioning whether Kate's role in it was completely innocent. She felt conflicted. She could empathise with her in one respect, yet she eyed her now with measured suspicion. She was a woman who had desperately wanted out of her situation. Was she desperate enough to kill a man? And what was it about the mention of the German gang that had scared her so much?

Anna decided to cut to the heart of the issue.

"Why did you shoot David Gallagher when you are a kickboxing champion and could have knocked him out?"

Kate met Anna's eyes again, and alarm flashed in them.

"How do you …?"

"I saw how you handled Gallagher's guy in the alley outside the Mad Hatter. I found your friend Pauline Forde's Facebook page and saw photos of you receiving your trophy. Don't lie to me, Kate!"

Kate sat back in the sofa again, having put the remains of her pizza slice back on the coffee table. Fear tingled in her veins. Perhaps this had been a bad idea. Anna knew so much about her. Even though she had been in hiding, the Gardaí and the Gallaghers knew where to look for her. Leaving Cork and living in peace with Natalie and the twins seemed like such an impossible dream now.

"I never meant to kill him!" she answered, her eyes on the tabletop, her voice barely a whisper. "He wasn't supposed to show up ... neither were the Germans!" She covered her face with her hands, and her shoulders began to shake. "It's all such a mess!"

Anna sat still. She dared not break the tension by speaking. Kate's shoulders were shuddering, but she made no sound. Anna heard her take a deep breath, and she finally removed her hands.

"I don't know where to begin."

"I find the start to be the best place," Anna said, parroting William Ryan's words – had it only been Friday that she had sat in his office and wondered if she was on to something with her theory linking the sexual-assault crimes? So much had happened since then. She rubbed at her temple, at the familiar pull of a forming migraine.

Kate smiled weakly. She knew now was the time to tell her story.

"David Gallagher has made my life a misery ever since Natalie met him. It's almost four years now, but he cast a curse on us, and I just couldn't break it! Natalie was completely enthralled by him from the start. She slept with him the first week they met – which was completely unlike her – and got pregnant. It was a nightmare. David was the worst excuse of a boyfriend ... everything you'd hate someone you care for to be involved with. He questioned why she needed to work, why she had friends of the opposite sex, why she spoke to me every day. He said we had an unhealthy bond and that I was obsessed with her!" She rolled her eyes at this. Her hatred of David Gallagher was etched in the tight lines of her face and the thin line of her lips as she spoke of him. "As I said, Natalie got pregnant really quickly. Gallagher was thrilled, and they moved in together. Whenever we met for coffee or a catch-up, he'd call her twenty times on the phone, really annoyed if she didn't answer immediately. She and I argued over him, about how possessive he was, about how fast they were moving – but she was pregnant and she said she loved him." She shrugged. "There was nothing I could do. But then she began to have bruises and burn-marks, and marks on her legs as if she had been kicked. I argued with her over it, but it was useless – she wouldn't hear a word against him. After the twins were born he started bringing women to the house while Natalie was at home nursing the babies … he had no respect. I tackled him in the end. He tried to hit me then. He had no boundaries." She laughed, a brittle sound. "He was a complete animal. I nearly broke his arm. Oh, that gave him a fright alright! But nothing changed. I reported him to the Gardaí over and over, but nothing worked. Natalie refused to press charges, and just went in and out of hospital, sorting her wounds and caring for the girls. It was as if she had switched off. She was lost inside herself. I was attacked in the street by some of his men, but it was as if she didn't care. My sister was gone, trapped by him."

Anna reached across the small space between them and squeezed Kate's hand. Her story was heart-breaking. And a motive to murder, Anna thought, her heart sinking.

Kate wiped her face, aware now that there were tears on her cheeks. She hadn't realised she was crying again. "Things changed in the last few months. Gallagher was high all the time … he took drugs every day. One day Natalie threatened to leave him, and he snapped. He took the twins. She rang me, hysterical. I was almost used to those calls by then." She smiled sadly.

"I remember that from the file at work," Anna said softly.

"He threatened to drive off the quay with the girls in the

236

back of the car. Natalie was beside herself. While David was whisked off by his father for a psychiatric assessment, only to keep him out of jail of course, she and I had a chance to speak. Something had changed for her. She'd had enough. I had sensed a change in her over the previous weeks, but this was it – David had threatened the twins, and for her a line was drawn, and she wanted out."

"That's great!"

Kate stood up and began to pace the small living room.

"If only it were that simple."

She leant against the mantlepiece and folded her arms across her chest.

"Natalie had done a one-eighty. She wanted revenge for what Gallagher had put her through. And if I'm honest, I wanted it too. He had caused so much pain … he deserved to pay! I was so happy she was seeing sense. We should have left it at that."

"What did you do?" This sounded like a confession. Anna groaned internally. She knew now was the time to call Detective Taylor, but she was lost in the flow of her story.

"Natalie and I convinced ourselves we had a chance of a better life, away from the Gallaghers. We owed it to the twins to get them as far away from David's family as we could. Tom Gallagher, David's father, was so overbearing, and his wife was worse – we knew we had to leave the country. But we needed resources. So, we came up with a plan. We decided to rob him and disappear, to start a new life. We needed enough money to stay hidden. We waited for the right opportunity. It took a while but we were willing to wait."

She sighed and began to pick at a cut on her hand, pulling the skin absentmindedly.

"David was always storing things. Stolen goods, money, drugs – you name it, he had it tucked away in the attic of the house, or cupboards under the sink. He was reckless. He used to boast about it when he was high. He'd say things like 'I have fifty grand under the mattress right now – what have you got?' – a complete moron. He liked to pull out big wads of cash from various gear bags, as if it would be some kind of bait to keep Natalie with him, not that he ever thought she would really leave. He did all his business openly in the house, never caring that Natalie heard him, or the twins either! I mean, they are nearly four – the things they have seen and heard!" She shook her head. "Natalie said the house was always full of people David was doing business with. Two weeks ago, he stored diamonds and cash for a group he referred to as 'The Germans'. He just left it stashed in the attic. I mean that's hardly secure, but he said it was so simple no one would even think to look. About ten days ago he was particularly pleased with himself. He began waving cash in Natalie's face and said there was plenty more where that came from, that he had hit on some big money-making scheme with a Dutch buyer. He said he had plans to show his father how real men made real money, not the small-time crap his father dealt in. There were tens of thousands of euro, all bound up in bundles, and he said that was only the first part of the payment. He stashed it in a bag and left it lying around. So … we decided to take it. David was supposed to be abroad on business and we didn't expect him to be back for a few days. The day before the shooting we saw an opportunity and took as much cash as we could. We stashed it in my house, and we planned to leave that week …" Her voice trailed off. She saw the shock on Anna's face and stopped speaking, unsure what was running through Anna's mind. "You have to understand! Natalie hadn't worked in years. I didn't have enough money for us all to escape and leave the country – it seems drastic, but it was necessary, I swear!"

Anna shook her head, trying to comprehend what she was hearing. "So, you robbed money from David ... and then what? Did he catch you?"

Kate held onto the mantelpiece now as if she was holding onto a lifebuoy. She felt faint. Recounting the story was draining her of all her energy. She stumbled to the sofa a few feet away and was surprised that frantic sobs escaped from her. She didn't care that David Gallagher was dead, yet she couldn't stop the tears from falling. Sinking into the soft cushions, she put her head in her hands and shuddered as tears poured down her cheeks.

Anna gave her space to cry. She was an emotional wreck. No doubt fear and exhaustion had taken their toll on her, not to mention the trauma of the night Gallagher died. Anna didn't know how to offer comfort – this was a terrible situation and she was still trying to gather her thoughts. She stayed where she was and watched Kate as she sobbed uncontrollably on the sofa. She wanted to believe that the girl she had known wasn't a cold-blooded killer, hadn't intentionally shot David Gallagher. But she had robbed him. And she had plenty of reasons to want him dead.

Anna felt a chill in the room and moved toward the stove to add more logs.

Kate's sobs subsided. She sniffed and looked at Anna who was standing beside the stove.

Kate took a deep breath.

"We planned to fly to Paris on the Thursday. He wasn't due back until Sunday. Then on Wednesday he returned unexpectedly and he was frantic. Natalie was terrified. David said the Germans had made contact – they wanted the gear he was holding for them and to complete the sale for the Dutchman. Whatever that meant. David was stressed that they had come in person. He searched the house but couldn't find what he was looking for. He never would have suspected Natalie of robbing him – he thought she was too beaten down. He left, and Natalie rang me, terrified. I convinced her to pack a bag and get the next flight out of Cork. I was at work. I went straight home. I packed a bag and gathered the money I had in my house and was about to join Natalie at the airport when David showed up."

"*Christ!*"

"He had gone home again, and realised Natalie had cleared out. So, he came looking for her at my house. He saw my packed case and he put two and two together. He was in a complete rage – his eyes were literally bulging out of their sockets. He told me John was on his way over. He was real nasty, pushing me around – well, trying to – but I'm not Natalie! I pushed back!"

"The crime scene report said David Gallagher suffered an assault before he was shot."

"It wasn't an 'assault' – they didn't see my injuries! My neck is still hurting where he half-strangled me – I have bruising all over my body! It was a fight, but I've had worse." She shrugged. "Yeah, I gave as good as I got, and he wasn't used to it. He pulled a gun."

Anna sat down next to Kate who had begun to tremble.

"He had the gun pointed at me," she went on, her voice shaking. "He said we would wait for John. I could have knocked him out cold if I could have got closer, but he kept the gun pointed at me the whole time. The threat of John scared me though – he's even worse than David. He's a sadist. David used to tell us things he had done, in revenge, or sometimes just for fun. I was panicking. I was terrified of David and John together. In the end, I had no choice. I had to get the gun. I lunged at him, taking him by surprise, and for a while we both had the gun, wrestling for it between us. The next thing I know, David is lying dead on the ground and everything is quiet."

Her voice faded into silence and she sat still, her eyes glazed, watching the film-reel of that night that wouldn't stop replaying in her mind.

Eventually, she sighed, her eyes firmly fixed at a spot on the floor.

"After I shot him, I panicked. I knew he was dead. I figured John would come for me, or the Gardaí. And I thought that if I was taken into the Garda station it was only a matter of time before his contact there would turn me over to Tom Gallagher. Or I could get convicted of manslaughter. I couldn't go to jail – Gallagher has employees all over the place, some of his female employees are in prison and still loyal to him. And that niece ... I'd be dead within a week!" She was leaning forward as she spoke, her hands trembling. She clasped them between her knees as she looked up at Anna. "I heard someone banging on the front door and I just ran. I fled the house. Forgetting my passport. I just grabbed this bag, which had a lot of the money in it, and fled. I hopped on the first bus that passed me and found myself wandering the streets in town. After what must have been an hour I checked into a hotel and continued panicking. But, eventually, I pulled myself together. I realised I had to get some fake documents and get out of Cork."

Anna stared at Kate, unsure what to say, feeling torn between shock and pity. She still didn't know what to think. She shivered involuntarily, despite the heat from the stove. What a mess her old friend was in! She had been through so much in such a short space of time. And her self-defence story was muddied now. She had admitted shooting David and robbing him too. Anna cringed. The charge of theft would surely be added to whatever Elise Taylor decided was the appropriate charge for killing David Gallagher. What had at first seemed to Anna to be a clear-cut self-defence case was now seriously a murky pool of uncertainty. Kate, a kick-boxing champion, had killed a man, robbed him, and left the scene.

Yet Anna didn't feel the woman sitting huddled on her sofa was a devious killer. She looked utterly wretched as she sat there, shivering, her shoulders hunched over. When she spoke of that night, her anger was obvious, but she looked scared and haunted by the memories. All she had wanted to do was protect her sister and nieces and escape the man who abused them. Now all she wanted was to escape this city and join them. Anna couldn't help but feel pity for her. Her good intentions had spiralled out of all control and now she was in huge trouble.

Anna rubbed Kate's hand. "This can all be sorted out, I'm sure of it. You were in a terrible situation – anyone could see that! And, really, it was an accident!"

Kate nodded and kept her eyes on the floor. Tears still fell, although gently this time, and she wiped them away occasionally with the back of her hand.

"So David was selling something to a Dutch buyer, and the Germans were somehow involved, and had come to collect?" Anna said. "Do you have any idea what David was selling?"

Kate looked up into Anna's face and nodded. She retrieved the bag from the other end of the sofa and rooted around in it for a few seconds. Pulling out a small USB flash drive, she handed it to Anna. "This, I think. I've no idea what's on it. I haven't had access to a computer. But I presume it was part of the deal. David was beside himself when he couldn't find it."

Anna turned the memory key over in her hand, intrigued. So, whatever was on here was enough to bring the Meier gang over to Cork from Germany, enough to make David attack Kate. Was it the reason John Gallagher

242

was missing? Was this the big money scheme David Gallagher had bragged about?

"There's only one chance of finding out – a slim chance as I expect it will be passport-protected. Come into the kitchen – my laptop is on the table."

Kate followed Anna through the archway into the adjoining kitchen.

40

"I have no idea what this is," Kate said.

Anna chewed her bottom lip as she clicked the mouse, moving between the pages of the spreadsheet in front of them, hoping for clarity to strike. She had to agree with Kate. She had no idea what they were looking at.

The contents of the memory key had opened without a security password, much to their surprise and relief. But they were clueless as to what the key actually contained, other than the fact that the names and Eircodes of all the major hotels in Cork were listed on one page of the spreadsheet.

Kate had had a lot of time to think in the confines of the small hotel room. As well as making plans for her future, hopeful plans involving Natalie and her nieces, she had sought to drive out her memories of the night she shot David by trying to figure out what was on the memory key. She had lain on the hotel bed for many hours, turning it over and over in her mind. All she knew for sure was that the contents of this memory key were the money-making scheme David had boasted about. But why had he cut his father out?

That part of David's plan had intrigued her the most. From what she knew of the Gallaghers, they were a tight close-knit family. They were ruthless with anyone who came between them, or anyone who disrespected one of them. She had been on the periphery of the Gallaghers' world for years and had watched as Tom brought David further into the business every year. He had trusted him with the nightclubs and had given him more and more responsibility. So why was David cutting him out? Why was David showing his father such disrespect?

"What's the point of anyone making a list of the city hotels and their coordinates?" she wondered aloud as she perused the page. All the city's four and five-star hotels were listed.

"Let's look at page two," Anna suggested, clicking on to the second page of the spreadsheet.

This page contained a list of initials in Column A, clearly referring to the hotels listed on the previous page – RL referring to the River Lee Hotel, IM referring to the Imperial Hotel, HM for Hayfield Manor, and so on. There was a list of eight hotels on page one, and a column of eight initials on page two, in column A. In column B, beside the initials of the hotel names, were further initials and codes. Column C contained even more codes.

"RL is linked to the initials TM in column B, which is linked to 'a. pers.' in column C," Anna said. "IM is linked to the initials AM in column B, which links to 'a. pers.' in column C. HM is linked to the initials LV in column B, which links to 'a. pers.' in column C. What on earth does it all mean?"

There were twelve lines in total, each one linking a city hotel with more initials and rows of question marks after 'a.

pers.'. One hotel was repeated, the River Lee, with more initials linked to that hotel than the others. Anna read all the letters aloud, hoping that by hearing them she might be able to decipher them. But her thoughts wouldn't go there.

She shook her head as though to clear it. "I can't make any sense of it."

"What's 'a. pers.' about?"

Anna sat, deep in thought. "I don't know."

Anna clicked open the third page which was a programme of some sort, listing activities by time: 11:30 press call, 12:30 lunch, 16:00 informal drinks, 17:00 dinner. It seemed innocuous.

Then Anna felt a tremor of trepidation creep into her consciousness. A simple programme of events . . . but why should David Gallagher or any other criminal show so much interest in it? This did not bode well.

"Click on to page four," Kate said.

The fourth page was a map of the city, scanned and uploaded. It had been drawn on with red ink. The city-centre hotels were circled.

Anna clicked on a fifth page and immediately felt a heightened sense of unease. This page featured a drawing: it appeared to show pipes or tunnels, with lines drawn here and there, and hotel initials written on it at different points in the same red ink. On a sixth page was the same map, but the Rebel Event Centre was circled.

"I've heard the name of the new event centre mentioned recently, but I can't remember the context," Anna said.

Suddenly she stood up.

"I need to get this in to work," she said. "This needs to be deciphered as soon as possible."

"Now?"

"Yes."

"You're leaving?" Kate asked, panicked.

Anna pulled on her boots and began to tie up her laces. "I have to. Who knows what's going on here, but it must be important. There's a guy at work, Myles, who's really good with computers. I'm sure he can help, even though he's really busy with this political conference that's happening on Thursday …"

Anna stopped suddenly, looking at Kate. Her mouth had fallen open in shock and her hands shook slightly. She felt as though someone had poured a bucket of ice-cold water over her head. *Of course!* She abandoned tying her shoelaces and jumped back onto her chair, clicking the mouse between the screens again.

"What is it?" Kate asked quietly. She knew Anna had figured it out but she wasn't sure she wanted to know the answer to this riddle.

"Jesus Christ," Anna whispered. She turned the screen so Kate could better see what she was pointing to as she spoke. "Column B lists the heads of state that are coming to Cork for the conference. Column A tells us what hotel they are staying in. I bet 'a. pers.' refers to whether they have armed personnel staying with them at the hotel, or in their immediate vicinity. Oh my God, this information must be classified. David Gallagher was going to sell it!"

"But where would he have got it?"

"He was a gangster – he could have got it anywhere."

"Why would anyone want it?"

The question hung in the air, but the answer was obvious.

"Someone wants to harm one of the politicians or compromise the whole thing. Anything politically sensitive has heightened security – criminals like David Gallagher don't usually have a download of the details!"

Anna pulled a notebook and pen from her bag which had been hanging on the back of one of the kitchen chairs.

She wrote down the initials one by one, drawing lines to connect them.

"See?" she said, turning the page to Kate. "TM must refer to the British Prime Minister Theresa May; she's staying in the River Lee hotel with armed personnel I'm sure. I bet AM refers to Angela Merkel, the chancellor of Germany. The letters refer to initials of politicians attending the conference. Oh my God!"

Anna pulled the laptop towards her again, shut down the spreadsheet and began to search the internet. With a few well-chosen search words, she quickly found an article about the upcoming political conference. She clicked open the webpage of the *Irish Examiner* and both women silently read the news piece.

On Thursday November 29th, the Rebel Event Centre will host a political conference, featuring heads of state from many European nations. Our Taoiseach, who lobbied fiercely and successfully for Ireland to be chosen as the venue for this timely event, said there has never been a greater need for unity in politics. As Brexit discussions enter a critical phase, it is hoped British Prime Minster Theresa May will attend, but her spokesperson has yet to confirm. The Mayor of Cork is proud that the city will play host to such a variety of nations. "Cork may not be Ireland's capital city," he said, "but our newly opened state-of-the-art event centre and our famed hospitality rival any capital city in the world. We are ready and waiting to welcome the European political leaders to Cork. Unity and international cooperation will be at the forefront of discussions. This is truly an historic event, happening on our own shores, and a wonderful way to close 2018 for Cork."

Cork city hotels will open their opulent doors to our

European visitors from Wednesday to Friday, with the conference taking place on Thursday and through to Friday morning. The visiting dignitaries will of course take in some of the famous sights while in the city, including the now famous English Market, visited by Her Majesty Queen Elizabeth II in 2011.

Anna abandoned the remainder of the article. She had read enough. There was no doubt. David Gallagher had somehow got hold of classified security details about the upcoming conference and was planning to sell it. This must have been how he had planned to make 'real money'. The Meier brothers were the intermediary, and had come to Cork to collect, kickstarting a chain of events which led to David Gallagher being shot dead. What mattered now was that this information should be taken to the right people, immediately.

Anna checked the time – almost seven o'clock. She knew the office staff in the Lee Street station would be long gone home. She wondered if Myles was still in the briefing centre with Janet McCarthy. She stood up and reached for her mobile phone. She texted him quickly before returning to the task of lacing up her boots.

"I'm going in to work. Please come with me. I should have alerted my supervisor you were here a long time ago." She immediately saw the fear creep back into Kate's eyes.

"Please, Anna! I can't. What if Gallagher's men see me? I can't risk it. As far as Tom Gallagher is concerned, I robbed them and killed their son. If he finds me I'm dead!"

She was trembling again, and Anna didn't think she could force her to go with her. What was she supposed to do?

Anna thought quickly. She pulled on her coat and scarf. "OK. Stay here."

Kate nodded at her gratefully.

"You can shower and rest – there's a spare room upstairs

on the left. Use whatever you need – take some of my clothes. Have a shower or grab some sleep, OK? But I'll bring a detective back here after I've handed this memory key over at work. Elise Taylor will help you, I'm sure of it. If you get this cleared up with the Guards, you'll be able to get your passport back, and go join Natalie. You could put this all behind you."

Anna had no idea how long that might take. And she didn't know if the detective would calmly speak with Kate, or just arrest her on sight. But she was sure she would treat Kate fairly, happy to clear this case from her workload.

Anna pulled the memory key from the laptop and stuffed it into her jeans pocket. Her mobile phone beeped to indicate a return message from Myles – he was still at the briefing centre. So that was where she would go.

"Anna!" Kate said. "Thank you. For everything. You've saved my life!"

Anna looked at her and smiled as she grabbed her car keys and bag. "I'll see you later."

As she pulled the front door closed, Anna couldn't help but feel that it sounded like Kate was saying goodbye.

Kate stayed where she was at the kitchen table for a long time, feeling cold in the empty house. She missed Anna now that she was gone – she didn't think they'd ever see each other again. She looked at the notepad where Anna had pieced together the contents of the memory key. So, this was what David Gallagher had stored on it. This was his get-rich-quick scheme. He had boasted of it so many times, always alluding to his big payday without giving away any details. David was a conman and a monster, and she was glad he was dead. She just had never imagined this situation, and never thought she could kill a man. Not that David had given her any choice.

She stood up. She was freezing. Anna had offered her some clothes, and she badly needed them. A hot shower and fresh clothes would make her feel better, she reasoned.

There had been so many lies. But it was almost over.

Picking up the notepad and turning to a fresh page, she wrote Anna a short message before she headed upstairs.

I'm sorry x

41

Anna was surprised to see snow had fallen thick and heavy while she and Kate were speaking. But the roads were thankfully safe; the daily traffic had created a safe passage and was now abated, and as Anna drove into the city she was able to pick up speed. She was panicking about the contents of the memory key, which seemed to burn inside her pocket.

While stopped at a red traffic light, Anna dialled the mobile phone number Elise Taylor had given her. It rang and rang, eventually going to voicemail. Anna hesitated slightly – had she really left Kate behind in her house? A woman wanted for questioning in the suspicious death of a man was in her home right now. She should have called the detective a long time ago.

After the beep she left her a voicemail:

Detective Taylor, this is Anna Clarke from work. Kate Crowley contacted me and gave me a memory key that she obtained from David Gallagher. I'm on my way into the briefing centre now to give it to Chief Super

McCarthy. **I'll discuss further with her, but I thought you'd like to know. Kate assured me she will speak with you. I'll ring you again shortly.**

With a shaky sigh she pushed her phone into her pocket and concentrated on the road. She hoped she wasn't in serious trouble for the length of time she had taken to contact the detective.

The car park at work was uncharacteristically, but understandably at this time of night, almost empty. Anna parked in the first available space and walked briskly along the street to the nearby briefing centre. Snow was compacted now on the footpath. Christmas lights illuminated her path and she hurried, not feeling the cold.

Chief Superintendent Janet McCarthy and Myles Henderson were sitting together at a large conference table in the centre of the briefing room. They were both reading from a screen and looked up as Anna entered.

Myles smiled in greeting, but his smile quickly faded as he took in her expression.

"Anna. What is it?"

Anna moved further into the room and put the memory key on the table.

"What's this?" Janet McCarthy asked.

"Kate Crowley came to my house this evening. She's still there."

"The girl wanted in the Gallagher shooting? Why would she call to your home?"

"I know her, well, I used to – we went to school together. She gave me this." Anna pointed at the slim metal key. "She took it from David Gallagher. We looked at the contents on my laptop – I think David was going to sell the information on to someone, a person he referred to as a Dutchman. She said that on the night David died he was boasting about having found a way to make some 'real money'. I think this is sensitive information relating to the political conference."

Janet McCarthy sat back into her chair and exhaled loudly. She looked pointedly at Myles.

Myles picked up the memory key and inserted it into the computer on the table in front of him. Both he and Janet began to peruse the information.

Anna sat down, watching them silently. She had expected more … shock.

"So it has surfaced. And it was David Gallagher, of all people!"

Realisation dawned on Anna – Janet McCarthy knew about the existence of the memory key, and its contents too. She felt a strange sense of relief, a welcome break from the panic she had felt as soon as she had realised what information was contained on it. If the Chief Superintendent wasn't too shocked by the revelation that the security details for the political conference had been stolen, Anna could only surmise that what was unfolding tonight did not pose a threat.

Anna watched their faces as they studied the information.

"See the question marks here?" Janet said to Myles, pointing at the screen with her pen. "They don't have the detail of how many armed personnel, just that there *are* armed bodyguards accompanying the heads of state."

"See how the maps of the underground pipes and tunnels have been added in. Note the areas circled here in red." Myles was excited now, leaning forward.

Anna, sitting silently, was growing confused by their calm evaluation of the situation. She thought of Kate back at the house, wondering if she was OK.

Janet rubbed her hands over her face. "There's almost enough information here to pose a serious problem! Hotel names, who's staying where, even queries about whether the VIPs will have armed personnel. Christ – access tunnels and a city map. This is very extensive research. I find it hard to see how it ended up in the hands of David Gallagher!"

"He must have someone on the inside," Myles said.

Janet frowned at him. "There's no way any of my detectives would have had anything to do with this!"

"I'm sorry, I really am. But it's the only explanation. The only way that information got into Gallagher's hands is by a security breach from inside. It can only have come from someone on the force."

Watching their exchange, it struck Anna as odd that Myles would be addressing the Chief Super this way – wasn't he here to sort out technical issues for the conference?

Janet exhaled loudly. "It would appear that there's no other plausible explanation. The national security arrangements are only accessible to a few. Certainly, within Cork, there are many detectives who are part of the team to keep the conference safe, but this information is kept classified." She groaned. "This is a disaster!"

Myles and Anna looked at each other. She saw the alarm she felt mirrored in his brown eyes. Janet had grown pale; she looked horrified at the realisation that one of her own team was responsible for stealing the data and providing it to a criminal. It allowed for the possibility that more information had been compromised. Janet picked up a pen and flicked it from side to side on the tabletop as she thought about what to do next.

Anna remembered what Kate had said, that she could swear the Gallaghers had their own information source within the Cork Garda force. She shifted uncomfortably in her seat.

"Are you sure Gallagher wasn't going to use the information himself?" Myles asked, keen to explore all angles.

Anna nodded. "Kate says he spoke about a buyer."

The Chief Superintendent whistled. "Even for the Gallaghers this is an ambitious reach. Tom must have thought he'd hit the big time!"

"No – Kate told me Tom Gallagher didn't know anything about it. David wanted to keep him out of it."

Janet McCarthy looked unconvinced. "Why cut out his father?"

Silence descended. The only person who could answer that lay on a cold slab in the city morgue.

Janet squared her shoulders. She had decided her course of action and was ready to press on.

"Anna, great work on realising the importance of this information. Is Kate Crowley safe? The last thing we need is for the Gallaghers to get hold of her – it seems they are as keen to find her as we are."

Anna nodded. "She's safe – they won't find her at my house."

"Right, we'll send a squad car there now," Janet said, rising to her feet. "OK! I need to get what we've uncovered here to some people, and urgently. The underground maps are an add-on, and it gives us a lead about what angle an attack might come from. I'll email it through to some colleagues and it'd be prudent to make a copy of this." She turned to Myles. "Do we have any spare USB keys here?"

Anna stood up and offered to get one from the storage room located near the room entrance. As she crossed the conference room Myles and Janet were deep in conversation, Myles pointing at something on the computer screen.

It took Anna a few seconds to locate the storage-room door again. "Stealth storage" was the right term. Anna finally felt the lip of the wooden door with her fingers, almost flush against the wall. She pushed against it gently and it popped open. The tiny room had no light but the conference room was well lit, so taking a deep breath she stepped inside. The door almost shut behind her and she propped it open with one foot as she searched the shelves packed with stationary.

As Anna's fingers settled on the slim metal case of a spare memory key on the middle shelf, she heard a soft, unusual noise.

Thwump! Thwump!

With one foot still propping open the door, she turned her head to look back into the conference room and saw Janet slumped over the table. Anna's heart stilled and her blood ran cold. Myles was staring wide-eyed in the direction of the door. With his left hand he fumbled at the computer and, with his eyes never leaving the door, he pulled the memory key out of it quickly.

"*No!*" he cried, before Anna heard the sound again, *thwump*, and Myles jerked backwards, falling from his seat onto the floor. He lay on his side, completely still.

Anna's hand shot to her mouth and she managed to stifle a cry. She quickly stepped all the way inside the storage room and pulled the door shut, praying the movement hadn't been seen.

The darkness inside the space engulfed her, suffocating her, pressing down on her chest. She had enough space inside the storage room to kneel and she did so, trying to steady her breathing and quell her panic. She could taste vomit in her mouth and hear her heart pounding in her ears.

Noises in the room outside the thin door drew Anna back to the present moment. Her thoughts began to clear, reality forcing its way into her consciousness.

It was a stark reality.

Janet McCarthy had been shot twice, and judging by the soft noises she had heard, Anna guessed that the sound of the gun was muffled with a silencer. Myles was also injured, having been shot at least once. Both were unconscious or worse.

Anna fought her rising nausea as she remained on her knees. Her palms pressed onto her thighs were sweaty on her jeans. She felt terror, a much greater terror than last night in her living room. It was a palpable, physical urge to run – but to where? Who had shot Janet and Myles? And why? Had she been followed here, by the Gallaghers perhaps? She knew she could defend herself from a physical attack, but not from a gun. A bullet could not be blocked or outmanoeuvred. Her breath caught in a gasp in her throat, her heart pounding.

Anna thought suddenly of her mother. Of her soft eyes and bright smile. Helen Clarke's face was never very far from her consciousness. She remembered her mother's gentle voice and how, whenever she listened to her favourite orchestral music, she would close her eyes, lean her head back and become lost, a tranquil look on her face. She remembered her mother urging her to have what she called "fortitude". She would say: *"Always face your problems, Anna, always be brave."*

Gulping air into her lungs, her thoughts finally began to focus. She was under attack. Two of her colleagues were shot and needed medical attention. And the shooter was in the briefing room with her, outside the thin storage-room door.

Anna pulled her mobile phone from her pocket and with shaking fingers dialled 112.

"Emergency, which service do you require?"

Anna whispered urgently, "Guards and ambulance, two people have been shot. The shooter is still here, in the building. Please hurry!"

"What is your location?"

Anna whispered the address and hung up, switching

her mobile phone onto silent mode. She put her phone and the spare memory key into her pocket.

She gave her full attention now to the room outside the tiny space she was trapped in, pressing her ear against the thin door. Someone was moving around, shoving things aside roughly. Anna surmised the shooter was searching for something they couldn't find.

Suddenly there was silence. Anna held her breath and waited. Her heart almost stopped beating when she heard a soft voice call out.

"Come on out, Nancy Drew!"

There was manic laughter. A woman's voice.

"Come out, come out, wherever you are!"

The singsong voice stopped just outside the storage room.

Anna had no choice but to push open the thin wooden door and step forward.

She blinked in the bright light.

She was face to face with Elise Taylor, who raised her gun and pointed it firmly at Anna's chest.

"Where's the fucking memory key?"

42

Anna's mouth was dry, her heart racing. She stared at the detective in shock.

Finally finding her voice she whispered, "Detective Taylor? What are you doing?"

"Hello, Nancy Drew. I'm surprised you haven't figured this one out already! So, the Crowley bitch turned up, did she? Two old friends reunited – how sweet. Now tell me where she is and give me the memory key. Let's end this sorry mess!"

Elise spoke with icy hatred, her hands steady on the gun. Her composure terrified Anna. She looked to be completely in control, and therefore she had just shot Janet and Myles in cold blood.

Anna's thoughts raced. Why did Elise want the memory key? How did she even know about its existence?

She looked past Elise to where they both lay. Janet was still slumped over the oak conference table. There was so much blood pooled around her head that Anna was sure she was dead. Janet and Elise had been colleagues – how could Elise have shot her? Her body was completely obscuring the computer and the contents of the memory key; the computer screen was on its side and under Janet's torso. Myles was curled into a ball on the ground at the leg of the table. Anna had seen him pull out the memory key and wondered if he still held it wrapped in his fist. There was a bloodstain on the shoulder of his shirt that was growing and seeping onto his back. He was losing a lot of blood. He would need help soon if he was going to survive.

Anna stifled a sob and looked at the detective in disgust.

"I don't understand," she whispered. "Why have you done this?"

Elise laughed. "Because I want to get out of this stinking town!"

The laugh faded on Elise's lips. Colour flooded her face as she stamped one foot on the carpet and spittle flew into the air as she spoke.

"I can't take it anymore! The filth, the blood, the drugs … we wanted a new life. And *she* ruined it! She shot David, and she –" The words seemed to catch in Elise's throat and a sob escaped her. "She shot David and she'll pay for that. I'll hand her over to Gallagher and collect the reward. Kate Crowley can rot in hell as far as I'm concerned!"

Anna couldn't believe what she was hearing. She realised they had all been duped.

Elise Taylor was grieving for David Gallagher.

Right now, Anna didn't have time to figure out why or to process what that meant. She quickly weighed up her situation. She needed to stall Elise, to give the Gardaí time to get here. The only way would be to keep her talking. But first she needed to attend to Myles.

"Please!" Anna heard the desperation in her own voice. "Please let me help Myles. He's losing a lot of blood!"

Elise's face was now bright red with anger. Her lips

were a thin, frustrated line as she turned her head to Myles, raised the gun, and shot twice more. One shot hit the leg of the large oak conference table. The second hit Myles in the upper thigh. He jerked where he lay and remained silent.

Anna's hand flew to her mouth, stifling her shocked cry.

Elise's smirk turned to laughter as she took in Anna's expression. Her laugh was loud and frenzied, and Anna was aware her own mouth was hanging open in shock and horror. She had underestimated the woman. DS Taylor was totally unhinged – she was intent on killing them all.

As Elise wiped tears of laughter and continued to sneer, Anna's shock and horror turned to anger. She could feel it coursing through her veins. She fought to quell it – her Taekwon-Do training had taught her that anger had to be controlled; it served no purpose. She knew most people lost all rational thought when angry. Jason had long ago taught her that anger allowed for quick mistakes and loss of control. She began to silently recount the tenets of Taekwon-Do and felt her heart rate slow down and her breathing return to normal.

Anna viewed her situation now with crystal clarity. She didn't care why Elise was doing all this. Anna only cared that Myles was bleeding to death … if not already dead … and that if Janet had any chance of survival, time was critical. She was going to end this quickly.

"Like I said, and I hate to repeat myself, Anna – where is the memory key?"

Elise now had the gun pointed at Anna's chest again, two hands gripping it tightly.

Anna wondered how many bullets she had left now that she had discharged five. It didn't matter – one would be all it took. She met the detective's eyes coolly.

"It's on the desk at the back of the room, near Myles' computer."

Elise jerked the gun in that direction, directing her to get it. Anna moved forward, her legs shaky, stepping past Janet and Myles at the conference table, keeping her eyes focused in front of her. Elise was at her heels, the gun pressing into her back. She could feel the hard metal jutting into her flesh.

Stopping at Myles' desk Anna made a show of searching the table, feeling around it with her hands, moving things here and there. The table was covered in printed documents, as well as two empty disposable coffee mugs and discarded paper bags bearing the Victus coffee shop logo. Anna fought a lump in her throat and blinked away tears that threatened to blind her. He was bleeding to death.

"Hurry up!" Elise barked, moving to stand in front of Anna, her eyes on the table and its contents.

Swiftly Anna pulled the spare memory key from her jeans pocket and tossed it at Elise.

As it soared towards her Elise momentarily lowered the gun, focused only on catching the small piece of metal. Anna snatched up the keyboard from the table with both hands and swung it wide and hard, striking Elise in the face.

Blood and spit flew through the air as Elise's head whipped to the left. She staggered backward in shock and pain, and Anna seized her moment. She kicked the detective with all her force into the midriff, two jabbing kicks, and as Elise doubled over, Anna kicked at her wrist. The gun flew from Elise's hand and skidded to a stop halfway across the carpeted floor.

Myles moaned from his position on the ground. The sound sent a jolt of happiness through Anna – he was alive!

Later – when the dust had settled – Anna would look back on this moment with huge regret. Without thinking, and forgetting everything her father and Jason had ever told her, she let her guard down. She turned and stepped towards Myles, her arms reaching for him.

263

Elise now stood upright again and took full advantage of the split-second distraction Myles had offered. With a scream of rage, she punched Anna in the face. The force of it was like a sledgehammer – Anna staggered and fell, striking her head hard on the edge of the conference table. She lay on the floor as stars danced in her field of vision, and tasted blood. The pain in her head was an intense pounding that brought bile into her throat. As she struggled to sit up, she felt herself pushed roughly back down, and became aware of a weight on her chest. Elise was sitting astride her, and she wrapped her hands around her throat.

Anna opened her eyes and, as her vision regained focus, she was seized by terror. Elise truly looked insane with rage. The older woman was heavier than Anna and had the upper hand. She squeezed Anna's throat hard, blood pouring from her own mouth.

"Ruining everything!" Elise was breathing heavily as she pressed hard onto Anna's throat, pushing down, determined to kill her.

Anna gasped and clawed at Elise's hands with her fingers. It was useless. Elise was so furious, extending all her energy into punishing Anna. Anna's head was pounding, and black spots appeared in her vision again. Time stood still, where the only thing Anna could do was struggle and gasp for breath. She was fighting to stay conscious. Her legs kicked and flailed, but everything was out of focus, all her efforts futile. She gasped, drawing precious air into her lungs, but it felt impossible.

Anna's father's voice rang loud in her ears. It felt like a physical push, and with it came the memory of their games in the small back garden, the ninja games he so loved to play. A film-reel of memories rolled through her mind. As Elise continued to squeeze and press on her throat, Anna felt that *this* was a game she had played before ... memories tugged her back.

Alex sat on Anna's stomach, his hands lightly around her throat, her own hands pushing at his shoulders but not strong enough to push him off. Her father smiling as he knelt beside them on the grass. "Good, Anna. Tuck your chin in, tuck your chin in! Now, put your hands over his, cross them over, your left hand on his left wrist, right on right ... that's it. Now jab down into the inner parts of his arms with your elbows – that's it, hard as you like – Alex can take it, can't you, son!" And then Alex's laughter, as his younger sister jammed her pointy elbows into the soft flesh of his arms ...

Anna opened her eyes, ready to replay the game. Only this time, there was no laughter.

She tucked her chin in and gripped Elise's wrists – left hand on left wrist, right on right – and jammed her elbows into the soft flesh of Elise's inner arms. Elise's eyes widened in shock; she groaned in pain and, for a split second, lost her momentum, the force of her weight no longer crushing Anna. The tight grip of her hands slackened on Anna's throat. She pulled the woman towards her and slammed her head upward into Elise's, connecting her own forehead with the detective's nose.

The crunching sound the bones made as they broke was sickening.

Anna pushed Elise off her and rolled to the side. She stood up and instantly regretted it. The conference room spun before her eyes and she heaved onto the floor, vomit and blood splashing onto her jeans and shoes, pooling at her feet. Anna became aware of Elise, crawling around the carpeted floor, feeling with her hands, left and right, moaning in agony. She was breathing heavily and in a lot of pain, and blood was pouring from her nose and mouth.

Anna, on her hands and knees on the floor, breathed

deeply, her nausea easing. Her throat ached. She wiped vomit from her chin and straightened up again.

Elise was standing again and once more had the gun in her hands, pointed at Anna, a smirk contorting her bloodied face.

Then Myles rushed at Elise from behind with such force the gun flew from her hand and through the air. Striking her head on the conference table, Elise crumpled into a heap on the ground.

Myles managed to pull himself up again – now he staggered and gripped the edge of the conference table.

"Myles!" Anna rasped as she moved toward him, struggling to stay on her feet. "Nice of you to help out."

43

William Ryan was having dinner with Gina in a very posh restaurant when the call came in. His eyes widened as he listened – a shooting in an office block near the Marina. In what he knew was the political conference briefing centre. He was within walking distance.

"Sorry, Gina!" he said, abandoning his fillet steak and pulling on his overcoat.

As he dashed from the restaurant, he heard Gina's annoyance as she called out *"I'll just pay again this time, shall I?"*

William winced – work had caused him to run out on too many dates lately. He doubted he could redeem himself this time.

He was at the building within minutes. The building's security desk was unattended, the lobby deserted. He raced across the tiles to the bank of lifts. As the lift ascended he could hear the wail of sirens and ambulances on the way. He was aware hordes of his colleagues would be en route – it wasn't every day a shooting was reported in Cork city. He knew that the Garda Emergency Response Unit would be on the way, and he knew he should hold back and let them go in first. He was first on the scene but, eager as he was to get inside the room, he decided it was best to wait.

Before he had time to reconsider, members of the Armed Support and Emergency Response Unit had arrived. He flashed his ID and was told to stay outside. In certain situations, William was good at doing what he was told. He stood back as they entered the room, weapons drawn, shouting for all inside to drop to their knees and put their hands in the air. He paced, his hands in his pockets, and waited. His phone vibrated in his pocket; Gina was calling, but William cut off her call and sent it to voicemail.

Very quickly, it seemed to him, he was given the go-ahead to step inside. The situation was under control. Walking into the conference room he was met by something resembling a scene from a Tarantino movie. A woman lay slumped over the large table in a pool of blood. She was clearly dead. A man sat on the floor, injured and bleeding heavily. A young woman knelt beside him. She had attempted to wrap makeshift tourniquets around his shoulder and thigh. She looked as though she'd been through two rounds with an MMA fighter. Her face was a mess. Both eye sockets were bruising, her lip was split and there were deep red marks on her neck where she had clearly been half-strangled. Somewhere deep in William's mind he registered all three faces – he knew these people surely? Shock was not allowing him to process the simple act of recognition.

It was the unconscious woman on the floor that caused William to step back and grip the edge of the table behind him in shock. Elise Taylor, his colleague, lay apparently lifeless in a crumpled heap. Her nose was obviously broken, and her lips were swollen. Her shirt was spattered with blood.

What the hell was going on?

William looked around him and the rest of the faces in the room slowly shifted into focus. It was the young woman from clerical staff, Anna Clarke, who was kneeling on the floor. The woman who had pieced together the clues to nail Dean Harris. Wasn't she at home resting from the events of the night before?

The man beside her winced in pain as he tried to move, his dark unruly hair even more unkempt than usual – Myles, wasn't it? The detective from Dublin, here to help with security for the political conference. It looked like he had been shot. Twice. William physically recoiled as he realised the woman slumped over the conference table was his Chief Super – Janet McCarthy – blood was pooling around her head and neck. She was surely dead.

"Detective Sergeant Ryan, isn't it?" Myles spoke from his position on the floor. The strength of his voice surprised William. "Myles Henderson, Special Detective Unit. On the table to your left you will find a weapon which was used by DS Elise Taylor to kill the Chief Superintendent," he gestured with his hand, "and shoot me. You'll find gunshot residue on Taylor's right hand and the bullets will match those removed from Janet and myself. Anna here was also attacked by DS Taylor. I suggest you take Taylor into custody. And we'll need that ambulance to hurry up!" He groaned and rolled back his head.

William was mute with shock. Elise was the shooter? He found that very hard to fathom. She was a respected member of the force. As far as he was concerned, everyone in this room, aside from his Chief Superintendent obviously, was a suspect. He attempted to swallow but his throat was bone-dry. He became aware of uniformed officers entering the room, standing behind him, taking in the scene. The ambulance had arrived.

He stood back while Myles was attended to by the ambulance personnel. Elise remained unconscious, and more medical staff moved towards her.

Anna became aware she was being gently pushed back on a stretcher. She refused and insisted she could walk. Her eyes followed Myles as he was stretchered from the room. She dared not look at Janet. The room was suddenly a hive of activity. Detective Sergeant Ryan was ordering no-one to touch anything and was now talking on his mobile phone. She could make out snippets of his conversation, heard the name Doherty, and a request for a forensics team. A Garda helped to keep her on her feet after she swayed a little. She wondered if she'd be able to walk out of here without vomiting again.

William stepped towards Anna as she stood unsteadily in the middle of the room. He noticed blood drying in her hair.

"Anna?"

She looked up at William quizzically, as if seeing him for the first time.

"I thought I told you to stay out of trouble?" he said.

44

Samantha cradled the mug of coffee in her hands for a moment and watched Alex and Chloe as they played on the floor. It was their daughter's bedtime. Alex was finished work for the day. He had read the newspaper articles about Dean Harris's crimes and arrest last night again and again. He now needed to spend time with his daughter, to immerse himself in her innocent play and laughter.

Alex lay on the soft carpet, propped up on one elbow, while Chloe lounged beside him. She was engrossed in a jigsaw puzzle. She carefully selected each small cardboard piece and looked at it closely, discarding some and choosing to work with others. Her tiny face was creased in concentration. Alex watched her with a smile playing on the edges of his mouth. Though he felt much more relaxed than earlier in the day, he was still troubled.

As she watched her little family, Samantha wondered if Alex ever really stopped worrying about other people. Especially his sister.

He looked up and smiled when he noticed her in the

doorway. She held out the coffee mug and he stood up, moving towards her. Chloe seemed not to notice.

He sipped the hot coffee and rubbed Samantha's arm. "You OK?"

"I was going to ask you the same question."

Alex's brown eyes met his wife's. He was tired. There were dark shadows under his eyes, and he looked peaky, the shade of pale he sometimes was when he hadn't slept enough.

Alex put his hand on her elbow and motioned to the kitchen. They sat at the table and he took Samantha's hands in his own, resting them in the centre between them.

"She could have been raped, Sam. That keeps playing on my mind!"

"Thank God she wasn't!"

"Yes, absolutely. Luckily she knows how to handle herself – my father taught her that."

Alex put his head in his hands, unable to continue. He had been over and over the articles about the series of sexual assaults today, and it had struck him how close Anna had come to being a victim of such an attack. It was doing him no good to keep reading about it, but he had been unable to stop himself.

Samantha rubbed his arm, seeming to sense his thoughts.

"Not everyone is like Dean Harris. You're not. There are always more good people than there are bad, Alex. Anna was just unlucky. Or lucky, really, depending on how you look at it."

He nodded. He knew she was right. He smiled. "You know, small as she is, I'd hate to cross my sister!"

"Do you know if she met with the private investigator yesterday?"

He shook his head – he had forgotten to ask Anna about it earlier. The events of Sunday evening had completely overshadowed her appointment with the man she hoped would shed some light on their parents' disappearance.

"Maybe you should tell her the things you told me, you know, about your childhood. About how your parents moved around a lot in England, about how your dad had so many different jobs."

"I don't see how that makes a difference now."

"Anna is searching for answers. And it seems that the two of you had very different childhoods."

Alex stood up as he heard his mobile phone ring, moving to retrieve it from where it was charging on the countertop.

"Maybe," he conceded.

He unplugged the charger as he brought the mobile phone to his ear.

"Alex Clarke."

Samantha knew immediately the call wasn't good news. Alex gripped the countertop beside him as he grew paler, his mouth hanging open. After a few seconds he seemed to rouse himself – he clicked off the call and sprang into action.

As he grabbed his keys and ran out the front door, his parting words shouted over his shoulder sent shivers down Samantha's spine.

"Anna's been attacked, she's at the hospital!"

45

After having a set of staples put in the back of her head and two stitches in her lip, and a thorough inspection of the inside of her throat, Anna was told to lie back on her hospital bed and apply the ice pack she had been given to her eyes and forehead. Concussion had been ruled out but everything hurt. Even her wrists, which had had a set of handcuffs placed on them for a while. William Ryan had been apologetic, explaining it was procedure. Anna understood. A uniformed Garda sat outside her door. Until she was cleared as the shooter, she was under suspicion. She had given William the memory key and told him everything she knew about its contents. She tried to rest, as the doctor had advised.

The nurse had given her some tablets, but she found it was too painful to swallow them. She had eventually been hooked up to a drip for pain relief. She'd had both hands swabbed for gunshot residue and the inside of her mouth swabbed as well. So far, it had been an eventful Monday night.

She lay back onto the pillow and closed her eyes, letting

her arms fall to her sides, the ice pack balancing on her forehead. She hoped sleep would come – she felt drained – but images of Myles and Janet plagued her. She knew Janet was dead. The nurse had confirmed it for her earlier. She had been shot in the head and bled out quickly. Anna had known, in her heart, that there was no hope for the Chief Super – there had been so much blood – but she still felt shock at hearing the nurse confirm her fears. Myles was in surgery, his two gunshot wounds needing urgent attention to save his life and give him any hope of walking again. Anna was struggling to accept this reality too. In fact, the whole thing was unbelievable. Somehow, Myles had mustered the strength to stand up and defend her from Elise Taylor. He had saved her life – but it had added considerably to his pain. Anna hoped his bravery had not further damaged his thigh.

How could DS Taylor have fooled them all so well?

How could she have done this to them, to Janet, her colleague of many years? Janet McCarthy had never been a dictator-type boss – as a Chief Superintendent she was fair and reasonable. Anna knew DS Taylor had been unhappy with resources on this latest case – but she also knew that that had been out of Janet McCarthy's control.

Had all this happened because of David Gallagher?

Anna lay in the hospital bed and wondered if there were signs she had missed, obvious markers she should have picked up. She was a statistician, not a psychologist. But as a human being, as a person capable of a reasonable amount of intuition, perhaps there was something about Elise Taylor's demeanour that should have raised an alarm.

Anna hadn't known the detective for very long, just three years, and their dealings had always been in a professional setting. She had often appeared moody to Anna and had been aloof with the clerical staff. She had a no-nonsense demeanour and was tough to deal with. Anna had thought nothing of it. She had assumed it was her job, and the nature of the cases she dealt with, that led her to be that way. And compared to some of the detectives Anna worked with – in particular Frank Doherty – Elise Taylor had seemed friendly. On this latest case she had seemed genuinely concerned about finding Kate – which was true. Just not to protect her, as Anna had assumed.

Thinking of Kate, Anna felt worry knot in the pit of her stomach again. She would be oblivious to all that had happened after Anna had left the house. She wondered if she was still in her house in Kinsale. At least there she was safe. She was central to a terrible crime involving people that were bad at their core – including the detective who had lied and had intended to turn her over to Tom Gallagher. Anna dreaded to think what would have happened to Kate if Elise Taylor had found her. Which would be worse? To be discovered by the detective or the criminal? Anna shivered – it didn't bear thinking about.

She longed to rest but sleep refused to come. She remembered how she had defended herself against Elise, how she had used her father's self-defence games. Her memories, and her love of Taekwon-Do, had saved her life. She realised she would not be able to teach her little Taekwon-Do Tykes this week, and that she would have to call Jason and explain what had happened.

Tears came then. For Janet McCarthy, and Myles. For Kate. For Michael and Helen, wherever they were. Anna let her tears fall.

46

In the dimly lit hospital corridor, William Ryan tapped the shoulder of the young Garda slumped on the plastic chair outside Anna's room.

"You can head off."

"She in the clear then?"

The Garda yawned and stretched, before strolling down the corridor.

William had the handle on the door to the private hospital room pressed when Alex Clarke grabbed his arm.

"Excuse me!" His face was pale – he looked wretched. "I'm Alex Clarke, Anna's brother. We met last night. What the hell is going on?"

William recognised Alex from the previous night outside Anna's house and at the station. He smiled at the man and put a comforting hand on his shoulder. "Hello again. Aside from finding herself in the wrong place at the wrong time – again – your sister is OK. She has only minor injuries. She's very skilled in self-defence, I believe. Once again it saved her life. I'm about to interview her now if she's up to it."

"Is she under arrest?"

"No. But I need to take her statement and collect her clothes for a forensics examination."

William had received the results of the gunshot residue tests back, rushed through as a favour by a colleague that had agreed to go into the lab, despite the late hour. Anna Clarke was not the shooter – in fact, William's own colleague was. Although the evidence had pointed that way, and Myles Henderson had given his account of the situation, William still found it hard to believe. He rubbed his face with both hands and exhaled loudly.

Alex felt sorry for the man – he looked like he'd had a terrible shock this evening.

"I still can't get my head around this." Alex shook his head, his voice cracking. "First the attack at home last night, now this! Poor Anna. It's like she keeps stumbling into trouble!"

William patted his arm again – he didn't know what else to do. He had so much to process and so much to do. He remembered the expression on Detective Superintendent Doherty's face as he had told him one of the force's senior detectives had murdered their Chief Superintendent and attempted to kill another detective. Doherty, instructed to take position as Chief Superintendent until further notice, had been unable to do more than shake his head in mute disbelief.

"Will you let me go in with you?" Alex motioned to Anna's hospital bedroom. "Please!"

William nodded.

Anna heard movement and removed the ice pack. Raising her head caused her nerve endings to scream in pain, so she abandoned the idea. She could see her bedside visitors from this angle anyway from the corner of her eye.

DS William Ryan and Alex.

Both men eyed her warily from the doorway.

278

"I'm fine." The croak of her voice surprised her.

Alex rushed to her side and took her hand. He sat on the nearby chair.

"Just about!" he said quietly. He reached out and touched the side of her neck, where the bruises were forming. "Anna, what happened in there? Why were you there in the first place? What's going on?"

Anna lay quietly – she literally didn't know where to start.

William Ryan sensed she was struggling to know how to begin.

"Anna," he said softly, "we need to get justice for Janet. And for Myles Henderson. If you're up to it, I need to know everything that happened this evening. Just start at the point where you brought the memory key to the briefing centre."

He smiled warmly at her, his notebook open and pen poised.

Anna pushed with her arms and sat up. She groaned in pain. Alex rearranged the pillows under her head so she was more comfortable. She pulled a cup of water from the bedside table towards her and sipped from the straw. She wanted every possible thing that could convict Elise Taylor recorded while it was fresh in her mind.

William Ryan shifted his weight and looked at her expectantly.

Sipping her water again to lubricate her aching throat, Anna took a deep breath and began her story.

Alex's hands shook. He could scarcely believe what Anna had got mixed up in. Sure, he understood the emotion behind wanting to help an old friend – Alex remembered Kate and Natalie too – but Kate had put Anna in danger.

As Alex looked at his sister, lying bloodied and bruised

279

in the hospital bed, he felt a rush of pride. She had just uncovered a potential terror attack or assassination attempt at the political conference. She had saved herself from a madwoman, and probably saved Myles' life as well.

As Anna had been speaking the detective in front of her had grown increasingly flushed with anger.

"I cannot believe one of our own did this. To kill another officer … Doherty is dealing with the memory key, so rest assured that's being taken care of."

"I think Janet already knew the information had been stolen. She didn't seem surprised by that fact, just that it was David Gallagher who had it."

"Seriously?" William looked sceptical.

Anna nodded. "Definitely. She wasn't at all shocked that the memory key existed."

William didn't say another word. Adrenaline pumped through his veins. Eager to uncover Elise Taylor's twisted motive, he looked forward to starting his investigation.

Hours later, as soon as the nurse had removed the drip in her arm and had left the room, Anna swung her legs out of bed slowly. She wanted to get out of here. Now that she had finished telling Alex and the detective all that had happened, she really wanted to get back to Kate. The woman was alone and probably fearful. Anna had been gone a long time. Her body felt stiff and sore, but when she stood up she was relieved her legs held steady.

"*Woah, woah!* Where do you think you're going?" Alex demanded. He had been dozing on the visitor's chair and was wide awake now, and not happy.

"Home," Anna muttered. Her voice was barely audible, yet she managed a tone that invited no discussion.

Alex ignored it. "That's up to your doctor!"

"Alex, I need to check on Kate! Detective Ryan has been

gone ages and I don't know if anyone went to the house! Please!"

Alex sighed.

William Ryan stepped back into the room and raised his eyebrows.

"Going somewhere?"

Anna sighed in exasperation. "Look, Kate is alone in my house. Shouldn't you be questioning her, detective? And the notes I made from the spreadsheet are on my kitchen table. They can help you piece together things on the memory key, if that's even necessary."

William Ryan had to admit he needed those notes, to collect all the evidence of this case if nothing else.

"I can drive you home. I'll get a uniform to follow in your car. You're going to need some clothes!"

Alex shrugged off his jacket and passed it to Anna. "I'm coming with you!" He wanted to accompany Anna everywhere she went for a while. Maybe he could keep her out of trouble. She smiled gratefully at her brother.

The doctor who had examined Anna was still on duty and needed a bit of convincing that she could go home. Only when he was satisfied that her brother would keep a close eye on her did he consent.

The nurse that had tended to Anna earlier managed to find her a T-shirt, a tracksuit pants and some slippers. With her bruised face and pieced-together outfit, Anna knew she looked a mess. She couldn't have cared less.

The three of them rode the forty-minute journey to Anna's house in William's car. Alex planned to collect his later. Anna closed her eyes and leant back into the cushioned seat. She felt nauseous again as the car sped through the city streets and on into the suburbs. Despite the cold she rolled down the rear window.

When they reached the Wild Atlantic Way route, and the sea air filled her lungs, she felt herself relax. She was almost home.

In the dark, it was easy to see that there were no lights on in the house when the car pulled up outside. Anna had a sinking feeling of dread settle in the pit of her stomach. She hoped Kate was sleeping upstairs, like she had told her she was welcome to do.

As she turned the key in the lock she contemplated calling out to her, but her throat felt too raw. Instead she moved from room to room, both upstairs and down, pushing her shaking legs forward. The house was empty. There was no sign of Kate, nor of her red bag.

William Ryan was in the kitchen, standing at the table, staring at something resting there. Anna assumed he had found her notebook and was reading her earlier attempts to make sense of the initials. Instead he was staring at the screen of her laptop. He looked up at Alex and Anna as they entered the kitchen, his expression almost apologetic. He turned the screen around. The laptop was almost out of battery, having been switched on since early evening.

"Your friend – Kate," William said gravely. "She's not as innocent as you think."

Anna leant forward and looked at the screen. It was the internet search history, and it was blank.

It had been wiped. Kate had searched for something online and then deleted any trace of it.

Beside the laptop was Kate's short note of apology.

She was gone.

47

Alex stayed in his childhood home that night. Anna hadn't wanted him to, had said there was no need, but he would not be swayed. Before midnight, when Anna had called the hospital, Myles had been still in surgery, and she had begun to pace the living room, consumed with worry. Her doctor had prescribed her a sleeping tablet and Alex had convinced her to take it, managing to swallow despite the pain. Sleep was a welcome relief from her thoughts. Before she fell asleep, she put her headphones in, and selected Bach's Cello Suite No. 1 in G Major. She was breathing deeply, lost in slumber, within minutes.

Alex stood in the door frame and watched her. He felt tired and very old. For ten years he had taken his responsibility for Anna very seriously and realised now that that was still the case. She was twenty-six years old, a graduate, with a career in front of her. But she was still his headstrong kid sister. Only now, as he watched her sleep, as his eyes roamed over the bandage on her head and the stitches in her lip, her bruising and swollen eyes, the marks on her neck, he couldn't help but feel an increasing amount of respect for her. He had been filled in on everything that had happened over the last few days.

He suspected that there was something akin to rage brewing inside his sister, that likely stemmed from the disappearance of their parents. Certainly, a dogged determination to get to the bottom of things. Alex wasn't sure. Whatever it was, she channelled it for the greater good. She had gone to extreme lengths to protect Kate Crowley and had placed herself in great danger. She had done the same to defend herself against Dean Harris. How many women were safe in their homes because of her actions? And the political conference – Cork could have gone down in history as the site of a significant terror attack or assassination but for her quick thinking and bravery. Alex knew their parents would be very proud of her. And so was he.

Alex's insomnia was back in full force and he wasn't surprised. How could anyone sleep after what he had seen and heard today? He checked in with Samantha, making sure she and Chloe were OK, letting her know he was staying in Anna's house tonight. He didn't tell his wife all the details of what had happened to Anna. He didn't know quite where to start.

Downstairs, he found a beer in the fridge and sat down at the kitchen table. She had plugged her laptop in to charge. As he sipped the cold beer he thought again of Anna's story. His leg bounced under the table with adrenaline, with fury.

He reached for the notebook on the table – William Ryan had torn out the pages Anna had written on earlier – and began to make notes. He listed the main players in this saga – Elise Taylor, David Gallagher, Kate Crowley, Tom

Gallagher … Alex had read about the two dead bodies found in a car and the burnt-out vehicle abandoned on Monastery Road, and he wondered if that had anything to do with this. Alex drew lines between the names, linking them together like a spider's web. In the middle of the names he wrote Political Conference. Alex drained the beer and fetched another as the enormity of today's events sank in – the city of Cork had just played host to a tale of epic intrigue, and his own kid sister had been right in the middle of it.

Detective Sergeant William Ryan decided the time was right to end things with Gina. There were now fourteen missed calls on his mobile, and a voicemail he didn't have the energy to listen to. He just didn't have the time for a relationship. His mind was too preoccupied with details, all of which he needed to piece together into a coherent report to present to his new boss, and fast. Gina had become just a distraction. He felt slightly unbalanced, as though he was walking through water. He needed the waves to part so he could get a clear picture of what exactly had transpired this evening, and over the past few days.

When William left Anna's house, he headed straight back to the building by the Marina. The conference room on the third floor was thronged with members of the Garda Technical Bureau conducting their forensic examination. They moved slowly and methodically through the room in their white suits. He put on shoe-covers at the door before he stepped inside. He didn't need to be here – he would receive their report as soon as it was ready, probably first thing in the morning. But he had his methods, and he knew he wouldn't be able to sleep until he had exhausted this demon.

He stood in the middle of the room and studied every inch of it, his eyes taking in every possible detail. The oak table was now empty save for a large bloodstain. The floor

Myles had lain on was also stained where his blood had pooled. Ryan observed the computer at Myles' workstation, its keyboard still on the ground where it had fallen after Anna had smashed it into Elise's face.

William struggled to see the entrance to the storage room in the wall opposite, but his eyes eventually located the slight outdent of the wooden door. He closed his eyes and inhaled, breathing the scene deep into his lungs. Anna's voice played in his head as though he had recorded her testimony and was playing it back.

William pictured Anna hiding in the storage room, Elise stepping inside the room and firing three shots, her victims falling. He turned one-eighty degrees, his eyes still closed, and faced Myles' desk where Anna and Elise had fought. He turned again to his right, to the end of the conference table, where Anna had fallen and Elise had tried to strangle her. He cut an unusual figure, standing in the middle of the room with his eyes closed and his arms by his sides, turning this way and that. None of the forensics team had witnessed the detective's strange method of absorbing a scene before; but they were professional, and it was late, and so they continued their work around him.

When William opened his eyes, it was with renewed clarity. He understood how the situation had unfolded. He strode purposefully from the room and pulled off his shoe-covers. There was much to do.

48

Tuesday

Anna woke late, the sleeping-tablets having worked as the doctor promised. When she first opened her eyes the events of the day before came to her as though it had been a dream. And Sunday night, the attacker in her home – had this all really happened? She felt sluggish. The pain in her head returned as soon as she sat up, and nausea crept quickly up her throat, but she persevered. She was anxious to telephone the hospital and get an update on Myles' condition.

Alex was downstairs and had turned her kitchen into a workstation. He insisted she sit on the sofa and he served her a breakfast of toast there – there was no room at the table – Alex had littered it with pages that were covered in his scribbled notes and figures. He was relieved to see her awake and looking relatively normal – albeit bruised.

Anna was somewhat annoyed that her brother appeared to have moved in. But she decided to park her irritation and resign herself to the fact that he was overprotective. She smiled at him and accepted his gentle hug.

As Anna attempted to eat the toast, Alex explained he

had been in touch with the hospital and with William Ryan.

"I had to pretend to be Myles' brother before they would tell me anything. Basically, Myles is going to be fine. The surgeons were able to repair the damage from the bullets. He's had blood transfusions and will be in hospital for a while yet. There's tendon and muscle damage, and he'll need physio. He's in intensive care and not allowed visitors."

Anna sagged against the sofa cushions in relief. She was surprised by the tears that clouded her vision. Blinking them away, she sipped the water Alex had given her – her throat was in agony.

"Detective Ryan said he'll be difficult to contact for a few days but to sit tight. He's following up with Myles to get his side of things once he can speak to him, and he's putting together a team to gather as much evidence as he can on Elise Taylor. Plus, there's major panic about the political conference. Ryan said that Chief Superintendent Doherty had been summoned to Dublin and we can expect to see a lot more security personnel on the streets this week and into Thursday!"

"So the conference is still going ahead?" Anna was surprised it wasn't going to be cancelled.

God, it hurt to speak!

Alex nodded. "Apparently so. There's been huge money ploughed into Cork for it, and the mayor nearly had a coronary when the idea of it being moved to another location was mentioned. I assume the security plans you found on the memory key will be changed."

I bet they've been changed all along, Anna thought, remembering Janet and Myles' lack of concern that the information had been stolen. They had seemed to her to be more curious about the fact that the information was in the hands of a Gallagher. It bothered her that Myles had seemed to know as much as the Chief Superintendent.

288

"Is there any news on Kate?"

Alex shook his head.

Anna nodded, feeling tired again. She stretched out on the sofa. Now that she knew Myles was out of the woods, she felt able to relax somewhat. Alex had lit the stove and Anna felt her eyelids closing. Sleep came quickly.

When Anna awoke again it was dark outside. She heard hushed voices coming from the kitchen and sat up, wincing at the pain in her head that just wouldn't quit.

Alex, Samantha and Chloe were sitting at her kitchen table, tucking into bowls of soup, dunking chunks of crusty white bread into them, chatting. Anna felt emotion surge within her as the sight of them brought back memories of her own parents, sitting with her and Alex after an outing somewhere, the four of them at the table with steaming bowls and torn chunks of bread. She moved gingerly into the kitchen and sat down on the remaining seat. The smell of tomato soup assailed her and compounded the crushing feeling of nostalgia.

"*Aunty Anna!*" Chloe squealed and abandoned her soup. She hopped onto Anna's lap and hugged her.

Alex made to stop her, but Anna indicated she was fine. She squeezed her niece back, inhaling the smell of her shampoo, feeling happiness rush over her in waves.

"You smell like strawberries!" she said, smiling, forcing strength into her voice, hoping she sounded normal to the little girl.

"Aunty Anna, what happened to your face?"

Alex and Samantha stopped eating and looked at Anna with bated breath.

Anna smiled at her niece.

"I fell off my bike, aren't I silly?" she lied. "But I'll be OK. Tell me all your news. Did you get taller?"

289

As Chloe chatted animatedly and bounced on her knee, Anna's thoughts drifted to Kate. She must have heard her twin sister lie to her own children many times about why her face was bruised and bloody. Anna could understand the level of hatred she would have felt for David Gallagher. She wondered where she was, and if she was OK.

Alex passed her a bowl of tomato soup and coaxed Chloe back to her own chair. Anna sipped the soup cautiously – it was lukewarm, and she was able to swallow it. She pushed away the tears that threatened to fall. She felt so emotional.

"Aunty Anna, I saw all the boxes in the hall and I took a peek!" Chloe giggled. "They're full of tinsel and sparkly balls for the tree. Can we decorate? *Please?"*

"Of course!" Anna beamed.

"Well, we'll need to find you a Christmas tree!" Alex's eyes were bright.

"Isn't it a bit early for that? It's still November!"

"It's never too early for Christmas!" Sam said.

Slowly, in the presence of her family, Anna began to feel like herself again.

49

Wednesday

Acting Chief Superintendent Doherty had not given William Ryan a moment's rest since the shooting on Monday. Even though he had been called to Dublin to get a dressing-down and orders to revamp security for the political conference, he had found time to harass the man several times a day. He was a demanding superior officer, and he wanted a full report. William had until Saturday morning to complete his investigation. The clock was ticking.

Elise had been charged with capital murder and one count of attempted murder for the attack on Janet and Myles. The charge of grievous bodily harm was added for the injuries Anna had suffered. William was still gathering evidence relating to the information contained on the memory key, but he fully expected her to be charged with conspiracy to sell classified information as soon as possible. She was facing the rest of her life in prison.

Elise was currently in isolation for her own protection. She had helped to put a large portion of the prison's population behind bars, and it would be inhumane to house her in with the other prisoners. There had been no application for bail but, even if there had, William was confident it would have been denied. She had committed capital murder – there would be no hope of leniency.

She had received stitches and treatment for her broken nose in hospital, and then been released into Garda custody, after which she had shut down. Elise Taylor had refused to say a word. She had remained completely silent, not even confirming her name.

William visited Elise on Wednesday morning. She sat at a table in the interview room, wearing a dark tracksuit, her hands cuffed at the wrists and resting in her lap. She glared at William throughout the visit, her eyes boring into his. William had had a sense she disliked him since his transfer into the station. This must be infuriating for her.

"I like your outfit," he said, opening the conversation. "Black really is your colour, it sets off your eyes."

Elise's mouth twitched but she didn't speak or break her stare into William's eyes.

"So was David Gallagher your boyfriend then?" William continued.

Colour rose in Elise's cheeks but still she remained silent.

"I wouldn't have thought he was your type. Maybe you like a bit of rough, eh? And we all know Gallagher was rough. Just ask Natalie Crowley. You took enough statements from her sister."

William knew he was wasting his time. Nothing was going to penetrate Elise's stony façade. He stood up, pushing in his chair, preparing to leave.

"A forensic examination of your apartment is happening as we speak. We'll find out everything, Elise. It would be better for you to cooperate. You're looking at forty years inside!"

Still silence.

292

"Why did you do it?" His voice was soft. "Janet didn't deserve that!"

Elise lowered her eyes.

William pulled a letter from his breast pocket. It had been pre-read, of course. He slid it across the table, saw Elise eye it with suspicion.

"It's from your sister. She's upset for you. She seems a bit lost without you."

Nothing. Elise was a wall of silence.

As William left the room, he thought he heard a tiny sob, but he could have been imagining it.

50

Thursday

The snow had abated, turning to slush. On Thursday, it returned in earnest. Beautiful thick flakes covered the ground. Cork resembled a winter wonderland. Alex finally left the house after breakfast. Anna had been encouraging him out for two days, but now that he was gone she realised she missed him. They had settled into a nice routine. He had worked at the kitchen table while she rested on the sofa. Her strength began to return as she was able to eat more, her throat no long aching.

Samantha and Chloe had come over in the afternoons and the house was filled with chatter and laughter. Anna's house was decorated to resemble Lapland thanks to Chloe's help. In the evenings, while Alex and Samantha cooked dinner, Anna played games with Chloe by the heat of the fire. She found herself laughing more and thinking about the events of Monday less. She pondered less on Kate's fate, resigning herself to the fact that the woman had made her choice to leave.

Now that Myles was able to use his mobile phone again, Anna was able to text him and make sure he was OK. He was seriously concerned he would fade away due to the tiny hospital food portions and he texted his concern with photographs of each meal. He still made Anna smile, and it was reassuring he was getting better. They texted as often as possible, growing closer every day.

William Ryan had called to the house to interview Anna again on Wednesday evening. He was still gathering evidence, but he promised to fill in the gaps for her about Elise's motives and intentions as soon as he could. Anna understood he couldn't do anything to jeopardise Elise's conviction. She could wait to learn Elise's motives. She again told William everything she could remember, and it was not hard to recall the details – the sounds and images of Monday night replayed in her dreams, a nightly terror she was relieved to wake from each morning.

The political conference took place at the Rebel Event Centre on Thursday as planned. The winter sun was bright and strong against the snowy backdrop of the city. It was televised and, as Anna settled down on the sofa with her comforter wrapped around her to eagerly watch it, she marvelled at how beautiful the city looked. Alex had lit the stove before he left and the house was cosy. Anna felt a lot warmer than the VIPs she saw standing on the steps outside the event centre. She recognised some of the politicians as they waved to the press and spectators gathered there.

She searched her TV screen for the presence of security guards, and it didn't take long to find them. Men and women in dark suits and glasses swarmed around the entrance to the building at the foot of the steps. She knew the enhanced security detail were all over the city, in the hotels and throughout the event centre.

She observed a tall, heavily built man in a long black trench coat standing at the entrance door of the event centre. His bald head was gleaming in the bright lights and he looked red and sweaty, despite the cold. Acting Chief Superintendent Doherty.

Now there was a man under pressure.

Once the VIPs were inside, the television coverage switched to inside the main chamber of the building and the opening speeches began. Anna switched off the TV, bored. She decided to head out and get some groceries. It was a while since she had stocked up her fridge, and she felt bad that Alex and Samantha were doing so much. Samantha had taken the week off work; she had wrapped up work on the project that had demanded so much of her time lately and was glad now to be able to spend more time with Chloe while Alex took care of Anna. But Anna felt better. And she longed to return to the gym and to her Taekwon-Do training.

As Anna was about to leave the cosy warmth of her living room, her mobile phone rang. Kristian Lane, the private investigator. Anna stared at his name on the screen, her heart pounding. He was no doubt keen to reschedule their meeting; he charged a hefty fee. With a determined sigh Anna cut off the call. At that moment in time she was undecided whether she wanted to dig up the past, but she knew for sure K.R. Lane wasn't the man to help her do it.

As she pulled on her coat the doorbell rang. Anna opened it and her breath caught in her throat.

"Vivian!"

Her best friend stood in the doorway, smiling. She looked just like her old self, albeit freezing as she stood in the snow.

Vivian's smile faded quickly as she observed Anna's face and neck.

"What the hell happened to you? I thought you said you knocked the guy out before he had a chance to –"

Anna smiled and pulled her friend in for a hug.

"We have so much to talk about!" she said, shrugging off her coat again.

51

Saturday

On Saturday morning Acting Chief Superintendent Frank Doherty sat at his desk and chewed on a large wad of gum. He was trying it out to help with his stress levels. Noreen hadn't been too pleased he was going in to work at the weekend, but she reassured herself it wouldn't be for much longer.

"When you retire they can pass the weekend jobs down to somebody else!" she had said before turning over and going back to sleep.

Frank Doherty loved his wife; she was the eternal optimist. But he had no intention of telling her yet that he was quite enjoying this semi-promotion.

There was a huge mess in his own camp. Elise Taylor was his subordinate and she had violated his trust, and Janet McCarthy's trust, in the worst way. Doherty knew Elise had had a tough childhood, but he didn't subscribe to the idea that that could shape her for life. Elise had been a fine detective, thorough and honest. At least Doherty had thought so. She had been a woman with choices; the fact that she had made the wrong one was her fault alone.

Doherty felt that he had taken his eye off the ball where his employees were concerned, and he wouldn't be going anywhere until he had this mess well and truly cleaned up. He was aware now that the security detail for the political conference had long ago been changed, once it was realised the files had been accessed and downloaded. The security breach had been kept quiet; the finer details known to only a handful. He felt slightly resentful to have been kept out of that particular circle of trust. After all the years of service he had given, all the sacrifices … he hadn't been brought into the loop … somehow, Doherty felt a renewed enthusiasm for the job, a vigour that had long ago abandoned him. He had something to prove again.

He had given William Ryan the least amount of time humanly possible to get the facts of this bizarre case together, and he was hungry for answers.

Doherty was still smarting from the dressing-down he had received, that one of his own detectives had stolen classified security details. It was still unclear how Elise Taylor had managed to steal the classified data – far more technical minds than Frank Doherty's were working on that. It was to his greatest relief that the political conference went off without a hitch. On Thursday and Friday, the European dignitaries didn't suffer so much as a toothache. Doherty wasn't normally a man for whiskey, but he had nursed one Friday night, savouring the way it burned in his throat and obliterated all other thoughts.

Doherty remained clueless as to how Elise had done it, or why. Clueless, and deeply rankled – someone he had worked closely with and respected had turned out to be a devious killer. Doherty had always thought of himself as an astute man, but maybe he was losing his touch. He wasn't ready to be put out to pasture just yet though – he had assured the top brass he'd have a full report in their hands before the weekend was out. So, he had put pressure on William Ryan, now his most promising detective. The man was due in any minute.

Detective Sergeant William Ryan was right on time. It was becoming one of his trademarks. Doherty spat the large ball of chewing gum into the bin under his desk and straightened up in his seat, shoulders back. He needed to command authority, even if he still felt shaken by the unprecedented violence Elise had wrought on the station. There were times Doherty found it hard to believe Janet McCarthy was dead. He shook a blood-pressure tablet into his hand, then added another for good measure. He had a feeling they would barely take the edge off.

"What have you got for me, Ryan?" Doherty stood and shook the younger man's hand. He gestured to the seat opposite his own and William settled into it.

"Everything, sir," he answered with an air of confidence.

Doherty eyed him with interest. William was dressed in a full suit despite the fact that it was Saturday. Doherty appreciated his professionalism. He wore a long dark woollen overcoat that looked like a good defence against the bitter cold.

Doherty nodded, said "I'm all ears," and waited as William sorted through the notes in his lap. William cleared his throat to begin. "So, this is every bit as bad as you can imagine. Elise Taylor has broken every code of this office in the most appalling way. The good news is, we have uncovered a vast trail of evidence that will secure a conviction, without question. Elise tested positive for gunshot residue on her hands. Her fingerprints are all over the gun, and the gun is confirmed as the weapon used to shoot both victims. It's not a Garda-issue weapon and it was fitted with a silencer. We can only assume she got it from her boyfriend. We'll know more on that in the coming days."

"The boyfriend. David Gallagher?"

"Yes, the younger son of Tom Gallagher."

Doherty exhaled loudly through his teeth.

"The gun is most likely stolen. Ballistics are trying to trace it now and are checking to see if it was involved in any other crimes. The fact that she didn't care to use gloves or disguise herself in any way perhaps shows us her mental state at the time. She must have known she could be identified. It stands to reason she planned not to leave any witnesses."

"Nor to stick around after the fact," Doherty interjected.

"Quite." William carried on in a tone that indicated Doherty would be best to stay quiet until he had finished his story. "Anna Clarke and Myles Henderson corroborate each other's account of what happened in the briefing room. We have no doubts about what happened on Monday evening."

"Right. How did Elise get mixed up in all this? And why?"

Doherty's tone was impatient – there were still so many unknown facts.

William took a deep breath. "This is where we had to dig a little deeper. We searched Elise's apartment, her workstation, her mobile phone. But it was while searching through her personal laptop that we struck gold, so to speak. The emails between Elise and David Gallagher yielded a lot of information, enough to convince us of *why* as well as how this happened."

Doherty leant forward.

"It would appear that Elise was assigned to a domestic violence case in late 2015. A complaint was made by Kate Crowley against her sister's partner, David Gallagher. Over the next few years, the instances of abuse continued, as did Elise's investigations. I say investigations, but really, there is strong evidence to suggest Elise informed David Gallagher after every report was made." William pulled a

300

typed sheet of paper from his folder and passed it across the table to Doherty. "This is just a sample. You will read here at the top of the page that Kate Crowley attended the Lee Street Garda station at 21:00 on the eleventh of January 2016 and made a complaint of assault against David Gallagher. She was interviewed by Elise for twenty-three minutes. At 21:41, Elise's mobile phone was used to call a number we have traced to David Gallagher. The call lasted four minutes. The pattern continued like that since then. Kate would make a formal complaint, not always interviewed by Elise, mind you, but Elise would always phone Gallagher shortly after."

Doherty looked flabbergasted. "Why on earth did she do that?"

"Because she was in a relationship with him," William answered matter-of-factly. He pulled a bundle of A4 size photographs from the folder and passed them across the table.

"We found these photographs on Elise's laptop. These are just a selection – there are hundreds. The dates vary, going between 2016 and up to six weeks ago, shortly before Gallagher was shot."

Doherty looked at each photograph in turn, his face growing paler with each one. Some he had to twist to a different angle in order to make out what was going on. They were all sexual in nature, and all featured Elise and David Gallagher. It appeared there was either a third party in the room with them, or they had set up a camera to take photographs automatically. After a few minutes Doherty passed the photographs back and cleared his throat.

There was disgust in his voice as he asked, "So she did all this because she was sleeping with him?"

He felt quite unnerved by the younger detective's composure – the man had worked with Elise too! – but he reminded himself that he'd had days to go over the

301

evidence, and he hadn't known Elise Taylor for as long as Doherty had. The shock of it all had surely worn off William Ryan.

"I think it was more than just sleeping with him. I think it was an extreme infatuation. We found emails Elise sent to David Gallagher, love letters really, begging him to leave Cork behind and start a new life with her. Gallagher's emails alluded to his intention to take over from his father and run the family business. He had no interest in ever leaving Cork. That intensified over time – he simply wouldn't even consider it. I think Elise viewed herself as Juliet and Gallagher as Romeo, star-crossed lovers on different sides of the tracks, unable to be together. By all accounts, Gallagher gave Elise just enough to keep her as his bit on the side, and his informant, for all those years."

"But what about the information she stole. Why did she get involved in that?"

"Ah!" William said with relish. "Here it gets really interesting. In David Gallagher's emails he bragged about dealings with the Meier brothers out of Munich. There's information in here that the German authorities will be interested in. Also, there's an intermediary in the picture."

William referred to his notes. "A man named Alan Ainsley, who Gallagher referred to as a middleman between himself and other gangs, and that includes the Meiers. Ainsley has been missing for two days, by the way, according to his wife. It seems David was storing stolen merchandise given to him by the Meiers, in deals arranged by Alan Ainsley. Anyway, Elise accessed the security arrangements for the political conference at work. She downloaded it onto an external hard drive. We now know that's the memory key. Our security systems had a major hole in them there, if you don't mind me saying. There was no fail-safe to prevent her downloading the data."

"She was a senior detective!" Doherty's attempt at bluster was half-hearted. He motioned for William to carry on.

"We have a series of emails and texts between Elise and David Gallagher that paint the picture for us quite neatly. Gallagher had Alan Ainsley enquire if the information was worth anything on an international level. Ainsley found that it was. A meeting was set up with the Meiers. It seems they too were intermediaries; they had a buyer lined up, a man Gallagher referred to in his emails as 'The Dutchman'. We have no other intel on who that might be. The deal was struck for David to sell them the data Elise stole. It would be unclear why David cut his father out of that deal except for part of Kate Crowley's conversation with Anna Clarke, where she stated David had boasted that he had planned to show his father how real men made real money."

"How much are we talking?"

"Half a million euro."

Silence descended on the small office. William stayed quiet while his boss digested the story so far. Doherty pulled a packet of chewing gum from his desk drawer and popped one into his mouth. He was aware his hands were shaking.

"Go on," he instructed, though he sounded as though he didn't want to hear any more.

"According to Anna Clarke, and this is based on her conversation with Kate Crowley, the Crowley sisters stole money and the intelligence data from David Gallagher. It's unclear how much money was stolen. Of course, the Crowleys had no knowledge of what was contained on the memory key, at least according to Kate Crowley. The Meiers attempted to contact David Gallagher personally to pick up the items, but it appears they took his brother John instead; David was dead and unavailable to them. The Meiers made themselves known to the Gallagher family, all in search of the memory key. We are looking into the killing of the Addams cousins, Gallagher's security men, in that respect. David was terrified of the Meiers, it seems, and made efforts to recover the memory key but found the whole lot missing. Natalie Crowley fled the country, but Kate was unable to leave, ambushed in her house by Gallagher. What followed was a confrontation with David Gallagher, in which he was shot. Most likely self-defence, if you ask me. She is still missing. But she did turn over the memory key to Anna Clarke, which seemed quite fortuitous for us. However, we know now that HQ were aware of the security breach and new plans were already in place."

"And all of us were under suspicion," Doherty muttered sourly.

"So it would seem."

Doherty exhaled loudly and clasped his hands together in front of him on the desk. It all made perfect sense when looked at with the benefit of hindsight. But Elise Taylor … mixed up with David Gallagher like that … he just couldn't believe it.

"OK, OK!" He held up his hands. "Why did the Meiers decide to come to Cork and not go through this middleman?"

"That's unclear, but I imagine time was ticking to the start of the conference, and perhaps the Dutchman was applying pressure. For whatever reason, the Meiers decided to pay a personal visit. We can confirm a farmhouse was rented not far from the city – forensics have been there since Friday morning. We believe four members of the Meier family stayed there. We should be able to collect enough DNA evidence to connect them to the samples retrieved from the bodies found in the burnt-out vehicle on Monastery Road, and once our German colleagues confirm a DNA match, we'll tie that up. In the farmhouse we have significant blood staining and evidence

304

of torture in one room. The landlord raised the alarm when he called to inspect the property – his statement has been taken. I believe John Gallagher was held and tortured there. He was presented at the A&E department in the early hours on Sunday night with significant injuries."

"Bloody hell!"

"Quite," William said. "I think the Meiers killed the Addams cousins as a warning to Tom Gallagher, to push him to hand over the memory key. Except, according to David's emails, Tom Gallagher didn't know of its existence. Elise played her role well, visiting Gallagher to further rattle him, requesting a warrant to search his house, seemingly investigating the crime from the point of view that Gallagher was responsible."

Doherty shook his head in disbelief at the deception that had played out under his nose. Elise had been so convincing.

"Of course, Elise had other avenues at her disposal," Ryan carried on. "Our background analysis tells us she had a tough childhood and grew up in a dangerous environment – but she has contacts all over the city. She wanted Kate Crowley found and she very nearly did it. She planned to avenge her lover's death, either herself or by handing Kate over to Gallagher. He had put a price on her head, a bounty if you like. Anna Clarke can confirm Gallagher's men were searching for Kate – there was a run-in in a club in town. Kate Crowley has disappeared."

Doherty's face was now bright red. He sat back in this chair, dreading how this report would read to his superiors in Dublin. He had heard enough.

"Well done, detective. You've been busy. So we are well covered for a conviction for Elise Taylor?"

"Oh yes, sir!" William said, rubbing his hands together.

Doherty could see the man was thoroughly enjoying himself.

52

One week later

Janet McCarthy's funeral took place in the first week of December. Anna was emotional before she even set foot in the church – the same day marked ten years since her parents had disappeared. Normally, on this date every year, she had felt a burning anger and disappointment that she *still* had no answers. But this year it had been quelled somewhat, replaced by the constant threat of tears and a trembling in her hands. However, Vivian's visit had revived and comforted Anna, and she was thrilled by the fact that her best friend was home for good. She was glad of her now.

Anna knew she was recovering from the trauma of the last few weeks. She had returned to the gym daily. Her body felt stronger and her mind clearer. She was teaching her beloved Taekwon-Do Tykes again. Everything in her life was almost back to normal, though she doubted she would ever feel normal again.

On the day of the funeral Gardaí lined the streets, stiff-backed and in full uniform, outside the church. Media cameras and personnel were present but kept outside. The service for Janet McCarthy was dignified, the church full of family, friends and colleagues. Government ministers and dignitaries were also in attendance. The church was packed full of people keen to pay their respects to a woman they held in high esteem. Janet was given the highest honour.

Anna stood between Myles and Alex during the service, in a pew behind Lauren and some of her other co-workers. Myles needed her support physically, and she was glad of the distraction that offered. His wounds were healing well, but slowly. He was lucky to be on his feet so soon. He had been discharged from hospital and was recovering at his mother's house in Dublin in between rounds of physiotherapy in Dún Laoghaire. He had travelled to Cork for the ceremony with his brother. Anna knew Myles had a long road of physiotherapy and pain management ahead, but he was characteristically optimistic. And happy to be home to enjoy his mother's cooking, seafood aside.

As Anna observed the mourners, she realised how little she knew about Janet McCarthy on a personal level. She had found her Chief Superintendent to be decisive and kind. Anna observed Janet's husband and two grown-up daughters in the front pew. She had sympathised with them before the service. Their faces still registered their shock at her sudden death. With tears blinding her, Anna turned away, unable to bear looking at their grief any longer. Anna had been present in Janet's last moments, and they haunted her dreams. She gripped Myles' hand and he squeezed hers back.

It was with some interest that Anna noticed the Taoiseach standing near the front of the church. He was flanked by security personnel and a number of his department staff. Two of the women beside him sniffed throughout the service, and a man that was part of his group wiped his eyes constantly. Janet had obviously made an impact in the course of her career, which didn't surprise Anna. The ceremonial aspect of the Garda funeral was very emotional; there wasn't a dry eye inside the church.

Reporters waited outside. Elise Taylor's crimes were national news.

Lauren removed her glasses to better wipe her eyes and sobbed loudly. Anna rubbed her arm. It felt good to focus on comforting her friend – it offered a welcome distraction from her own emotions, which still threatened to overwhelm her. Continuously she drew deep breaths into her lungs, focused on her breathing; it distracted her, and steadied her nerves.

Anna was intrigued by the fact that the tall man to the Taoiseach's left greeted Myles by name as they moved slowly from the church after the ceremony. He was dressed in a black suit and put on a pair of dark sunglasses as he exited.

"How are you recovering, Mr. Henderson?"

Anna stopped and let Myles and the government official walk on, Myles shuffling with his walking stick. She wondered how they knew each other. They exchanged words for a few minutes, then Myles turned to Anna again and smiled. She moved towards him once more, and they continued their slow pace back to his brother's car.

"Who was that guy? Have the Men in Black finally come to take you away?" she asked lightly. She was intrigued to see a slight blush creep into his cheeks.

Detective Sergeant William Ryan appeared beside them and interrupted the moment. Myles exhaled in relief – and it wasn't lost on Anna. William made small talk for a few minutes, enquiring about Myles' recovery, rubbing his hands together in the cold.

A mountain of a man approached them; noting his

stressed-out expression, Anna assumed the newly promoted Chief Superintendent Doherty was in his usual form. He looked down at her, his bald head gleaming in the winter sunlight.

"How are you, Nancy Drew?"

Anna met his eyes and found they were kind; his huge meaty hand gripped her arm and squeezed gently.

"You take your time coming back to work – there's no rush."

As quickly as he had arrived, Doherty was gone. He walked briskly towards a group of suited men standing at the edge of the carpark, his trench coat flapping in the breeze. William Ryan made his excuses, and he left them as well. Anna watched him go. He had been good to her and Myles over the last week, filling them in with as much information as he could. William was confident there was enough evidence to lock Elise up for the rest of her life. Anna knew that Elise still refused to speak, even to her legal counsel. Anna wouldn't lose any sleep over the fate Elise had carved out for herself.

Myles smiled at Anna, and they continued their slow pace.

When they reached Myles' brother's car, he turned to her, his brown eyes heavy with tiredness. The physical exertion of attending Janet's funeral had taken a toll on him.

"Can we get together after Christmas?" He pulled open the car door.

"Sure." Anna smiled at him.

Myles bent his head and kissed her on the cheek, then disappeared into the car.

Anna spotted Alex waiting for her to the left of the church entrance. He linked arms with her as they walked to his car.

"You doing OK?" he asked, his voice full of concern.

Anna felt a rush of love for him – her amazing big brother, who had lost his parents ten years ago today too, was always worried that she was alright.

"I'm getting there," she said, squeezing his arm. "You?"

"Getting there," he replied softly, and they walked on.

53

Kate Crowley stepped from a train at the station in Chartres, France. It was dry and bright, the winter sun high in the sky. She rolled her neck from side to side and leant to the left and right, to stretch out the joints in her body that had sat upright for far too long. Slinging her red bag onto her shoulder, she stood on tiptoes to better see over the heads of the alighting passengers. There was no sign of Natalie.

It had taken her over a week to get here and she had been in contact with Natalie the whole time. Purchasing a mobile phone was one of the smartest things she had done lately. It felt good to be able to text or call her sister whenever she liked, and to have access to the internet. She remembered how she had been too scared to buy one when she was still in Cork, in case it led to her being arrested or found by the Gallaghers. She realised she should have taken the risk – the Gallaghers had been able to find her anyway.

She had read with interest online details of the cold-blooded murder and attempted murders committed by none other than Elise Taylor. The very same detective who had been so reassuring to her whenever she had reported David Gallagher's attacks on Natalie. The same woman who had convinced him to let Kate's nieces out of the car when he had driven them to the quays and threatened to drive into the water. She felt little consolation from the fact that she was proved right that there was an informant in the Lee Street Garda station. And she felt huge sympathy for Anna Clarke, the girl who had helped her so many times. Her old friend had been attacked and almost killed – she assumed she was the unnamed woman who had been seriously injured in Elise's attack.

Every time she thought of Anna, she felt a large pang of guilt settle in her stomach. It was difficult to shake off. Her childhood friend had saved her life, taken her in and offered her a safe place to stay. And she had lied to her, betrayed her trust and left without explanation.

She told herself she'd had no other choice. She could not turn herself in. And Tom Gallagher's gang was everywhere, surrounding the city. Time was pressing on and she was no closer to getting a passport and a way out of there. For her, it was an easy decision.

Once Anna had left the house that Monday over a week ago, Kate had made full use of her internet. Her searches confirmed what she already knew – she needed a passport to get into France. Briefly, she had felt despair. But she'd had to fight for so long, the last hurdle could not be the one where she faltered. Every avenue open to her was difficult, but nothing was impossible. She had survived worse than this.

She was proud of how her sister found the courage and stuck to the plan. Natalie had fled with her children, and then it was her turn to run.

When David came to the house, she had been packed, almost ready to leave. David had been like a man possessed; his face was a shade of grey she had never seen

312

on anyone before, his eyes bulging and red-rimmed. She knew he could hardly believe Natalie had robbed and left him. It must have been a huge shock – that thought had made her smile many times. She had seen fear in David too. He had shouted about buyers trying to contact him – or perhaps he had said "Meiers" – he had slurred his words – and said he needed the memory key. He had spoken of nothing but the key.

She remembered her words that afternoon. David had stood opposite her in her living room, his fists balled up, his whole body shaking.

"My sister has left you, you piece of shit, and taken her children with her. *You can rot in hell!*"

David had bellowed in rage, a guttural sound borne of fear and anger and disbelief. He had launched himself at her and wrapped his hands around her throat. For a split second his eyes had terrified her. Then she remembered her own rage at this man who had put her sister through so much ...

The autopsy report was right – David Gallagher had suffered a vicious assault before his death. But so had she – David's knuckles would surely bear evidence of that. When he had pulled a gun and told her he had called John to come over, she knew it was his life or hers.

She had lied to Anna about the struggle for the gun with David Gallagher that day – it had been easy to disarm him. Whatever drugs he had taken that morning were probably wearing off, and their fight had exhausted him. She was a skilled kickboxer, and David was suffering for it. Pointing the gun at him, she had felt nothing. She had him where she had always wanted him, yet she felt empty. There were six feet between them, and little threat to her when she pulled the trigger. David's lips were moving, but she couldn't hear anything but Natalie's voice.

"I fell down the stairs … yeah, I'm so clumsy!"

"I burnt my hand on the stove."

"Yes … OK… it was David. Please, Kate! Just leave it!"

"It's my fault, I should have known he was tired."

"Kate … help me! He has the girls!"

When she pulled the trigger, David Gallagher was midway through shouting a threat at her, spittle flying from his mouth and sweat coating his face. She heard none of it.

She would never regret what she had done. All she regretted of that afternoon was not taking her passport so she could get the next available flight out of the country before the Gardaí knew to look for her.

As her neighbour had banged on the front door, she had fled through the back door, assuming the noise at the front door was John, and was still running.

And as Elise Taylor pulled the trigger and shot Janet McCarthy dead, she was in the back of a taxi, en route to the city-centre bus station. From there she boarded an overnight bus to the town of Rosslare and had never looked back.

When she had arrived in Rosslare, she quickly realised she had missed the next available ferry to Cherbourg in France and had days to wait until the next crossing. She checked into a small hotel, feeling safer than she had in days. She was still careful – she assumed the Gardaí would be watching the ports, but she felt able to relax a little. The worst was over. She went out the next day, bought some new clothes, and had her hair properly styled.

Mostly, she ate and slept. It had been too long since she had fulfilled both of those basic human needs properly. She finally purchased a mobile phone, feeling less anxious in Rosslare than she had in Cork. Her first call was to Natalie. It was so good to hear her sister's voice! And speaking with her only fuelled her desire further to make it to France. In the dead of night, when she woke suddenly amid nightmares of David Gallagher's face, she thought of all the mistakes she had made. The suitcase and passport left behind, the near-suicidal attempt to buy a passport in the Mad Hatter. And the most fundamental mistake of all: they should have taken the money and fled the same day. It was reckless, all of it! She knew she was lucky to be alive, and not in Garda custody. There had been so many mistakes – she was determined to make sure every move from now on was bullet-proof.

On the final evening in Rosslare she found him. She was having dinner at the Sole Diner, a busy pitstop for truckers and drivers before they crossed the channel to France. She had been looking for a specific type of man, and here he was. He wasn't too tall nor too heavily built. And he was wearing a gold band on the ring finger of his left hand. So, she assumed he was a family man. She sat down opposite him as soon as his food arrived and offered to buy him dessert. He declined, looking slightly mortified, his cheeks reddening.

Bingo.

The man wasn't a deviant or a pervert and he wasn't so big she couldn't defend herself if things got difficult between them.

She explained what she needed. She slid one thousand euro across the table under a red chequered napkin. The man looked nervously around the diner, but no-one was bothering to look at them. Everyone was engrossed in their own meals, distracted by the toils of their own lives. She left his table shortly after and walked in the direction of the ferry port. She took care to walk as close as she could to the edge of the road; it wasn't made for pedestrians, and the road was congested with traffic.

Shortly, his blue-and-white Arctic truck pulled up

alongside her and she hopped into the passenger seat. Without a word, and without making eye contact, she climbed into the sleeper in the back. She pulled the blankets over her head and began to pray.

The ferry crossing took almost eighteen hours. While they were sailing, she tried to relax with the gentle sway of the ocean. She was cramped and uncomfortable. She slept a little and ate a little of some food she had brought in her bag. She saw no sign of the driver, and her heart pounded loudly in her ears every time she heard a noise nearby. When she had to, she moved from her hiding place to urinate into a small plastic bucket in the back. Once she added vomit to its contents. The eighteen hours felt like days. Sparks of hope kept her misery at bay.

Eventually the driver climbed back into the cab and wordlessly started the engine. She assumed he must be nervous – security checks were stringent these days; searches for migrants were commonplace. As the truck drove on, stopped at what she assumed was a security checkpoint, and on again, she waited with bated breath. Eventually it stopped completely, and she climbed gingerly into the passenger seat again. She nodded briefly to the driver, put another thousand euro on the seat, and left the truck. No words had passed between them since their encounter in the diner.

She smiled as her feet hit the concrete of the road. David Gallagher had done everything while he was alive to drive her and Natalie apart. Now two thousand euro of his stolen cash had brought them together again.

It was mid-afternoon when she had arrived at Cherbourg. A Google search on her new phone told her that her sister was almost six hours away by train. She needed another hotel. She was growing tired of being alone, but she knew the end was in sight.

She chose the most rundown hotel she could find – she had no form of identification and wanted to answer no questions. As soon as she shut the door of her room she called Natalie.

"I'm in France, in Cherbourg. I'll catch a train to Chartres tomorrow."

Natalie was unable to speak, sobbing into Kate's ear instead. They had never gone this long without seeing each other, and now they were almost together again. When she ended the call, she couldn't stop the tears that poured down her cheeks. All the pent-up fear and anxiety of the last few weeks came flooding out. She curled into a ball on the bed, hugging her knees, while her body shuddered with exhaustion and relief. She slept better that night than she had in months.

And now here she was in Chartres, waiting for her sister at the train station. Sitting on a wooden bench, she clutched the red bag to her chest. She consoled herself that the train was a little early, that Natalie could be delayed for a variety of reasons – perhaps the twins had needed the bathroom. The minutes ticked on and felt like hours.

Suddenly, there she was. Natalie. Her green eyes swam with tears as she ran up the platform to her sister. They embraced tightly, each reluctant to let go. Natalie's long red hair whipped in the wind and she studied her sister's face, held between her own hands. Never had either sister felt such happiness.

Natalie had left Rhea and Rachel with a hotel guest she had befriended, an elderly lady who appeared to dote on them. She greeted Kate warmly when they went to collect the twins. The woman made no remark as to how alike Natalie and Kate were, which was a first for the Crowley twins. Kate realised how different they looked now, with her hair cut short and died a darker colour. Or perhaps it was that the events of the last few weeks had aged her so much.

She was a little crushed that her nieces didn't recognise her straight away. They were shy, hiding behind their mother's leg. With gentle coaxing and lots of stories read to them on the small sofa in Natalie's hotel apartment, they eventually came around. By the end of the day the twins were calling her 'Aunty Kate' again. Her heart soared.

Once the girls were asleep Natalie and Kate settled into their armchairs in the small living room. Natalie had opened a bottle of wine, and Kate filled her in on everything that had happened in Cork, and then Rosslare. She gasped as Kate recounted her run-ins with Gallagher's men in the Mad Hatter and the Kingsman hotel. Natalie hated that she had suffered so much, but they both knew it could have been far worse.

Kate told her sister of her encounters with their old friend Anna Clarke.

"You owe Anna your life," Natalie stated, and Kate nodded solemnly. "Do you think you'll contact her again?"

"No, I don't think so. I hate the way I left, and from what I read in the papers, she was almost killed over that memory key. I don't think she'd want to hear from me!"

Natalie nodded, and stared into the distance. "So, is it over now?"

"Almost," Kate replied. "We need to leave France. The Gardaí and the Gallaghers will continue searching for us. We'll leave here as soon as we can."

Setting her wineglass on the small coffee table, Kate moved into the kitchen and pulled the sharpest knife she could find from Natalie's cutlery drawer.

"Where are they, Natalie?"

With an excited smile Natalie walked into the girls' room. She emerged moments later with the two blue teddy bears they loved so much and passed them to Kate without a word. Kate carefully cut the four glistening eyes from the teddies and laid them on the coffee table.

She and Natalie sat and looked at the four diamonds for some time. They were perfect, in the twins' opinion. They were oval in shape, almost all the same size, and glistening brilliantly in the light. Presently Kate took a photograph of each of them on her new mobile phone. She sent the image to her old college friend and waited. After a few minutes, the phone beeped, and Kate's face broke into a smile.

"Hannah is on board. She will fly in from Antwerp later this week. She's finalising a price."

The twins clinked their wineglasses and sat back in their armchairs, relaxed and hopeful about the future. A future without David Gallagher, whose stolen goods just kept giving and giving.

Epilogue

The new year dawned as cold as the last had ended. Anna was on extended leave from work, at the insistence of the new Chief Superintendent Frank Doherty. She was recovering well and was keen to return to her desk. She missed Lauren and the others, missed her morning coffee in Victus, and the busyness of her days. For now, though, she was relishing her time away from the macabre case files that usually marred her day.

Anna continued to train with Jason and teach her Taekwon-Do Tykes. Some things she was not prepared to give up for longer than absolutely necessary. The martial art had saved her life, and she had never felt more fully alive than when she was practising and teaching.

After her trips to the gym, she spent her mornings listening to music on her father's record player, cello pieces mostly, in her living room. She lit the stove early and sat with a book and a coffee, savouring that fact that she had little else to do. She knew this couldn't last much longer. Her bruises were completely faded. In truth, she felt the familiar stirrings of restlessness push into her relaxation. She would go back to work soon.

The first Sunday of the new year found her at Alex's house, immersed in the raucous squeals of five-year-old princesses, racing up and down the narrow hallway and into the living room again. Chloe had turned five and her only wish was to have a *Frozen*-themed party. Ten mini-princesses had turned Alex and Samantha's home upside down. Anna had painted tiny fingernails and braided hair as best she could, ever the dutiful aunt. She sipped mugs of coffee with Samantha in the kitchen while the girls raced around, both women lamenting that it wasn't glasses of wine in their hands. At five o'clock she stood up and kissed her brother and his wife goodbye.

"You absolutely cannot leave us!" Alex protested.

Anna confessed she had plans. She observed the slight intake of breath, the furrow of eyebrows, as her brother digested this. He was always worrying. It didn't grate on her anymore – she understood it was his way, and she didn't need to give him a hard time over wanting to protect her.

"Just coffee with Myles," Anna reassured him, patting his shoulder.

Traffic was light into the city. It was Sunday, in the first week of January, and the temperature was almost freezing again. Anna felt weary of the weather – Lauren had asked her to go abroad for a week, to get some vitamin D and a suntan before her wedding. Every time Anna went outside and had to layer on her thick coat, scarf and hat, she edged closer to agreeing to go.

Myles had texted Anna and asked her to meet him in Victus, but it was closed. Anna wasn't surprised. They opted for a city-centre hotel instead. Anna found parking on the street on the South Mall and walked quickly to the hotel, savouring the heat that blasted at her as soon as she stepped inside the lobby. She was early. And excited. She hadn't seen Myles since he had visited Cork for Janet McCarthy's funeral many weeks ago. Their relationship was conducted through technology lately, and Anna couldn't wait to see Myles' warm brown eyes and broad grin in person.

She sat alone at a table-for-two by the window and looked out into the city lights. The Christmas lights were still shining, and Anna lost herself in memories of her childhood, of family Christmases when everything had been so much simpler. She had spent Christmas in Alex's house, sleeping over in Chloe's room, and had allowed herself to get lost in her niece's magical joy. She had smiled for almost two days straight.

The waitress brought her coffee just as she observed a tall dark-skinned man walk with a slight limp past the window and into the hotel. He was dressed in a suit and thick coat, carrying a briefcase. She couldn't be sure until he stood beside her and grinned his hello, but it was Myles. He looked so different. She had barely seen him in anything other than skinny jeans and sweaters. His formal clothes confused her. His hair was longer, swept back into a bun at the nape of his neck.

Anna couldn't contain her surprise.

"Myles, you look so different!" she said, rising to return his hug. She noticed his right arm was still stiff, not able to rise as high as the other.

Myles laughed and sat down. "I'll take that as a compliment, shall I?"

They settled into easy conversation, each asking questions of the other: how have you been, how are your family? Myles had spent Christmas in the bosom of his large family, and Anna laughed as he told stories of his brothers' antics over the festive holiday. At some point the waitress brought coffee to Myles and refilled Anna's cup, but they were too lost in each other to notice much else.

Eventually there was a lull in the flow of their conversation, and Anna caught Myles' brown eyes. "Are you going to explain the suit?"

"I'm working."

"On a Sunday? Where?"

Myles set down his coffee cup and looked at Anna seriously. She felt a shiver of anticipation – in the time she had known Myles, he had never looked so solemn. His grin was gone, his mouth a thin line.

Anna decided now was as good a time as any to bring up something that had bothered her lately.

"OK, you can answer that later. But I've been meaning to ask you something about the night Elise attacked us. When I brought you and Janet the memory key."

"What about it?"

"You and Janet already knew the security detail had been stolen. I'm right, aren't I?"

Myles scratched his head. He looked around the hotel, playing for time or weighing up something. Eventually, he leant across the table and spoke in a soft voice.

"Yes, you're right."

"I get why Janet would know that information, she was Chief Superintendent. But not you …"

"Do you remember I said I worked for the Special Detective Unit?"

Anna thought of the man in a dark suit and glasses outside the church a few weeks ago. She realised she was holding her breath.

"Well, I do," he said, "but I work a little higher up than I originally let on."

He stopped and swallowed a lump in his throat.

"I'm not in a position to elaborate about my job any further. Let's just say I work for the State and leave it at that."

"Excuse me?"

Myles groaned. "Oh, come on, Anna!"

"Do you work in Phoenix Park?"

At the mention of the Garda Headquarters location, Myles shook his head.

"That's classified, sorry."

"Are you in the Defence Forces? Or in military intelligence?"

Myles shifted in his seat, and Anna couldn't tell if it was because of their conversation or if his injured leg was making him uncomfortable.

"I was stationed in Cork to assist with security for the political conference. That's all that's relevant really."

Anna narrowed her eyes and Myles had the good grace to look contrite.

"I guess there's no harm in telling you what I can. I was undercover. We knew there had been a security breach, and that the security details of the political conference had been both accessed and downloaded. What we didn't know was by whom. Or why. We were very keen to establish who the buyer for the information was, and even more interested in knowing who the target was. We still *are* very keen to find that out. Hopefully, Elise Taylor will start talking, especially if it means reducing her sentence."

Anna was stunned into silence. She realised her mouth was opening and closing repeatedly, and she made a conscious effort to stop. She couldn't believe what she was hearing, and she suddenly felt incredibly sad. She had never seen or heard Myles so serious, and so professional. She missed his brown eyes dancing with laughter, his relaxed conversation. She wondered if she really knew him.

Suddenly he reached across the table and grabbed both

of her hands, holding them firmly in his own. He smiled at her warmly.

"I didn't lie to you, Anna. I could only tell you what I was permitted to. And besides, nothing's changed. I want to keep meeting you for coffee, and dinner, and whatever else you'll meet me for!"

He raised one eyebrow and a large grin spread across his face.

Anna shook her head, fighting the smile that pulled at the corners of her mouth. Myles was so fun, so intriguing, and someone she wasn't ready to stop seeing yet. Whatever his job, she knew she wanted to be around him. But her smile quickly faded … the last few weeks had taught her that no one was who they seemed to be.

Anna was still intrigued about Kate's true motive and questioning her innocence. She tossed and turned at night, wondering what had become of her childhood friend. Then there was Elise Taylor, a respected detective; she had let down those who trusted her, in the worst possible way. Now Myles, the carefree surfer and casually dressed detective, was a serious intelligence officer, and had hidden the truth, albeit for good reason.

Myles sat back and let Anna's hands drop, his expression thoughtful. He seemed to be weighing something up in his mind again, trying to come to a decision.

Anna silently watched Myles reach down and pull a file from his briefcase. He sat now with his hands over it, an expression on his face that, if Anna hadn't thought better, was nervous. Myles looked at her with something akin to apology in his eyes.

"What's wrong?"

Myles inhaled deeply and adjusted his glasses. He sipped coffee and fussed with his napkin, folding it over and over.

Anna sat still, quietly waiting, unable to look away from the file on the table. She was terrified to speak in case he changed his mind about telling her whatever it was he was debating telling her.

Finally, he was able to speak.

"Anna, I remember what you told me about your parents – how they are missing now ten years, how you wanted to hire a private investigator to search for them. In the course of my job I have access to files and records. I hope you'll forgive me … but … I looked up the file on their disappearance."

Anna's blood ran cold. She could feel her heart beating inside her chest, pounding a quick rhythm.

"And?" she whispered, not sure she wanted the answers she had craved for ten years.

Myles closed his eyes for a few seconds. He appeared to be steadying himself.

"I could get fired for this, but … the investigation looks solid. Every lead was followed up, and every angle was covered. The detective in charge was as baffled as anyone, and he made entries in the files right up until he retired."

Anna's shoulders sagged – she had hoped for something more.

"It's just …" Myles adjusted his glasses again. He took a deep breath. "You said your parents were English?"

Anna nodded. She kept her hands folded in her lap to stop them shaking.

"And you have no other family alive today, apart from your brother?"

Not trusting herself to speak, she nodded again. It was little more than a jerk of her head – she was beginning to feel paralysed by fear and anticipation.

When Myles spoke, his voice was so soft that Anna had to lean forward to hear him.

327

"Your mother disappeared before, Anna. What I mean is, that night ten years ago was not the first time she disappeared."

Anna was aware of a loud buzzing noise in her ears.

"Do you know your mother's maiden name, Anna?"

Myles' question threw her into confusion – what a strange thing to ask! She was about to answer that of course she did, until she realised that she didn't actually know the answer. Her mother had always been Helen Clarke. Anna had been too young to ponder on anything else. Myles sensed the truth and didn't press her. Instead, he answered his own question.

"Your mother was born Yelena Vasilieva in 1956 in the Russian town of Omsk. She was the daughter of a successful businessman. When she was a child the family moved to Moscow, where her father gained more prominence as a supporter of Khrushchev. Your mother was a promising cellist. She played with the Moscow Orchestral Reserve throughout her teens. In her early twenties, she visited London with the orchestra and some time on the night of September 4th 1978 she disappeared."

Anna was unable to breathe. All the sounds within the café ceased to exist.

Myles slid the file across the table. Anna unfolded her hands and picked it up, willing her shaking fingers to work, to open the file. Her vision felt out of focus.

Inside was a photocopy of a newspaper article. The headline drew her attention.

Moscow Orchestral Reserve Wow at the Royal Albert Hall

The words danced and flashed before Anna and she made no further attempt to read the short article. Set under the headline, and taking up most of the page, was a black-and-white photograph of a group of what were presumably the musicians, standing outside the Royal Albert Hall. The men and women stood there smiling broadly, dressed in an array of thick coats and fur hats.

Anna instantly found her mother's face. Yelena Vasilieva was of average height and build, with soft features, and large oval eyes. Her hair was bundled into a fur hat, but Anna had no doubt it was her mother. Her coat was thick and knee-length, with four large black buttons. Although the image was black-and-white, Anna knew that coat was a bright, fire-engine red.

Anna touched the image of her mother with a trembling finger. She had never seen her mother this young. There were no photographs of her mother's childhood, because she had always said she left them behind her, and now that her parents were dead, she had no way of retrieving them. She wondered if that part of her story was true. If anything she knew of her mother was true.

Her face suddenly felt wet; she touched her cheeks and found them moist with tears. She wiped them and turned the photocopied page over. A second sheet, another photocopy from the same newspaper, was dated one week later, and featured a photograph of Yelena Vasilieva, alone, standing beside her cello. It appeared to be a promotional shot, perhaps used in advertising for the orchestra. The headline was thick and bold:

PROMISING RUSSIAN CELLIST DISAPPEARS

Closing the file, Anna stared at Myles with dry eyes. After ten years of tears and anguish, enduring a cruel mystery, here lay secrets she could never have imagined. Lies were unfolding into truth on the pages before her. Lies that had kept her blind for too long. Her heart hardened, her back stiff, Anna made up her mind.

It was time to discover the truth.

Printed in Great Britain
by Amazon